The Ex-Perimento

The Ex-Perimento

Maria J. Morillo

BERKLEY ROMANCE
New York

BERKLEY ROMANCE
Published by Berkley
An imprint of Penguin Random House LLC
1745 Broadway, New York, NY 10019
penguinrandomhouse.com

Book design by Ashley Tucker
Title page art by IFM Design/Shutterstock

Library of Congress Cataloging-in-Publication Data

Names: Morillo, Maria J., author.
Title: The ex-perimento / Maria J. Morillo.
Description: First edition. | New York, NY: Berkley Romance, 2026.
Identifiers: LCCN 2025027107 (print) | LCCN 2025027108 (ebook) |
ISBN 9780593955246 trade paperback | ISBN 9780593955253 ebook
Subjects: LCGFT: Romance fiction | Novels | Fiction
Classification: LCC PR9333.9.M67 E9 2026 (print) |
LCC PR9333.9.M67 (ebook)
LC record available at https://lccn.loc.gov/2025027107
LC ebook record available at https://lccn.loc.gov/2025027108

First Edition: February 2026

Printed in the United States of America
1st Printing

The authorized representative in the EU for product safety and compliance is Penguin Random House Ireland, Morrison Chambers, 32 Nassau Street, Dublin D02 YH68, Ireland, https://eu-contact.penguin.ie.

For Mami and Papi—
I know it's not a university degree,
but isn't it so cool?

Para mami y papi—
sé que no es un título universitario,
pero ¿verdad que está cool?

CHAPTER 1

SPECIAL OCCASIONS REQUIRE SPECIAL DRESSES. And special dresses are often the ones that don't let you *breathe.*

I shift in my seat at the Aula Magna de la Universidad Central de Venezuela, trying not to call attention to myself. The *crunch, swoosh* of tulle over linen doesn't help. But the dress was a gift from my boyfriend, and even if Alejandro can't remember which fabrics give me a rash, at least he was thoughtful enough to get it for me in the first place. Plus, it's his graduation. The right thing to do was to suck it up and wear the thing. That's what love is.

To my right, an elderly woman with a soft cloud of stark-white hair gives me a sympathetic look. She pats my knee over the armrest between our seats with a wrinkled yet perfectly manicured hand. Her golden bracelets click with the movement. I attempt an apology but the warm lights of the auditorium dim, a subtle *shut up* to everyone present.

The auditorium is charged with an atmosphere of eager solemnity. Vibrant, billowing banners float against the white of the vaulted ceiling, a perfect contrast with the classy elegance of a theater, like a marriage between the modern and the timeless.

I can't help but grin as dancers dressed in folklore attire take the stage, the opening to the grand event. The last time I was in this room, five years ago, it was for my own graduation. I walked across that stage to receive my journalism diploma. The sense of accomplishment I felt back then, the pride at having something mine and mine only remains unmatched. There is nothing quite like crossing an item off your list of plans, knowing you're on track to building the life you want.

Tonight is no different. I'm not the one becoming a doctor, sure. But Alejandro's achievement feels as much mine as it is his. We're in this together.

After several performances and graduates being called one by one, it's Alejandro's turn. His stride is long, precise, and calculated. Just like him. Every step he takes—now and any other day—is premeditated, careful. It's why we get along so well, how we've managed to stay together four years. It's a quality that has only ever worked in our favor.

I hold my breath as the medical school faculty director slides the medal over his head. My chest swells with pride. He did it. For the last four years, I've seen how hard Ale has worked for *this* moment—the sleepless nights, the tears of frustration, the never-ending exhaustion and strict diet of caffeine and protein. No one deserves it more than he does.

Jumping to my feet, I join the eruption of cheers. From the stage, Alejandro seems to find me amid the crowd and everyone else in the auditorium disappears. I know it's impossible, I'm not remotely close enough, but I can still pretend it's just the two of us here. I can fantasize that the grin splitting his face, so wide he can barely keep his eyes open, is directed at me.

Alejandro swallows hard before he blinks, looking away.

He marches tall and proud offstage, followed by another graduate whose name I forget as soon as it's said.

My eyes sting as I take my seat. He did it. For the past several months, ever since he told me his graduation date, I've pictured what the rest of our lives will look like. Now we're one step closer. The plans we've discussed and dreamt of while he was studying on my apartment floor late into the night are taking shape before my eyes. Him: a respectable neurosurgeon. Me? An arts journalist. International recognition, of course. A house in La Lagunita (the best neighborhood in Caracas); three kids (two boys and a girl); and a golden retriever named Scott (in honor of the toilet paper). It's all mapped out.

Not until after I graduate, though, Ale would say whenever I brought it up.

Well, he's graduated. Our future is starting here, tonight. I'm sure of it.

ALEJANDRO HOLDS ON to my hand as we get out of the taxi to join his graduation party. He's ditched the robe for a dashing baby-pink button-down. He's rolled his sleeves up to his elbows and is wearing a brown tie to match the khakis he decided to wear. And I'm . . . still in this scratchy dress.

I check the time on my phone: 9:32 p.m. We're going to be here for about two and a half hours. Alejandro will want to leave at midnight, because he leaves every party at midnight. That means in approximately three hours I'll be in the comfort of my own bed, wearing pajamas, and watching an episode of *New Girl* to calm my mind down. I can do this.

"No phones tonight," Ale says beside me. "You promised."

"No, I know." I put my phone back in my clutch purse and smile. "It's your night."

Ale squeezes my hand in response. I squeeze back, inching closer to wrap my free hand around his elbow. My job is probably our only sensitive subject. As the metaphorical face of *Ellas* magazine, one of Latin America's biggest online platforms, I need to be on my phone all the time. Not to mention I also give relationship advice, which means getting a little personal about my own relationship. But I don't expect to be a reluctant influencer/love guru forever. This job is leading somewhere; I've been working my way toward a promotion. It's just a matter of time.

Ahead of us, the venue waits in all its romantic, rococo, French glory. Tall ceilings, white walls, and Ionian pillars face us head-on. Gold filigree shimmers where it's hit by headlights from oncoming cars. Booking Casa Versalles for tonight was nearly impossible. I had to promise them a feature in any of our future "best spots to . . ." lists, but it was worth it. Finding the perfect venue for Alejandro's graduation party was the only thing his parents asked me to do. I had to do it right.

Music engulfs every inch of the premises. Below our feet, the bass shakes the ground with the beat of an old reguetón song that I haven't heard in like five years. It's 100 percent ruining the vibe. Imagine stepping into Pemberley and Georgiana Darcy is playing Bad Bunny.

We zigzag, dodging furniture as Ale stops every five seconds to greet someone.

"This place is a damn laberinto," he yells over the too-loud music. "Who picked it?"

I trip over my shoes. "You don't like it?"

"No, I—*hey!*" Ale interrupts himself when he spots his parents across the hallway.

Their faces immediately brighten at the sight of their son, ditching the scowls that will latch on to my memory forever. His mother, Bárbara, opens both arms to him, pulling him down for a hug that yanks his hand from mine.

As Ale's mother turns to face me, her ruby-red lips curl downward and her eyebrows knit together in a disapproving frown. She lets out a sigh before speaking. "Maria Antonieta."

I try not to flinch at the use of my full name. Before I can say a word, she turns to her husband and whispers something I can't catch due to the damn music, but I know it's about me.

Suddenly, the dress I'm wearing feels too . . . everything. Too short, too tight, too wrong, too much. I should have worn something else, something classier. Never mind that I didn't even pick out the dress.

The shade of lipstick I chose is probably wrong too. It's too dark. She probably thinks it's wrong for my olive skin tone (it isn't) and that I should have picked something more along the lines of *her* lipstick, but she's always right and I'm always wrong. And who wears purple on their lips anyway? Also, it's not matte, it's bound to smudge. I'll be forced to drink champagne, the lipstick will stain the glass, and they'll all say I'm trash.

I run my sweaty hands down my dress. My second mistake.

Alejandro's mother follows the trajectory of the movement with her eyes, fixing her attention on my godforsaken outfit. Her gaze moves slowly back up until our eyes lock. I attempt a smile. She does the same. We both fail.

Anxiety flares in my chest. Squirming under scrutiny is not how I pictured tonight going.

"Mauricio is here?" Ale asks, making me jump. "Give me a second, I'm gonna—" I grab his forearm, keeping him in place. He turns to me with an amused smirk. "It'll be two minutes. Mi mamá doesn't bite."

"She hates me," I whisper. In case the last four years haven't been indication enough.

His eyes soften as he inches closer, grazing his fingers along my chin, a ghost of a touch because his parents are right there. "She doesn't hate you. No one could hate you."

I huff, thinking of my boss, half of my teachers, and my ninety-year-old neighbor from across the hall.

Shaking his head as if he could read my mind, he smiles and takes one step back. "Dos minutos. You'll be fine."

Before I can beg him to stay again, he's gone.

It's his night, I remind myself. He can talk to anyone he wants to. And I'm used to being alone at events. It's part of being a journalist.

I turn back to his parents. "So, how—"

Aaaand I'm talking to no one. They're gone. Perfect.

Choking back my own words, I make my way to the garden. I actually like the mazelike distribution of the house. I like the stone floor and the tall trees with fairy lights hanging from the branches. Surrounded by Alejandro's friends and family, I can't help but think of the future. Again. My friends and family aren't many. A *future* event here would mean adding maybe thirty extra guests, paying a little more for food, and of course, creating a classier ambience than a graduation party needs. There was one particular spot that made me fall in love with the venue. The gazebo. As I make my way toward it, my heart mimics the *boom, boom, boom* coming from the speakers. Purple strobe lights reflect across the grass; I watch squealing children chase the little dancing dots in overflowing delight.

The black dome of the gazebo rests on six Ionian pillars adorned with delicate carvings at the top. I'm captivated by the way their intricate flower design resembles lace. I run a hand over the white iron railing as I walk up the concrete steps, and cold seeps through my skin. Moving to stand at the center, I imagine myself as a bride. I imagine my mother wiping her tears with a dramatic flourish of a vintage handkerchief. My current stepfather will probably give me away, since there is nobody else, while the setting sun hits the golden details on the ceiling at exactly the right angle. It'll look like gold is raining on us. Then, Ale and I will share our first kiss as husband and wife. I imagine my mother clapping. I imagine *his* mother forgetting she hates me for all of one minute.

Sure, timing your wedding to the last second is not something many people do, but this is *us* we're talking about. Ale and I time everything to the last second. Why should our wedding be any different?

Not that he's asked me to marry him. Not yet, at least. But how could I not indulge, being here? Alejandro said the building feels like a maze, but maybe if he stood here with me, allowed me to guide him through my vision, he would change his mind about the venue.

My phone vibrates in my purse, an imperceptible sound to anyone else, but I'm so in tune with it, it's like I can sense it on a molecular level.

I sit with my back to the party. Please, God, don't let my dress rip open. Or let Ale find me on my phone.

It's just a text from my mother. A photo of a bright orange suitcase on a bed. Her not-so-subtle way of reminding me she's arriving in a couple of days.

YO: all set?
MAMÁ: Sí. Are you still picking me up from the airport?

I roll my eyes at that. Like I have an option. She would never let me live it down if I, her only daughter, didn't bother to pick her up at the airport. This is the same thought process that made me offer her my guest room for twelve weeks while she's in the city hosting a children's singing competition. Considering she's a national treasure (Miss Venezuela, then Miss Universe, model, actress, daytime TV host, radio host, author, and I *think* she even tried to become a singer at one point) and has a dazzling career stretching longer than three decades, I think she could be working at an international network if she wanted, but no. Instead, she's coming back to Venezuela to host this talent show—supposedly the saving grace of a local network that's bound to die anyway. But I work as a fabricated online persona for a living, so who am I to judge?

YO: of course I'll pick you up
MAMÁ: thank you, mamita

I sigh, dropping my phone back into my purse, and stand. I turn and push forward over the gazebo railing, scanning the sea of faces for the one most familiar to me. People stand in tight circles across the garden. Some are laughing while others dance to the quick rhythm of tamboras and trumpets as the DJ plays a merengue mix. I catch a whiff of cigarette smoke as a group of guests walks by. Waiters dressed in white are spread out, all of them carrying trays of either alcohol or far-too-fancy hors d'oeuvres.

Finally, I spot Alejandro talking to his mother under a large mango tree illuminated by delicate torches and fairy lights. Ale's mother tells him something that makes him throw his head back and laugh, drawing a smile out of me. He blooms when he laughs, like a flower growing out of a crack on the sidewalk. It's a glimpse of his true self breaking out of his signature stony exterior. A wave of affection for him hits me square in the chest. After four years, the butterflies are quieter than they used to be, replaced by a lazy house cat that lounges in the living room day upon day. Sure, it doesn't move a lot, but you know it's there—breathing, eating, messing up your rugs. You can count on it. And then, once in a while, something takes the little monster by surprise and it startles. Like right now.

My smile freezes when Ale's mother pulls a little box out of her purse and hands it to him. Velvet? Leather? I can't tell from this far, but when Ale sees the box, his expression shifts to something between a frown and a smile. He opens the box. His eyes snap up to meet his mother's so fast it makes me let out a silent gasp. He's speaking, but I can't read his lips. His mother shrugs. It takes him a full two seconds, but he grins, wrapping her in the biggest hug I've ever seen him give anyone. Including me.

I watch the entire exchange, which can't have taken more than three minutes, in shock, which slowly evolves into fear and then excitement. The box is exactly the right size for a ring. And the moment is exactly the right moment to give a ring to your adult son to give to his girlfriend of four years. But it might not be a ring. It might be a . . . really small watch. Right?

Alejandro and his mother break apart, and in that brief second when they're still kind of holding each other, his eyes find me.

I look away, pretending I was stargazing the whole time. The movement is so fast my elbow knocks over a discarded champagne glass someone left on the railing. It shatters on the tile floor, splashing my shoes.

Great. Now my toes are wet and my shoes are slippery.

"There you are."

The lazy house cat jumps again at Ale's voice behind me.

"Hi!" I turn to him, grinning. I can't help but stare into the green eyes I know so well, get lost in them like I did when I was twenty-three and couldn't think about him without giggling. "Are you enjoying yourself?"

Don't mention the box, don't mention the box, don't mention the box.

"I'd be enjoying myself more if you weren't hiding in the gazebo." He looks up at me from the other side of the railing. Then he offers me his hand. "Come on. Dance with me?"

I grin. I love dancing, but Ale hates it. He's not great at it, so he avoids it as much as possible. But not tonight. Tonight is different.

This right here is the vision, the dream: him, asking me to go with him. Go dance, go eat, go back to bed. Go to a fancy party at his parents' place or to McDonald's after a long day. It doesn't matter. The answer will always be the same.

"Yes."

CHAPTER 2

IT'S BEEN THREE DAYS. NO PROPOSAL. NOT EVEN a mention of the box. If it wasn't a ring, then why hasn't he shown it to me? Who keeps a random box a secret? From his mother, no less. I think a graduation gift from your mother is the kind of thing you would show your girlfriend. I know if my mother had gotten me a graduation gift, I would have shown it to him.

"Marianto?"

Blanca—my co-worker and best friend—is looking up at me with doe eyes, a perfectly wild spray of brown curls framing her heart-shaped face. She seems to have been talking for a while.

I blink at her. "Yes?"

"Are you talking to Eugenia today?" she asks, and her tone indicates she's repeating herself.

"Oh." I shake my head. "Bad timing."

She turns back to her laptop and starts typing. "What's so bad about it?"

I scan our office's layout before leaning over her desk. Our workspace looks like a Swedish furniture store—minimalistic desks in pastel colors with cushioned chairs to match. Mine is a soft turquoise with a touch of baby pink, and the one next to mine is apple green. The waiting area, however, is bright and gleeful, almost like a preschool classroom; it sports a striped carpet designed by iconic artist Carlos Cruz-Diez, with abstractly shaped fuchsia and ocher chairs resting on it. Portraits of famous journalists and influencers hang from every wall—the only place you'll find Barbara Walters, Marta Colomina, and Kylie Jenner in the same room. I love the orchestrated mess of it all. It fuels creativity.

"I think Alejandro is proposing," I whisper, after two coworkers from the Advertising Department (whom we suspect are having a forbidden romance) walk past us.

Blanca's eyes double in size. "*Qué?!*"

"*Shhhh!*" I lean even closer, fighting a grin. "I don't want to get ahead of myself—"

"You already are."

"*But,*" I continue, "at his graduation party, his mother gave him a little box, which I'm pretty sure holds a ring."

Blanca narrows her eyes, sipping water from a Stanley cup she takes everywhere. "And you're ready to say yes?"

"Of course I am. I've *been* ready." I try to keep the nervousness out of my voice.

Blanca sighs, taking another sip of water. "Well, then, I don't see how that's bad timing to ask for a promotion. You've worked your ass off for five years."

"Weddings are expensive" is what I say because the truth is a horrible thought.

"All the more reason to ask for a promotion now," Blanca says. "More money."

"I know, but—"

At that exact moment, two things happen: My phone vibrates with a text notification, while Blanca's laptop chimes with another.

Mine is a text from Ale.

ALE: are you free for dinner tonight?

My heart jumps. I glance over at Blanca, who isn't paying attention to me anymore and is busy with her laptop.

I quickly type a response.

YO: Sí!
YO: of course I am.
ALE: ok. I'll pick you up at 7. Is Taiko okay?

I don't feel like eating Japanese food, so I suggest we to go Moreno instead.

ALE: sure. See you then.

We haven't had a dinner at a fancy restaurant in so long. Ay, Dios, what if today is the day?

As soon as the thought enters my mind, I can feel it in my bones. Soon, we'll be in our dream house in La Lagunita, having a late dinner because he had surgery that went longer than anticipated. But it's good, the guy made it, Ale saved his life. Our dog will be barking in the yard at the little frogs that never shut up. And the two of us will be together and anchored. Forever.

When I turn to Blanca, she's already watching me with something akin to urgency in her face.

"She's coming."

Around us, the entire office moves like clockwork. Two seconds later, in true Venezuelan-Miranda-Priestly fashion, Eugenia Fajardo—CEO, editor in chief, and complete badass—makes a straight line toward her office. Her hair is pulled into her signature silvery ponytail, not a strand out of place. She looks immaculate.

"Buenos días," Blanca and I mumble as she walks by Blanca's desk.

We turn to each other, wide-eyed, when Eugenia ignores us.

I watch her disappear around a corner, her step sure, and think back to the last five years. Eugenia will never promote me out of my current position if I'm engaged. My job as the current Ella consists of three elements: one, showing our followers and readers that the lifestyle we advertise is actually possible; two, running *Querida Ella*, our weekly relationship advice Q&A segment, which is currently what brings in the most engagement; three, doing the previous two through the magazine's social media. In the twenty-five years *Ellas* has existed, no one in my role has gotten engaged or married. She'll see it as validation, an opportunity to show her little love guru's advice actually works. She'll want it all documented.

I have one shot. If she says no, I won't be able to ask again for a long time. I'd have to quit. I can't risk losing this opportunity to impatience.

"I won't talk to her about the promotion today," I decide. "The timing isn't right."

"Maria Antonieta!" I jump at Eugenia's sharp command.

"Go, go, go," Blanca whispers, rolling her chair over to push me away.

I follow Eugenia to her office. People scatter, rushing to get to their desks and out of our way. Her personal assistant is waiting inside with coffee, sitting on Eugenia's chair to warm it like she does every morning. I stop before crossing the threshold. Quick outfit check—mom jeans, wine-red tank top, navy blue blazer, and my brown hair falling in soft waves to my elbows. It's effortless chic. It took me an hour to put it together.

I do my outfit run-through in the time it takes Eugenia to cross her office and sit at her desk and for her assistant to walk out.

"Good mor—"

"I don't see this week's schedule anywhere," Eugenia greets me. Her desk isn't pastel like ours. It's black-and-white. Blanca says it's to assert dominance over the rest of us. She's the mother and we're the babies, so our desks are baby colored. And fortunately/unfortunately, I'm her favorite kid.

Panic beats in my chest. "That's odd. I sent it on Friday. Like I do every week."

I did this right before I left for the weekend. A thorough, detailed social media plan for each day of the week, along with the graphics I'm going to post and the topic for Wednesday's "Hablemos de . . ." I'm pitching "Low-Budget Things to Do in Caracas." It's all planned out.

"Please, make my life easier and send it Monday morning before I make it to the office," she says. "I need it to be the first thing I see. I don't want to have to look for it two hundred emails down."

"Very well." Mental note: *Don't send emails Friday afternoon, even though you've been sending emails Friday afternoon for the last four years.*

But there are worse problems to have. Eugenia is incredible. To be the person she's taken under her wing is an honor.

After a couple of clicks and taps on her laptop, Eugenia looks up. "'Low-Budget Things to Do in Caracas'?"

Her already narrow eyes study me in what I *think* is confusion. Or murderous intent.

"Yes." I clear my throat. "I was thinking—"

"No," she cuts me off. "We don't do low-budget, you know this. And where's the romance in that? Make it about . . ." She snaps her fingers as she thinks. "Oh! 'Perfect First Date Spots in Caracas.'"

Not again, I think. Please, no more quirky, overpriced restaurants the government uses to launder money. Low-Budget in Caracas is something everyone can do. It's an opportunity for outsiders to explore the city when they come and for those of us who have been living here since the dawn of time to use to reconnect with it. I wish I could make her see that vision.

"Didn't we already do that last year?" I say instead.

"Yes, you're right." Eugenia taps one finger to her chin, then perks up. "I've got it! 'Perfect *Fifth* Date Destinations in Caracas.'" *Fifth date?* Fifth dates aren't a thing. "Make sure you don't repeat locations."

I blink. Once, twice. "Okay."

Because if I tell her it's not a thing, she's going to tell me to *make it a thing, then*. I don't want to spend the next month writing articles about how "he doesn't love you if he can't remember your fifth date anniversary."

"Everything else looks good." Eugenia ushers me away with bright red nails. "Get on it."

"Of course."

Back in my pastel cubicle, I go through the graphics I have prepared for each day of the week and choose one. These little affirmations are like our horoscope. There's a myth in the office claiming that whatever I post on Mondays will dictate the mood for the rest of the week. At first it was just for fun. Five years later, it's become weirdly accurate.

Today's affirmation reads *Do not beg for what does not want to stay* in cursive brown letters against a soft pink gradient background. Minimalist, cute, clean. Perfect to become someone's lock screen if they so desire.

I hesitate before posting it. Not quite sure why. But then I shake my head and follow it with a text story that says, "No begging esta semana, damas y caballeros." We're independent human beings, damn it, and that's the energy we're bringing to the week.

I turn to my laptop and log in to my work email. An ugly "237" welcomes me, signaling how many unread emails there are, all of them starting with "Querida Ella." At 8:00 a.m., the day already feels thirty hours long.

Squaring my shoulders for the second time today, I crack my knuckles. Time to tell people how to be just as happy as I am.

CHAPTER 3

I THINK I'M GONNA THROW UP. IN A GOOD WAY, IF such a thing exists.

Sitting on a bench outside my apartment building, I run both hands down my legs, smoothing the folds of the soft pink pleated skirt I decided to wear. I paired it with a silk spaghetti strap top in an effort to achieve a sophisticated yet casual look. That said, the night is chilly and since I didn't have a jacket to go with this look, I'm starting to freeze.

I double tap my phone to check for notifications, but it's empty. The time reads 6:57 p.m. Ale said he'd be here at seven. That's in three minutes.

The weight on my chest doesn't lift at that thought. If anything, it grows heavier. I don't know how to tell my body that this is a good thing. Why am I so anxious? I can't wait to marry Ale. I can't wait to have his cologne next to my perfume in the closet, for the hallways in our home to still smell like him even twenty minutes after he's left. I can't wait to buy groceries for two instead of one. I can't wait to say, *Oh, I have to check with my husband.* My husband. My family. Bound together by love and law, but most importantly by choice.

I double tap my phone again. 7:03 p.m. Still no messages.

The pavement glistens under the streetlights. Thick white clouds crown the peaks of the mountains circling the valley that is Caracas. The cold wind bites my cheeks, making my hair dance.

I check my phone again, by inertia, and see it's only been two minutes even though it's felt like two hours. Maybe Ale is late because he's driving carefully, or traffic today is particularly bad. Or maybe he died.

His car finally rounds the corner at 7:22 p.m., after I've called him five separate times. As soon as I make out his frame through the windshield, all is forgotten. The butterflies in my stomach bat their wings, the clouds part above me to let the stars and moon shine. I'm sure I even hear a bird chirping.

I push to my feet, smoothing my skirt again, as he slowly pulls to a stop. Legs shaking, I approach with a half grin. I pull the door open, flipping my hair over my shoulder, and find Alejandro . . . still in scrubs.

My grin falls as my elated heart drops to my stomach in disappointment.

"Hey," he says, while scrolling on his phone. "You look nice."

How would you know? the little duende living in my head asks, but I shush it. He knows because he saw me as he was pulling up. There's no reason to think he's lying. There must also be a good reason why he hasn't changed out of his work clothes, which, as I climb into the car, I notice have specks of blood on them.

"Was there traffic?" I try not to sound upset, because I'm not upset. Traffic is not abnormal in Caracas. In fact, it's the rule. It's a possible reason for why he was late.

But he shakes his head, shifting the gear to get us back on the road.

I study his profile the way I do every subject Eugenia asks me to write about. Analyze it. His jaw has a bit of stubble, unusual for him but not unheard-of. His posture is so stiff his back isn't even touching the seat. He's nervous. Or stressed. Or both. I've only seen him like this two other times.

The most recent was the day before his graduation. Ale couldn't even eat. The other was when he asked me to be his girlfriend, four years ago.

It was January 27 and we'd been texting back and forth for months. We'd gone out a couple of times with friends we had in common. Every time my phone chimed with an incoming *anything*, my heart would gallop. It didn't matter if I was at work, or my apartment, or the bathroom. Ale gave my life a much-needed buzz of excitement that I hadn't felt in so long.

That day, we'd been texting nonstop. I'd had the most horrible day at work and he'd failed a test. It had been raining in Caracas all day; every inch of the city was cold, even the birds were hiding away. Ale had asked me out the day before, just the two of us for the first time. I had been waiting for months for Ale to gather the courage to ask me out. Now, after this horrible day, I looked out through the window at the thick, white clouds looming over the mountains visible from my building and almost wanted to cry.

Then he texted:

ALE: what do we do?

Hands shaking, I replied.

YO: what do you want to do?
ALE: I want to go out with you.

YO: I want to go out with you too.

ALE: I'll be there in 30

Back then he didn't have a car. When he let me know he'd arrived, I rushed down and met him outside. He was standing in front of my building, still as a statue, soaked to the bone, out of breath. His lips were almost blue. The moment I opened the door, he climbed the steps two at a time. He reached me, softly grabbed the back of my neck, and drew me to him, sealing our lips with the most romantic kiss I'd had in my life.

An incoming neighbor cleared his throat, startling us. Ale jumped back, blinking as he moved out of the way.

"Perdóname," he panted. "I needed a win today."

I don't even remember what I said. But we decided to stay in, and later that night, sitting cross-legged on my living room carpet, after having dinner delivered and laughing until we forgot why we were stressed in the first place, Ale asked me to be his girlfriend, and I said yes.

It's that same stiffness I see in him now as he drives in front of Plaza Venezuela and flags hanging on tall poles wave in the wind outside. He's about to do something that scares him.

I almost ask, *Are you okay?*, but he reaches for the stereo and turns up the music before I have a chance, and the rapid stringing of a banjo followed by a heavy bass booms in the car. I recognize the tune as my favorite song by the band Caballo de Troya. The fresh combination of pop rock with folk instantly puts me in a better mood.

Alejandro quickly changes the playlist. To reguetón.

I narrow my eyes at him. For someone who knows how much I don't like música urbana, this is certainly A Choice.

A notification pops up on my phone.

BLANCA: tell me EVERYTHING!

Right. Tonight is special. It's just a song. It's probably a ploy to distract me—being late, the scrubs, the music . . . it's like he's not being romantic on purpose. A classic move.

"How was your day?" I ask, because I can't be alone with only my thoughts and Bad Bunny saying *Tití me preguntó si tengo mucha' novia'* as company.

"Good," he says without even a quick glance.

His response stings. I get that he doesn't want to seem romantic, but he doesn't have to be rude.

And because Ale is nothing if not thorough in all his endeavors, he turns up the music. No more talking.

Fine. The city streetlights casting their warm reflection on my window are all the company I need. I love Caracas best in the dark. There is nothing like a big city at night. Tall buildings, so many lit-up apartments that it's impossible to count. I might as well be living inside a Christmas tree. Everywhere you look, it feels like you're there for the first time. It's more exciting, more enticing. That's Caracas: wild and carefree by day, sophisticated at night.

The car is silent except for the soft hum of the sound system as one song follows another. I steal a glance at my future husband. He's staring ahead, eyes on the road, but seems lost in thought, so I let the wormhole that is Instagram suck me in. I log in to my personal account, which is private and which I hardly ever check anymore, considering my entire following is from *Ellas*. I'm swiping mindlessly from story to story until I land on Caballo de Troya and see a familiar flag. I sit up too fast, and the seat belt yanks me back. The colors are right—yellow, blue, and red. Horizontally. In that order. I count the stars forming an arch in the middle; they're all there. It's the Venezuelan flag. Posted by Caballo de Troya. In a black-and-white picture, lead singer Simón Arreaza is looking down at the camera, strong eyebrows raised in silent question.

The next story is a comment box.

If, hypothetically, one of us went to Venezuela, where should he go?

Holy crap. All sweaty hands, I'm typing a reply before I register what I'm doing.

Caracas. I'll give him a hypothetical tour.

My phone vibrates when Alejandro parks in front of a restaurant.

Oh god, I've been acknowledged. Not that it's hard. They have a little over fifty thousand followers, which sounds like a lot for a regular person, but for a band . . . *Ellas* has ten times that.

A smile escapes me when I see the response: another black-and-white photo depicting Simón Arreaza with his signature messy hair and Caballo de Troya hoodie, giving me a thumbs-up.

"Are you okay?" Ale asks from the driver's seat.

Face flushed, I lock my phone almost guiltily, even though I didn't do anything. "Yup."

Alejandro kills the engine with a sigh. "Okay."

He gets out of the car first and walks toward the restaurant with his hands deep in his pockets. Still in the car, I catch him sigh for what has to be the tenth time tonight. He blinks to the sky and swallows. I feel bad for him. I really wish I could end his misery, but I can't ruin this moment for us with my impatience. He planned for this proposal, he deserves to do it the way he wants to. Whatever he has up his sleeve, when he finally asks, I will say yes. Alejandro is perfect for me. Smart, funny . . . ish. Responsible, reliable. Marianto friendly. He's not an artist, which is a plus. Growing up with an actress who was constantly traveling for work made me realize two things early on: that I wanted to settle down young, and that I'd never be happy sharing a life with someone in the same line of business as her. I want an anchor, not a hot-air balloon. Ale is my anchor. He has been for the last four years.

The lazy cat in my stomach stirs as I get out of the car and Caracas's crisp February air wraps itself around me like the world's thinnest blanket.

I walk up to Ale and intertwine our arms. "I love this place."

The restaurant has an air of elegance and aristocracy. As Ale leads us in, my boots click softly on chessboard floors. The scent of herbs and spices wafts through the air, mingling with the fragrance of simmering sauces and soups, wine, coffee, and desserts. My stomach growls and I remember I forgot to have lunch. All I'm running on is coffee and anticipation.

A waiter is at our side immediately, smiling from ear to ear. "May I offer you a table?"

"Yes," Alejandro replies, then turns to me. "I need to use the bathroom. Can you take care of this?"

"Of course."

Ale untangles my arm from his and disappears down the hall, scratching the back of his neck.

I stare after him.

"Señorita?"

I blink, giving my head a soft shake, and focus on the waiter. "Table for two, please."

He leads me to the center of the restaurant. I would have chosen something closer to the windows so I could see the garden outside, but there isn't one available in that area. I let the waiter pull out a chair and take the seat with a smile.

"May I bring you something to drink in the meantime?"

"A virgin piña colada for me." I return the drinks menu. "And my boyfriend will have a Guinness."

He nods once, gracefully.

I wait for the waiter to leave, then fish my phone out of my purse like I'm a spy on a mission. I want to get my proposal on camera. My mother will want to send the video to all her friends. Plus, it's the kind of moment I'll want to relive over and over until the actual wedding happens.

Okay, what do I have at my disposal?

I remember my therapist's method to beat anxiety and put that to work, except instead of finding five things I can see, four things I can touch, and three things I can hear, I'm trying to find at least one thing I can use to hide my phone *while* filming a video at the same time.

I scan the table:

-The napkin holder.
-Salt and pepper shakers.

That's it, that's all we have on the table.

It'll have to do. Thank God for my white phone case, it'll camouflage with the napkins.

I curse when the phone slips from the napkin holder for the third time with a *smack!* but no one seems to notice. I see a light at the end of the tunnel when, with only a corner of the camera out, it stays in position. The video will be crap, but it'll do. Now I simply have to pray Alejandro doesn't need a napkin at any point in the night.

As if summoned, Alejandro pulls out the chair across from mine, startling me.

"Hey." He sits.

I start the recording through the napkin holder and pretend to forget about it.

I smile. "Hi."

Silence follows. My hands start to sweat. Not in a good way.

I wipe them on my skirt and clear my throat. "Um, so—"

"Marianto—" he says at the same time.

The waiter comes back with our drinks. Alejandro blinks up at him, confused. He places the glass of piña colada in front of me and the beer in front of Ale.

Ale stares at his bottle. "Uh—"

"Yeah, you're driving so I figured you wouldn't want too much alcohol," I say.

"Enjoy." The waiter steps back. "Let me know when you're ready to order."

"A toast?" I offer once he leaves.

Alejandro's eyes snap up to meet mine. "Marianto—"

"To the future?" I add.

Alejandro grabs the beer and drinks at least half of it in one gulp, eyebrows pinched together, his skin glistening with sweat. Now, *that* didn't happen when he asked me to be his girlfriend.

"Are you okay?" I ask.

Alejandro sets the bottle down on the table, eyes fixed on me. "Maria."

My throat dries at the name. Sure, it's my name, but with him I'm never Maria or Maria Antonieta. I'm Marianto. Maria is what my mother calls me when she's angry. I don't even introduce myself to strangers as *Maria.* I don't think any Maria is just *Maria*. That's like half a name.

I sit up straighter, trying to seem calm. No, I'm not calm, but he doesn't need to know that.

Ale casts his eyes down, fidgeting with his fork, trying to mask a guilt so evident I can't believe I didn't see it sooner. He's scared all right. He's probably about to confess he cheated on me with a colleague. Doctors are serial cheaters, that's what all the telenovelas and my mother say.

Alejandro finally looks at me, lips parted to speak, but his expression shifts from guilt to a panicked frown before anything comes out.

"Um, Marianto?" Ale's voice is hesitant.

"Qué."

He points to my hand. I'm clutching the butter knife as if I'm getting ready to stab him.

I unfurl my fingers and the knife lands on the table with a loud *clank*. I didn't even realize I'd grabbed it.

"What's going on?" I ask. Ale swallows. Tries not to look away. Fails.

"Mira, this isn't how I planned on having this conversation but—"

"What conversation?" I press.

"Marianto, I'm . . ." He pauses. Swallows again. I can physically feel time pass.

"What?"

"I'm trying to say it!" he snaps. Curious eyes around the restaurant turn to our table. He's never raised his voice at me before. "God, this is why I need a break. I feel like I can't even exist around you sometimes."

The world stills. *Not* in a good way. There's a ringing in my ears that drowns out every other sound in the restaurant and I think, *I must have heard him wrong.* I must have because I *think* my boyfriend of four years just told me, in a public place, that he needs a break from me. But that can't be. This is Ale. He checks every box.

"I'm sorry," Alejandro continues, eyes softer, so in contrast with what he's saying, while mine start to burn as soon as those words are out of his mouth.

It doesn't make sense. We're good. We're more than good.

"No entiendo. I thought . . ." He was going to propose. I thought he loved me. I thought he wanted me. I don't say any of that. "You brought me here." My voice is pathetically weak.

"You picked this place," he retorts, as if that's the point. "Which is so . . . perfectly us. I ask you to dinner, you pick the place, you don't even care if I like it or not—"

"You asked me to—"

"—*You* call the shots and I'm just along for the ride."

I shake my head, fighting tears because Camacho women don't cry in public.

"That's not true," I whisper.

"It's not?" He lifts both eyebrows. "You decided we'd get married four months after I graduated. You didn't ask me. You have a Pinterest board for our wedding I haven't even seen. You decided where we'd live, you have a spreadsheet for how much we have to save so we can afford it. You probably already know what our kids' names are gonna be. I've never had a say in anything. La Lagunita is the most expensive neighborhood in Caracas, Marianto. Do you even know how much I hate Caracas?"

"Why are you talking about marriage like I'm forcing you into it?" I ask.

"Because you are!" Ale exclaims. "I know that's what you expect now that I'm done with school, but I can't." He slumps back in his chair, running a hand down his face with a frustrated sigh. I watch from my chair, trying to file all this information into categories so I can understand. "I *just* graduated," he continues. "I need a break, okay? For most of the four years we've been together, I've followed your lead and I've done so happily. I was busy with school, so it was easier to let you take care of the details, but now things are different. People have expectations, I have decisions to make, I'm under enough pressure as it is and . . ."

He pauses to catch a breath or think, I don't know. He's speaking too fast, saying too many things, but all I hear is: I'm not sure about you.

Does anything else matter if he's not sure about me?

A tear slides down my cheek. I wipe it away before he notices.

"There's a job opportunity back home in Barinas and my family is begging me to take it," Ale adds. He makes an attempt to grab my hands over the table, but I yank them back. He flinches and nods, a movement so small it would be invisible if I hadn't been witness to it a million times before. "I know that doesn't fit into the plans you've made for us, or what you want for yourself. I need . . . time. To figure out what *I* want. I can't do that if we're together. I have to do it on my own."

And he stops speaking. Is he done?

I suppose the pause is for my benefit, but I'm waiting for the realization to hit. It doesn't. It's like he's a stranger. No, I didn't know he hated Caracas, he never told me. I also didn't know I ruled our relationship like a dictator, or that being with me was so awful, or that I basically stripped him of his free will. I didn't know *our* plans were actually *my* plans. I didn't know.

But I don't say any of that.

"So I'm the problem," I say instead.

Alejandro deflates. "*No.*" He grabs my hands across the table. This time I let him. "You didn't do anything wrong." Never mind that he just listed off every one of his complaints about me. "Marianto, I can't jump into the kind of commitment you want from me without being sure."

Those words are a needle to the bubble I was apparently living in. My biggest fear becoming a reality: He's not sure. After four years. I don't think I need to hear anything else.

Blinking fast, I push to my feet. The wooden chair I'd been sitting on screeches. There's rustling in the restaurant as all the noise rushes back to my ears, disorienting me for a second. People shift in their seats, pretending they weren't watching us. They're most likely thinking their dinner was ruined. Yeah, well, mine too.

"Marianto," Alejandro says, but doesn't do much else to stop me. "I just need some time."

Yeah, I got that. Hearing him say it again doesn't make it easier to digest.

I grab my purse and phone from the table. Damn, it's still recording. I stop the video, walking toward the exit. I've taken maybe five steps when I halt. There's something I need to know or I won't be able to sleep, obsessing over it. So I turn back and muster enough dignity not to retrace my steps. "Can I ask you one thing?"

Ale, shoulders slouched, turns at the sound of my voice, eyes clouded.

I look at him, study him like I did in the car, detailing the face I've seen from up close so many times before. The beautiful emerald eyes I love to get lost in, the bronze complexion I was always a little jealous of. I know him and I don't.

Ale nods.

I clear my throat. "At your graduation party. What did your mother give you?"

He frowns, tilting his head to the side. "My grandfather's graduation ring."

He lifts his hands to show me a grotesque, thick band of gold with a big topaz glinting front and center. It's on his right hand, index finger. I hadn't noticed it until this very moment.

So it *was* a ring. At least I got that part right.

A bitter laugh escapes my lips. I turn on my heel without another word and leave.

CHAPTER 4

FOUR YEARS. THAT'S HOW LONG ALEJANDRO AND I have been together. Gone in a ten-minute conversation. Was it even ten minutes? My XXL bag of Doritos crinkles when I hug it to my chest. I'm moping as I walk out of my kitchen, crushing the chips in the process. Caballo de Troya is blasting so loud I feel the sound waves moving around me. Helping me. Healing me.

"PORQUE YA NO TE NECESITO,
Y SI TE LLEGO A EXTRAÑAR POR UN DESCUIDO,
ESO AL RATO SE ME PAAASAAA!"

I yell the lyrics at the top of my lungs. Tears prickle my eyes. The words that shattered my reality mere hours ago are echoing inside my brain. The pressure in my chest makes it hard to breathe, and I have to remember the exercises I learned back when I was in therapy.

Inhale. Hold it. Exhale. Repeat until your eyes suck back the tears.

I groan and tear the bag of Doritos open with such strength that it explodes around me. Some land on my head, but most of them fall unceremoniously to the floor. I drop to the living room carpet and start eating them. I don't care. My eyes burn again. Small pieces of Doritos stab my knees. Getting them out of the carpet is going to be a pain. Ants will infest my apartment. I'll have to call a professional to get rid of them.

I angrily wipe the tears that escape. None of this was part of the plan. Tonight was supposed to be happy. It was supposed to end in tears of joy, not in this hole in my chest the size of Venezuela. We're supposed to be calling our families with the happy news. What about his birthday? It's coming up in a few weeks. I'd already made plans for it. I paid a deposit. I hired a caterer. Am I supposed to cancel that? And what if he regrets it before then? What will happen to his birthday party? What's going to happen to the rest of our plans? The house in La Lagunita, and the kids, and the dog, and the vacationing in Los Roques, which he still doesn't know about because I didn't get a chance to tell him. We're people who stick to the plan, we always have been. So why didn't he?

The usually comforting four walls that make up my tiny living room now feel suffocating, and I have to remember to breathe again. In and out, in and out. But breathing just makes it harder to keep the tears in.

Somewhere in the apartment, my phone vibrates.

Alejandro.

I crawl to the couch and start throwing pillows aside until I find it, wedged between cushions.

EUGENIA FAJARDO: Maria Antonieta, where is the Q&A you promised our followers for today?

My eyes fall shut. "Oh no."

This is what does it. In a matter of seconds my anxiety skyrockets; no technique is going to help me now. Tears stream down my face, my chest heaving as sobbing makes my entire body shake. How could I forget? It was supposed to go live at nine, but I have been having a breakdown since eight thirty. I send a quick reply: *I'm sorry, I'll do it right away.* Through teary eyes, I find the video and click *post.* Hopefully I can now mourn the pause on my relationship in peace.

God. A break. Like Ross and Rachel. We all know how *that* turned out. The urge to google "what to do when your boyfriend asks for a break" is strong, so I lock my phone and put it back on the couch where I found it. I walk down the hall to my room, switching off the lights as I go. I climb into my bed, then lie on my side as I pull the covers all the way over my head.

I hate crying, but all the willpower in the world wouldn't help me stop now. I cry, and I keep crying until I fall asleep.

THE PIERCING CRIES of macaws cuts through the still morning, stirring me awake. I sit on my bed, rubbing sleep from my eyes. My skirt has rolled up to my waist, leaving my legs bare. My top is attempting to strangle me. For a second, I'm confused as to why I fell asleep in last night's attire. Then I remember.

The scrubs, the restaurant . . . the break. I was hoping it'd all been a dream, but my swollen eyes confirm it wasn't. My chest hurts from sobbing, I didn't know that was possible—to physically feel a pain that should only be emotional.

My throat closes up again, and I hug my comforter closer. After last night, you'd think I wouldn't have any tears left, but you'd be wrong. I'll have to call in sick; there's no way I can show up to work like this.

I drag myself out of bed. I need to feed the birds, I need to find my phone, tell Eugenia I'll be working from home today and won't be showing my face.

At the kitchen, I grab two bananas. Then, in the living room, I pick up my phone from the couch, where I left it last night, and head to the balcony. I peel the bananas and place them on the railing before sitting on my lounge chair, grateful for the morning sun and its warmth.

There are four macaws here today—three yellow and blue, one green and red. They ruffle their feathers as they eat. Two of them are familiar, my regulars. I call them Marta and Pedro Luis. In my mind, they're married. The other two are smaller and new. They need names, in case they come back.

I'm stalling. My phone is cold in my shaking hands and I'm trying to ignore the stabbing pain of my soul, even though I feel it in my chest. What if I find a text from Alejandro saying we should turn this *break* into a *breakup*? I'm even more terrified I'll find nothing at all. At this point, I don't know what's worse.

I have maybe thirty minutes before I have to start getting ready for work if Eugenia says, *Absolutely not, if you're not here in five minutes you'll lose your job.* And she would. I wonder if that time would be better spent in blissful ignorance or if I should rip the off the Band-Aid.

As if deciding for me, my phone lights up with an incoming call. My heart picks up speed anticipating Alejandro, but Blanca's name flashes on the screen instead. I forgot to update her on yesterday's events.

"Aló?"

"Ay, gracias a Dios, you're awake," Blanca says. "Where *were* you?"

I frown. "I was sleeping."

"You haven't checked your phone since last night?" Blanca asks, her voice urgent.

"Not since posting the Q&A." I clear my throat. "Things . . . happened with Alejandro."

"I know. I'm so sorry, reina."

"Yeah, he—" I sit up. "What do you mean you know?"

On the balcony railing, Marta and Pedro Luis bicker with the other two birds.

"There is no easy way to tell you this, so here goes." Blanca pauses. "Marianto, you didn't post the Q&A, you posted a video of Alejandro breaking up with you."

My stomach drops. I stand up so fast I knock over a small succulent I've been trying to keep alive.

I deleted it. I thought I deleted it. At the restaurant. Didn't I? Please, God, let me have deleted it. But when I log in to the account, hands shaking so much that keeping a steady grip on the phone is a whole separate task, the video is there. Eight minutes, twenty seconds long. First thing on our feed. I move to my photo gallery, and sure enough, the Q&A video is sitting happily next to it with a bright pink thumbnail.

This can't be real. I stare at my phone in shock for I don't know how long. I'm hoping I'll wake up and confirm I didn't actually post a video of Alejandro breaking up with me on the magazine's account. Please, let this be a dream.

But numbers don't lie. My notifications confirm it. Over a thousand messages on Instagram. Thirty-five missed calls from Eugenia. And one solitary text from Alejandro:

Did you get home okay?

I sink to the floor, clutching the phone to my chest. It's all too much. Alejandro hitting the brakes on us, on our plans, saying I'm controlling, pressuring him to get married . . . and now thousands of people know about it. Eugenia knows about it. I haven't had a chance to internalize it, let alone tell her.

God, my mother probably knows about it already too. It's like I built my life on a sandcastle I woke up to find crumbling.

Respira, I remind myself. In and out, in and out. I'm about to hyperventilate. I can feel it. And I'm alone.

"Marianto?" Blanca says, still on the call.

This is bad. This is very bad.

My mouth dries. I try to swallow my anxiety, along with the urge to get in the shower and cry. I need water. I'm probably dehydrated from crying so much and from all the sodium in the unholy amount of Doritos I consumed last night. So, water. And then I should eat a banana. And then I need to . . . move to a deserted island? And hope no one ever finds me.

But first I take the video down. The stats hit me like a brick. Eight hundred thousand views. I don't even know if we lost followers because we gained like fifteen thousand more. Five thousand comments.

"OMG I WOULD DIE!"

"Why would ANYONE break up with their partner at a fancy restaurant?"

"Is it too soon to ask if he's available? Demasiado bello!"

"Ay, mami, pero es que tú también . . ."

Nausea builds in the pit of my stomach. I'm going to throw up. Or faint. Or both.

Dios.

I need to shower, get dressed, and go to the office—there's no way I can stay home now—but I'm paralyzed on the cold floor of my balcony as the birds, my loyal companions, fly away one by one.

CHAPTER 5

BLANCA LOOKS UP, STARTLED, WHEN SHE HEARS the door open. Her expression is pinched with concern as I march past her. The office smells like freshly printed paper and coffee. The ever-present hum of many voices whispering at once, pitched high and low, suddenly disappears as I zigzag my way between cubicles toward Eugenia's office. It is painfully obvious they were talking about me. It is even more painful to know they will keep talking about me as soon as I'm out of earshot. They'll probably talk about this for a while.

"Sweetie, are you okay?" Blanca's voice is soft behind me. I wasn't aware of her following me. "You look a little . . ."

I stop and turn to her. She assesses me, her brows furrowed. I know my choice of no makeup, hair pulled into a messy bun, *and* sneakers instead of some type of heel makes me look like I came straight from the gym, but I didn't have the time or energy to stage a whole production like I do every morning.

"Yes?" I demand.

She swallows. "Unhinged."

Perfect. Just what I was going for. "I'm fine," I lie. "I need to talk to Eugenia and then I'm going to take the rest of the day off."

Blanca winces. "Babe . . ."

"It'll just be a second." Hopefully.

I turn back toward Eugenia's office. This time Blanca doesn't follow.

I find my boss sitting behind her desk, not one single strand of hair out of place, typing furiously into her phone. A fresh wave of nausea hits me. I break out into a cold sweat. I don't know what I was thinking. She's going to tell me this meeting could have been an email, even though it absolutely couldn't have. I shouldn't have just come, I should have called first. I should have apologized profusely and asked if she'd be willing to meet with me.

I'm thinking about bolting, but before I have a chance to make a run for it, she looks up. The only part of her body that moves are her penetrating black eyes.

The fear that settles in my chest is like nothing I've felt before. Her black-on-black-on-black attire, her hair pulled back, and her bloodred lips make her seem positively murderous. Yeah, this could have been an email.

In a movement that is almost feline, Eugenia puts her phone down as she reclines on her chair, crossing one leg over the other while lifting her left hand to support her chin.

I make myself walk in. There's no reason to be afraid. I made a mistake. No one gets fired over one solitary mistake. And I'm not an intern, fresh out of college. I've been working here for five years. That's not nothing. She's not going to fire me. And showing my face here today instead of hiding at home shows professionalism.

"Maria Antonieta." Her voice is sharp, cutting, as she utters my name. "I didn't think you'd be showing up to work today. Or ever."

I swallow hard. Okay, maybe there is a little reason to be afraid. "Eugenia, I understand you must be furious. I would be too. But if you let me explain—"

"No." She stops me. "No explaining. Sit."

I obey. The cold metal of the chair presses into my arm as I lean forward in anticipation.

"You're fired," she says. My eyes go wide, my body shooting forward. It's a simple statement, like telling someone today is Tuesday. "Effective immediately."

My mouth is instantly dry, like cotton, as she falls silent with a smile. A lump grows in my throat as the reality of my situation dawns on me. Five years, wasted. Getting coffee, getting yelled at, being promoted to columnist, Eugenia taking me under her wing and making me a less menacing version of herself. I did it all in the hopes that she'd see the potential in me and allow me to cover events, meet artists, write reviews, give a voice to the talented voiceless. Like she does. And now I have to start over.

"Eugenia," I try. *Be reasonable*, I want to say, but I have a feeling she won't take that well. "I know I messed up. I will issue a public apology. I'll do whatever you want. If you give me another chance, I swear nothing like this will ever happen again."

She huffs. "Do you really expect me to let you give love advice to my readers after this?" I wince. "In case you forgot, you violated the sanctity of our Ella. We sell people dreams, a promise of a happily ever after, and now you've ruined that. You broadcast your breakup to our entire readership and left it up for twelve hours." Eugenia picks up a pen from her desk and starts clicking it. "You write a relationship column, Maria. Last night you lost all credibility. No one is going to take advice from a woman who got dumped for being too controlling. Your breakup, unfortunately, is now a liability to the company."

"But we didn't break up." I don't know what force of hell propels me to say this. "We're on a break. Didn't you hear what he said?"

Eugenia tilts her head to the side. "Querida, *everyone* heard what he said."

"Then you know." I run both hands down my jeans to wipe off the sweat. "We'll be back together before you know it. This is just a temporary setback." But she's already shaking her head. I grip the edge of her desk. "Please don't fire me. I really need this job. I love this job!" I hate how desperate I sound, how my voice is coming out all shaky. "All publicity is good publicity."

Eugenia leans forward, pins me with a look I can't quite define. She's studying me, searching for I don't know what. Silence falls over us like a wet blanket. My hands are sweating again. Sitting on this uncomfortable metal chair under her scrutiny makes me feel like a child in the principal's office.

I can't take it anymore. "Please, I'll do anything."

Her eyes get lost somewhere behind me. Her thinking face. Or her *I'm about to screw you over* face. They're interchangeable.

"Muy bien," she finally says. I perk up. "Since you're so sure your ex is coming back, I want you to document it. What you said, what he said, who begged who. What works and what doesn't work. I want insight into the process of mending your broken relationship."

I deflate. Oh no. Alejandro tolerates my "influencer" lifestyle. He doesn't condone it, and he definitely does not encourage it. The only reason he's not actively against it is because my identity is kept deliberately vague. As a result, so is his.

"I'm not sure I can do that." I picture Alejandro's face when he hears I want to document our way back to happiness. It's not very happy. "It's not just my privacy, it's Alejandro's too."

"Then talk to Alejandro." As if it were that easy. "Unless it's a definitive breakup and you're trying to con me into giving you your job back. In which case, you can forget about finding work anywhere remotely reputable. You need a good reference from me, which, at the moment, I'm not too keen to give."

"No!" I jump to my feet. "No, we're definitely getting back together. This is temporary."

I remember his text, which I still haven't answered because I'm dealing with *this* dumpster fire first. He sent it last night and he didn't sound angry, so chances are he sent it before the video went viral. And he asked if I got home okay. That means he still cares.

"It's settled then." Eugenia's narrowed eyes are almost predatory. "I can see it. It'll be just like *How to Lose a Guy in 10 Days*. Except it's 'How to Win a Guy Back.'" My eyes widen. "We can't use 'How to,' though. Too cliché. We need another format."

I blink, hoping she'll stop talking long enough for me to make sense of what she's saying. But she simply waves the title problem off with a nonchalant, "I'll come up with something." She smiles that wolfish smile of hers, sending chills down my spine. "If you pull this off, I'll give you your job back."

"I'm still fired?" I ask, my voice pathetically soft.

"Of course you're still fired." Eugenia laughs. "You broadcast your breakup on the company's social media."

I wince at the reminder. It's what I deserve. It's what anyone else in Eugenia's position would have done. But I'm still shocked that after five years of working for her, four of those years under her personal tutelage, Eugenia would let go of me so easily. I'm about to walk out of her office—which I helped decorate—without a job. A strange force possesses me. Perhaps it's the freedom of knowing that I have nothing left to lose, or a brief psychotic lapse, but even I'm surprised to hear the words that tumble out of my mouth next:

"What if I don't want my old job back?"

Eugenia's eyebrows shoot up, surprised for the first time since I sat here. Probably for the first time since I started working here.

I continue. "What if I want to write the kind of articles *you* write?"

"You want to be in Arte y Cultura?" she asks.

I nod once, half nervous, half nauseated.

Eugenia smirks, resting her back against her chair with a chirring sound as she twirls a pen between her fingers.

"All right," she finally says. "Write the article, prove to me you've outgrown writing love advice, prove to me you're ready for bigger pieces, and I'll consider promoting you to the Arts and Culture team. It'll be your swan song before you move forward."

A part of me says, *No, you're better than this*. But am I? I need a job. And I don't want to spend three years climbing a new ladder. This is just a bump in the road. Nothing but a nightmare I'll soon wake up from. Before I know it, everything will be back to normal. There's no good reason why Ale should refuse. He let me share little insights into our relationship before, albeit begrudgingly. Why would this be any different? Why shouldn't I accept? I'll be back here next week. I won't even have to break into my savings.

"Okay. I'll do it."

Eugenia grins. "Perfect. You have two months."

She rises to her feet as she offers me her hand. I take it. "It won't be that long."

Eugenia releases my hand. "I should hope not."

Sitting back down, she taps her iPad and it blinks to life. A clear dismissal. As I leave, I don't give myself time to become nostalgic. Soon, I'll be back in this office telling her my plan for the week. *No*, I'll be back here telling her about a new band, a new restaurant, a new event. It won't take two months.

Outside, I fish my phone out of my purse to check the time and my heart soars when I see I have a new message from Alejandro.

ALE: you posted our breakup on Instagram?!

CHAPTER 6

I DON'T HAVE ENOUGH TIME TO PROCESS ALE'S text before he's calling me.

"I can't believe you went and posted our breakup on social media," he says as soon as I pick up. No *Hello*, no *How are you holding up?* Nothing.

The word *breakup* hurts in my gut. I thought we were "on a break."

"It was an accident," I tell him.

"An accident?" He huffs. "An accident is when you butt dial your doctor, Marianto. What the hell were you filming us for?"

Three steps short of my car, I stop. His words are fists squeezing my heart. I feel my cheeks warm. I'm such a fool. I was so excited, hiding my phone in the napkin holder, missing all the signs.

A light breeze grazes my skin. A dog is barking in the distance while I tune out the sound of people talking as they move around me. The sky is a striking blue, no clouds in sight. The outline of El Ávila—the mountain that rounds the valley that is Caracas—is perfectly visible, and I look to it for strength. Part of me doesn't want to answer Ale's question and make an even bigger fool of myself. The other part says, *Hey, it's Ale, we can tell him anything.*

This is the part that wins. "I thought you were proposing."

The line goes silent long enough that I manage to get into my car, but I know he's still there. I feel him as if he was sitting beside me, fumbling with the A/C so the airflow doesn't hit him in the face, the way he always does.

Alejandro curses under his breath, almost in defeat. I'm not sure he even meant for me to hear, but to me it's like he whispered it into my ear. It takes me back to that first time he kissed me outside my building. To his hand cupping my face, his thumb drawing circles on my cheek; his out-of-breath, rapid one-word responses, and the smile that followed.

I swallow through the lump in my throat and blink until my eyes don't sting anymore.

"I'm sorry about the video," I whisper. Ale sighs, but stays silent. "Do you think we could . . . I don't know, talk about it over coffee or something?" I force a smile into my voice. "My treat."

Ale clears his throat. "I don't think so."

His words knock the air right out of me. "But last night . . ." I attempt. "You texted."

"We should probably not see each other for a while." His tone is final.

"Ale."

"Goodbye, Maria."

He hangs up before I can get anything else out. I stare at my phone, needles prickling my eyes. Even though I'm sitting in my car, I feel like I'm falling. I've been pushed off a cliff. My future is nothing but fast-approaching waves crashing against sharp rocks, and there is no one to catch me.

Inhala, exhala. Do not cry.

People in Caracas mind their business, they hardly stop for anything. So there's no reason why I should believe they would stop for me, but I do. I picture an old man bent outside my window, telling me to get it together. I picture a little girl asking her mother why the lady in the red sedan is crying.

My phone vibrates in my hand. My heart races, hope igniting in my chest, before I realize it's just an alarm.

Pick up Mamá at the airport.

"Perfect," I mutter, laying my head on the steering wheel. I don't care who's watching.

MY USUAL OLIVE coloring is gone, replaced with pale, tight skin, like a mask. My hair is tangled and matted from tossing and turning all night, pulled up in the messiest of buns. The cloud of defeat around me is dense. I can't believe I marched into Eugenia's office looking like this. I can't believe I'm going to let *my mother* see me like this.

I groan, looking into the rearview mirror at the line of cars behind me. I see a couple jump into each other's arms, a cutesy airport reunion that makes me nauseous. Thirty seconds later, there's a knock on the passenger side window that makes me jump. My mother waves enthusiastically. She's in a green velvet jumpsuit, a travel pillow resting on her shoulders.

No llores, no llores, no llores, I repeat in my head five hundred times as I unlock my car and climb out to help her with her luggage. It's amazing that I have any tears left. You'd think I'd have run out by now. But as soon as I'm out of the car, she rushes to my side and pulls me down by the neck, wrapping me in a soul-crushing hug I had no idea I needed this much, and I break down. I'm twelve years old again, waiting for her to come home from shooting to let her know my best friend died from a stroke. I'm fifteen, begging her to come with me to find my dog, who escaped while I was taking out the trash. And she was not able to make those things better; my friend was still dead and my dog was still missing, but she hugged until there weren't any tears left. She held me like she knew. Now, in this parking lot, clinging to each other in the midst of the busy airport, the thrum of engines and whirr of propellers from planes taking off above our heads, she holds me like she knows.

Mamá takes a step back, her deep brown eyes—the very same ones I have—searching my face as her thumbs brush over my cheeks, drying my tears. "Mamita, are you okay?"

My throat closes up again at the sound of a voice I'm more used to hearing over the phone nowadays. She stands a couple of inches shorter than me: Her newly dyed caramel hair frames her tanned face in soft waves, baby highlights catching the sunlight, giving her a youthful look. In my current state, she must seem like my younger sister.

I nod. "I'm okay. I missed you."

It's a lie. She knows it's a lie. I wait for her to push, to call me out, but she doesn't. She simply accepts it, pats my cheek a couple more times, and says, "I missed you too."

"OKAY, SO THIS is the kitchen." I point at it from the hall. "Mugs, plates, glasses are all in the top cabinets. Cleaning supplies are under the sink. And the oven doesn't work, so I use the air fryer."

I live in a two-bedroom, two-bathroom apartment. The kitchen is two strides away from where we're standing in the living room, which is the first thing you see when you walk through the door. I'm renting it from Blanca's elderly great-aunt. It smells slightly of dust and mothballs, which made me develop a severe addiction to allergy medication. It's located in Altamira, which gives my online persona an air of sophistication. To maintain the illusion, I only take pictures on the balcony, overlooking the city. Inside, the apartment is mostly wood and orange tile floors that will clash with every single item someone might bring in. It's like living inside a pumpkin.

Beside me, my mother frowns, assessing. "How do you make a cake?"

"I don't."

I buy cake. One slice, because I am one person, and my boyfriend doesn't eat refined sugar.

Ex-boyfriend, my brain immediately corrects, and the weight in my chest returns.

"And how will *I* make a cake?" my mother asks, bringing me back before I drift too far.

"Do you need to bake a cake?"

She shrugs. "I might."

"We can buy a cake," I reply, taking a step down the hall toward her bedroom.

Out of all the things we could be talking about . . .

"Unacceptable," she says. "I'm going to get you a new oven."

I halt. "Why?" I don't need a new oven. Hell, if we tried to fit a new *anything* in this apartment, a wall might fall on us. It is that old. "You really don't have to do that. I don't cook that much."

"Why not?" She steps into the kitchen and starts measuring my stove with her hands.

"Well, because my job—"

The realization hits me before I can finish the sentence. *My job.* No more coupons or collabs with restaurants and coffee shops. If Alejandro and I don't get back together soon, I'm going to have to start paying for food. Or worse. I'll have to learn how to cook.

I clear my throat. "Anyway." I point to the door down the hall. "That's your room."

Mamá beams, rushing to my side. "I get my own room?" She grabs my shoulders and squeezes me against her before walking around me to get ahead. "I thought we were going to bunk together in your room like when you were chiquitica."

When I was little we had to share a room because that was all we could afford while she was out trying to become an actress, but I don't remind her of that. She made it. And made it big. Now she can afford to buy me a new oven and everything. That's what matters.

I follow her into my guest room. It's bigger than mine; it came with a closet, dresser, and a king-sized bed. The only reason I didn't take this room for myself is because Blanca said her great-uncle passed away in his sleep on that bed. I don't tell Mamá this.

"Do you think my podcast set would fit in here?" Mamá asks.

"I'm sorry, your what?"

"My set," she explains. "For my podcast. Can you help me set it up?"

"Uh—"

Goodness gracious, an oven *and* a podcast set. My left eye twitches. This is fine. It's not like my life is falling apart. It's not like I'm notoriously bad with change.

She springs up with a clap. "Oh! Would you be my guest?"

God, help me.

"My daughter, the influencer, ladies and gentlemen." Right. "We'll talk about how growing up in the entertainment industry shaped your brilliant future." She pulls me down for what has to be the tenth hug in the last three hours. "I am so happy to be here with you." Her embrace tightens. "This is going to be just like the old days. You and me against the world. Aren't you excited?"

I gulp. I suspect my shortness of breath has less to do with her grip around my shoulders and more to do with the dread settling in the pit of my stomach.

But she's my mother. So I answer her question. "Ajá. So excited."

CHAPTER 7

DAY ONE OF TRYING TO WIN MY BOYFRIEND BACK starts as any other day: with my laptop and a spreadsheet. Research tells me couples get back together reasonably fast if the issues that led to the breakup are minor, which I believe ours are. If you really think about it, we're not even broken up, we're on a *break*. And breaks sometimes get fixed. Like when Rachel regretted the break immediately after. It's a horrible example. The thought makes my throat close up, but it does happen.

It's only been three days since the restaurant, I remind myself. This is all normal. Crying is not a sign of weakness. It's a sign of being alive. It's a sign of holding too much love inside your heart and realizing it has no place to go. Everyone in my position would cry. And I'm alone. I'm allowed.

I need to keep these facts at the ready, to pull them out whenever I need to. *It's normal, he does love you, you didn't make it all up. It's temporary, couples get back together reasonably fast when the issues are minor. Our issues* are *minor. They* are.

Outside my bedroom, the *clank!* of something metallic hitting the ceramic floor reminds me that I am, in fact, not alone. That my mother could barge into my room at any second, so

I'm not allowed to cry until she leaves because the last thing I want is someone fussing all over me.

I focus on my spreadsheet again. It's empty. How am I supposed to plan an article on how to get my boyfriend back when the only thing I want is to call him and beg him to come to his senses? That's not very *Ellas* of me.

Groaning, I lean back on my chair. A soft squeak echoes around my bedroom, a sound I'd never noticed before, and I realize I can't remember the last time I sat at this desk with enough time to lean back, enough time to look up at my ceiling and notice a crack by the top right corner or the cobweb on my lamp. It's past eight in the morning. I should be at my pastel cubicle, a cup of steaming coffee next to me, giving people advice on how to live their best lives, how to spice their relationship up, what kind of gift to get for the one-week anniversary. I should not be sitting in my bedroom at an old desk, on a squeaky chair, plotting how to get my life back with a tightness in my chest like God is choking me.

What is it old ladies say? *Dios aprieta pero no ahorca.*

"God squeezes but doesn't choke, my ass," I mutter.

I sit back up. The screen is still empty. My brain is empty too. And the only person I want to talk to about this wants a break from me. The urge to call him is so strong, I feel it radiating from every pore, electricity coursing through my body, making it almost unbearable to sit still. I just need to feel some kind of familiarity. I've been falling into a dark hole for the last three days and there seems to be no bottom, nothing to hold on to, nothing to anchor me or steady me.

Screw it.

I move from the desk to my bed. Sitting cross-legged, I grab a pillow and place it on my lap. Before I can regret what I'm doing, I pull up his contact and compose a text.

YO: this is so hard.

I study the words, their edges and curves, and the little arrow by the corner waiting for me to tap it and hit *send*. The last time Alejandro and I talked was two days ago, but each painful minute has felt like an eternity.

I hit send before I can regret it.

The next few seconds are excruciating, adrenaline burning just under my skin. I know Ale is awake. I know he's most likely sitting at his breakfast table, pretending plain coffee is a meal before he rushes out the door to the hospital. I know he drinks coffee while reading the news on his phone. And I know that when he's done, he catches up on any messages he might have received while he was going through his morning ritual. *So, come on, Ale. Read it. Catch up with me.*

"Cariño, I'm leaving!" Mom announces from the hall, startling me. "Dios te bendiga!"

A gush of air escapes my lips as I press a hand to my chest. "Okay, have a good day!"

My phone vibrates in my palm. I hadn't noticed he was typing back.

ALE: I know.

He knows?

I push the pillow aside. Hope flares in my chest. Maybe I won't even have to write that damn article. Maybe he's having his Rachel moment. And I didn't sleep with anybody, so we should be fine. He knows. It's hard for him too. And if it's hard for him too—

Another text comes through.

ALE: but it's for the best

No. It isn't.

ALE: you may not realize it now, but we both need this.
ALE: it'll be good for us. You'll thank me one day
YO: are you sure about that?

It takes him a full minute to reply. I hold my breath for the entirety of it.

ALE: no

I stand. Pacing my bedroom, I conjure a message that will convince him of what an awful idea this is. We belong together. Everyone thinks so. By everyone I mean me and my readership. If he's not sure, then whatever issues he thinks we might have, we can work through together.

ALE: I have to go, my shift starts in ten minutes and I haven't left the house.

My text is only half done. I backspace until it's gone.

YO: okay. Have a good day.

I wait five full minutes. He reads the text but doesn't reply. The lack of response stings, but not enough to dim the realization that this so-called break is as hard on him as it is on me. I can work with that. All I need to do is remind him of the days when he was so sure about me that he didn't mind entertaining my silly dreams of marriage and kids and homes; the days when he didn't mind making himself the hero in all of them. I don't know how well this will work out, this . . . experiment. But it's the first spark of an idea I've had since walking out of Eugenia's office.

Standing in the middle of the room, still clutching my phone for dear life, my spine straightens. That's it. As soon as the word "experiment" crosses my mind, I see my article. Not a "How-To." An "Experiment." Adrenaline courses through my body as I yank a drawer open and grab my notepad and a pen and start scribbling.

The Get Your Ex Back Experiment.
The Felices Para Siempre Experiment.
The Ex-Novio Trials.

These are all terrible, but when I tell Eugenia, we'll figure it out.

The excitement of a sparkling new idea is enough to make me forget about the reasons why I need to write this article in the first place for all of ten seconds. My previously blank brain is not blank anymore. I pitch the idea to Eugenia before I have time to overthink it. She replies within seconds.

EUGENIA: no

I deflate. Then another text follows.

EUGENIA: El Ex-Perimento.

My eyes skim the words over and over until they sting. I feel myself smile. It's perfect. A series of experiments, trial and error, with one goal in mind: happily ever after. Slowly, it takes shape in my head: a walk down memory lane—a throwback to the happiest moments of our relationship—highlighting some of the most romantic spots in Caracas. Eugenia will have no option but to promote me after reading it.

I start listing the places we'll visit first, my heart pounding as my hand cramps. This will work. I know it. My life will be back to normal in no time.

CHAPTER 8

THE EDGES OF MY PHONE DIG INTO MY PALM, TATtooing a fine red line on the inside of my hand. My leg bounces up and down as I sit on the couch. I'm hunched over the phone, holding it so close to my face it can't possibly be good for my already decaying sight.

It's been twenty-four hours since I launched Experiment #1: ***Evoke a memory.*** I decided to start small by posting a picture Ale took of me when we went to La Colonia Tovar to celebrate our first-year anniversary. In it, I'm surrounded by sunflowers, my hair is shorter than it is now, and bangs frame my face, giving me a rounder look. I'm wearing a yellow sundress. I match the flowers. Two seconds after he snapped the photo, I got stung by a bee on the cheek. It's a cute memory.

My personal Instagram account is private, but the post has had enough engagement that the possibilities of Ale not seeing it are virtually zero. Three of his cousins have liked it. One went so far as to leave a comment. Five yellow hearts. That means something. But Alejandro? Nothing. This was supposed to remind him of brighter days when we were young and drunk with love, celebrating that we'd made it through a year, and if we made it through a year, we could make it through two or three or four and so on forever.

I bite a corner of my lower lip, considering my next move. It's been twenty-four hours. There's no way he hasn't checked his socials in twenty-four hours. He takes his phone to the bathroom, for God's sake. With a few taps, I go into his profile and find our mutuals, all seventy-nine of them, looking for someone who posted around the same time I did. I find the cousin who left the hearts. Her last post was eighteen hours ago. She has thirty-four likes. He's one of them.

Seeing his name sends a shot of pain through my chest. So he *has* been checking Instagram. He just decided not to engage with me.

To say this experiment is not going the way I planned would be an understatement.

A rattling sound comes from the kitchen, telling me my mother has started the dishwasher.

"Come on." I shake my phone. "Say something."

"*—I know, I'm so worried about her—*" My mother's voice reaches me from the kitchen.

Slowly, I sit up. Who is she talking to? And more importantly, does she think I can't hear her? We're sharing a matchbox of an apartment.

"*—you know how many times I tried to tell her he wasn't good for her.*" Oh, God. Unwittingly, I've risen to my feet, inching closer to the hallway leading to my kitchen, where I can hear her pacing. The dishwasher stops running. A cupboard is shut. A plate is placed on the granite. "*Of course I'm not trying to pick a fight, François. I'm keeping the peace.*"

Anger ignites in my chest. Ever since the breakup my emotions have been at surface level. Hearing my mother talk about me like I'm a child who doesn't know better is the last thing I need. I'm no longer a child, and this is my house. That I live in. That I've been paying for on my own for the last five years. By myself. She can't talk about me like that in my own house.

I have half a mind to march into the kitchen and tell her exactly this, but I can't. She's my mother. The only one I have. The only one I'll ever have. Good children respect their parents, and I am a good daughter. *Talento V*, the show she's here to host, starts shooting on Monday and it will only last twelve weeks. Eighty-four days. Then she'll go back to her life as a Venezuelan in Miami, living it up with her French husband and only seeing her daughter once a year in Cancún or Puerto Rico, for no more than a week. The way God intended. By then, Alejandro and I will be back together, I'll be working at *Ellas* again, and everything will be in its rightful place.

"Twelve weeks," I whisper to myself.

I swallow my anger, grab my keys from the dining table, and leave. This doesn't have to bother me. So, it won't. I have work to do.

EXPERIMENT #1 WAS a disaster. No interaction whatsoever. Not even a pitiful like. Nothing.

I'm hoping Experiment #2: ***Be unpredictable (so he knows I'm not a control freak)*** works better. Since I can still see Alejandro's location on my phone, I tracked him down to a new sushi place in El Hatillo where he's having dinner. It's not weird if he hasn't turned it off and I use it to my advantage.

"Remind me why we're doing this?" Blanca says from the passenger seat. "You hate sushi."

Untrue. I've never tried sushi because I refuse to eat raw

fish. I'm allergic to the majority of seafood, so I can't take risks when it's also uncooked. But Ale loves sushi, and what better way to show I'm unpredictable than choosing, out of nowhere, to try his favorite food for the first time at the new place where he also happens to be?

"Because love will triumph in the end," I tell her. "Who knows? I might like it."

I park in front of the restaurant. The first thing I notice is that instead of windows, it has giant fish tanks filled with fluorescent little fish that must have been genetically altered—yellow, blue, pink, orange, and purple. I bet they glow in the dark. Beside me, Blanca also stares at the fish.

"That must be illegal." She undoes her seat belt.

"Yeah." I grab my purse from the backseat, find my EpiPen, and hand it to her. "You're responsible for this."

"You mean for your life?"

I nod, unbuckle my seat belt, and climb out of the car.

Blanca walks in before I do, pushing against the heavy metal door. Inside, the ambience is dark. There are mini fish bowls on every table as centerpieces. The ceiling is lined with LED lights, changing color according to the beat of the music. "We Can't Be Friends" by Ariana Grande is playing, so the changing of the lights is slow but perfectly timed. A woman stands beside the door, holding an iPad. Blanca engages in conversation with her, but my attention is on the familiar figure sitting by the bar. The music, the lights, the fish fade into the background. The space that physically separates us seems to disappear as well. We're the only two people to exist here. We're the only two people to exist in the universe.

Alejandro hasn't seen me. He's sitting with his back to the door, one arm propped on the bar, leaning on it. He's wearing a baby blue button-down, the sleeves rolled up like always. He's untucked his shirt. This is relaxed Ale. The sight makes my heart ache.

"Marianto?" Blanca grazes my elbow with her fingertips. "They have a table for us."

"Oh, great!" But I'm not even looking at her. Ale's posture is slouched, he's balancing on a barstool, a beer beside him. He never slouches. But one of his friends says something and he throws his head back and laughs. He doesn't look tired or heartbroken. He seems happy.

Blanca has to drag me away from the door. Away from Ale.

Once we're seated, I've lost visibility of Alejandro. The screens and bamboos won't let me see.

"We're stealing these, right?" Blanca asks, tapping the bowl housing two pink GloFish.

I scan the restaurant, making sure no one heard her. "Of course not."

Blanca laughs. "Relax. You're very tense."

"Of course I am, I'm about to try raw fish for the first time," I say.

"Did you know you need a reservation to eat here?" Blanca taps the fishbowl again, startling the little guys.

I had no idea we needed a reservation. "How did we get a table?"

"I name-dropped *Ellas*," she says. "She's your fan. Said you saved her relationship."

My eyes widen as I lean forward. "My *fan*? I don't want fans. Since when do I have fans?"

"Since you revealed yourself to be the mastermind behind *Ellas*' account and your breakup went viral online." Blanca shakes her head as if to say *Silly girl*. "Also, I might have told her that you'd write a piece on the restaurant."

"Are you crazy? I got fired. I can't write a piece on this restaurant."

"Well, if you decided to make social media your business, you could write pieces without *Ellas*. You could write a blog, you could start a YouTube channel. You could run around Caracas filming videos galore and make a living out of it. You have no idea how much you don't need any of this."

I know that. But I never dreamed of living off social media, being an influencer. I want to be a journalist. Running the *Ellas* account and the column was great because people didn't know who I was. The spotlight has never been an aspiration for me. I want to put others there.

"It doesn't matter, I'll be back before you know it."

Blanca opens her mouth, but a waiter materializes next to our table before she has a chance to add anything else. I let her order for us because she has more experience.

For the next ten minutes, I pretend to listen to Blanca talk. I've actually been stretching my neck as much as possible to catch a glimpse of Alejandro, to see if maybe he's still at the bar. I have no way of knowing without being conspicuous. I think Blanca is talking about something Gustavo, her boyfriend, did. I *think* she's not happy about it.

"I hate to interrupt you, Blanquita, mi vida, I really do," I blurt out. Blanca cuts herself off abruptly, as expected, and watches me like I've grown a second head. "I can't sit here anymore. Could you pretend to go to the bathroom and see if Alejandro is still there?"

She watches me in silence for at least five seconds.

"You're a terrible friend," she deadpans.

"I know."

"Really terrible," she adds, in case she wasn't clear.

"But you love me."

She rolls her eyes. "I do."

"So could you please . . . ?"

Blanca begins to stand.

"Marianto?"

Blanca and I freeze. I look to my right, where Alejandro is standing just a couple feet away, a look of surprise on his face. Blanca slowly lowers herself onto her chair again.

"Ale!" I don't even have to act surprised. "Hola!"

I need to tone it down a little.

I push to my feet, careful not to seem too eager. I need to be nonchalant, collected. The epitome of a sane woman.

"Hi," he says, though it sounds more like a question. Right on cue, our waiter brings out our food. Ale scans the table with a frown, his eyes going from the sushi platter to me. "Since when do you eat sushi?"

"Oh, Blanca convinced me to try it," I lie.

His eyebrows shoot up in surprise. "Did she?" He turns to her. "How did you manage that? I tried for years and she never budged."

Oh no. Abort. Abort. He hated when I made it seem like I didn't value his opinion. I was supposed to look relaxed and go-with-the-flow-ish. There are a number of other things I could have said. *I decided to try something new*, or *I thought I'd see what all the fuss is about*. Literally anything else.

Blanca clears her throat. "You know Marianto." She shrugs. "One day she just wakes up and she says yes to sushi."

"Right." He nods. "Well. Enjoy your dinner." He pauses. Stares. Damn it, this is a disaster. "I hope you like it."

He puts both hands deep into his pockets and disappears from our view with three steps. I watch the space Alejandro was just occupying, replaying all the ways I could have executed that better. He was surprised to see me. Surprised enough he approached. He didn't seem displeased. In fact, I think if I'd asked him to sit with us for a bit, he would have. Until I practically told him I value Blanca's opinion more than his.

Defeated, I sloppily sit back on the chair.

"He'll call," Blanca assures me. I stab a piece of sushi even though I'm not hungry. I made it this far. I will at least do what I came here to do.

I pop the sushi roll into my mouth. It's salty and sweet and bland, all at the same time. Plus, it's not hot or cold. Everything in it is mushy.

"You hate it?" Blanca asks.

"Yup."

I swallow. Not ten seconds later, I'm clearing my throat. Great.

"EpiPen?" she asks then.

"Yup."

But the moment that finally breaks me isn't Alejandro leaving while thinking I don't value his opinion, or having to stab my own leg in public. It's when Blanca calls for the check and has the waiter prepare our food to go. I gasp at the amount of money we have to pay. We could've gone to McDonald's three times for that amount. And the only thing I managed to do was risk my life.

"I got this," Blanca says. "I'm eating most of it anyway."

I nod, agreeing. Never mind that it's too much money for her to cover on her own, or that I dragged her here. I have no fight left in me. All I want to do is go home, eat cereal, and ignore the reality that this is unsustainable. If science class taught me anything, it's that experiments aren't cheap. Keeping this up will drain my bank account faster than I anticipated. I need a job.

CHAPTER 9

••••••

LAST TIME I WENT TO A JOB INTERVIEW, I WAS A lost twenty-two-year-old, fresh out of college. I think things were less scary back then. I don't remember sweating this much or my heart pounding this hard.

The man sitting across from me hasn't stopped smiling the entire time I've been here. He's not old, early forties at most, and I'm only making that assumption due to his receding hairline. The thick beard gives him a sophisticated look. He's the editor in chief at a local news outlet. They had an opening for a junior position in the Sports Department. Not ideal, not what I want, but once inside it's easier to move around. Besides, it's a temporary job. I might be gone before my trial period ends. But it pays weekly per word, and what I need right now is quick money.

The man caps the pen he's been using throughout the interview, scribbling away I'm not sure what. If the purpose is to intimidate me, he's succeeded.

He sets the pen aside, intertwines his fingers, and sighs. "Do you mind answering one last question?"

"Not at all," I blurt out, too quick.

"How come you're changing your lane from Lifestyle to Sports?" he asks.

I anticipated this question. I've gotten it at every other interview in some shape or form, so I've perfected my answer by now.

"A career change is always good," I say. "I don't want to be perceived as merely a love columnist. I want to expand, learn, grow. Five years doing the same job is hardly the way to do that."

It's a half-truth. If he asked me on a deeper level, I would have to tell him this job is just a means to an end. I would have to disclose my goal of becoming an Arts journalist. I would have to tell him the real reason I'm not at *Ellas* anymore and that I'm in need of money. But no one discloses those kinds of details while trying to impress their future boss.

He nods, still smiling. Extending a hand to me, he pushes to his feet. I take it, standing as well. "Thank you for coming, we'll be in contact."

The other six interviewers have said the same thing. They haven't contacted me yet. I understand it's a long process—it's always a long process—but I don't have the luxury of going through a two-month hiring process.

"Will you?" I find myself asking.

I'm immediately horrified.

His smile finally falters. "No." *Oh.* To his credit, he looks like he's just as surprised to hear himself answer that question as I was hearing myself ask it. "It's nothing personal, you simply lack the experience for the position we're looking to fill. You have mostly worked with social media. My advice, if I'm allowed to offer it? Look for a job in that field. Your experience is extensive and impressive."

I take a step back with a nod. "Thank you for your honesty. And the advice. Have a great day."

WHEN I GET home, I fall face-first on my bed with a groan. I scream into my pillow as Caballo de Troya blasts from the speakers in my bedroom, drowning out the sound of my misery.

It's official. I'm like one of those actors who are typecast as their most famous role and no one ever hires them again for anything different. Sure, I'm talented. Sure, I'm impressive. Sure, I'm good at my job. But apparently I won't be good at any other job.

I groan again before tossing the pillow to the side, flipping over to lie on my back. I'm starting to run out of breath.

The ceiling has scars drawn by time and decay, but I trace every line, every humidity stain, in an attempt to regulate my emotions. I try to find three truths to focus on as music plays in the background. One, I'm young, I have plenty of time to find another job. My career is not over at twenty-seven. Two, it's not the interviewers' fault that I need a job tomorrow. It's my fault, for posting that video on *Ellas*' account. A hiring process can take months, they're just looking out for their company. And even I know I'm not the right fit—I'm planning to leave within a month. Three, tomorrow is another day, another opportunity to go out, try to land another interview, try again. There. Three truths. They're all BS and they do nothing to soothe me.

A knock on the door makes me sit up, my bones shifting under my skin, telling me I'm not a teenager anymore and that I need a new mattress. My mother pokes her head in my room, holding her phone away from her face while she covers the lower part, like it's a landline.

"Mamita, do you mind turning the music down? I'm on a call," she says.

I do mind. I want to sulk in my misery. But she's my mother, so I obey with a few taps on my phone. There's nothing quite like sharing a living space with one's parent to make one feel like a teenager again.

Mamá winks at me and whispers, "Gracias," before ducking out. But her voice, previously drowned by the music I was blasting, still reaches me.

"*—did they already hire one of those TikTok kids?*" she's asking someone. "*My stepson taught me how to do it . . . I know, it's a real time-suck . . . we need to find one fast. I don't think anyone even knows it's happening. It's a kids' show, we need to get on whatever the kids are doing these days.*" She pauses. I sit up. "*Well, clearly what they're doing isn't working. Last time I asked, we didn't even have contestants.*"

Curious, I grab my phone and go through the *Talento V* tag in every platform I can think of. My mother told me shooting should have started days ago. To not have contestants is bad. When I dive into the content they've been putting out, I understand why. Each graphic looks like it was created using PowerPoint and WordArt. There is no mention of where, when, or how to apply. Their TikTok is nonexistent. There is no intention to their Instagram feed; it's just a bunch of pictures that, when seen together, make no sense. It doesn't feel like an organic experience. It looks like the profile of a government facility. Which should be a compliment, but isn't.

My mother must have moved to the balcony or to her room because I can't hear her anymore.

Maybe you should try for a job in that field. That's what the last interviewer said. And maybe I should. I'm running out of options. For a temporary job, what does it matter if it's running social media accounts? Hell, what does it matter if I'm working as a bartender? I won't be there forever. There's no shame in working. I've been supporting myself since I was eighteen. I've been an assistant, I've been a waitress, I've been a social media manager, I've been a love advice columnist. I can be whatever I find first. However, asking my mother is not an option. For one thing, I would never hear the end of it. For another, I'm not in the mood to throw almost ten years of emancipation out the window.

I move to my chair, google *Talento V*'s contact info and send in my CV. It's perfect. The job ends in twelve weeks. I could do it remotely for most of the time, pick a couple days a week to make content, and then come home and create magic. It won't even feel like I'm working with my mother. Worst-case scenario? I don't get the job. There's nothing to lose.

Thirty minutes later, my mother pokes her head back inside my room to ask if I want to go out for lunch. I take us to where they make my favorite roasted chicken. Because it's rush hour, parking is next to impossible. When we reach the doors, a young woman tells me there are no tables available. And then she sees Mamá standing behind me and a table is magically offered to us.

We're in the restaurant for an hour. I snap no less than forty pictures of my mother with various types of people as our chicken grows cold on our plates. I do it without complaining because my mind isn't here. I don't know what song is playing in the background, or what my mother is saying to the couple of women standing next to us. My mind is on my inbox and the notification for a new email I just got, waiting for me to give it the attention it deserves. I'm afraid to do it here and have my face betray me.

After the last picture is taken, Mamá announces she has to go to the bathroom and I take her absence as my chance to check my email without making her feel her company wasn't enough to entertain me.

Hunched over my phone, I read the email, muttering to myself, skimming through the initial hello in search for any crumb of hope I could cling to.

"*. . . thank you for your interest . . . impressive . . . excited . . .*" I stop. My spine straightens. "*Could you come in tomorrow?*" I read the words over and over, just to make sure I'm reading them correctly.

I type a quick response confirming I can meet with them tomorrow. I need to put together a plan, a vision, the way I did every week at *Ellas*. If my mother's call was any indication, they are desperate to find someone. And the truth is, they *need* to hire someone sooner rather than later. Hopefully, that someone will be me.

CHAPTER 10

THE LAST TIME I WALKED THESE HALLS, I THINK I was thirteen or fourteen. Mamá had landed the antagonist/villain role in a telenovela written by Leonardo Padrón. She played a housewife whose husband fell in love with a much younger woman. Tried to kill the protagonist a couple times throughout the show. Ended up in a mental asylum with third-degree burns I don't remember how she got. I smile, remembering being with her on set, meeting the actors, doing my homework surrounded by cameras and lights. VeneTV's main building hasn't changed in that time. The walls are lined with posters from their productions, old and new. My mother's face is in some of them. She's been a talk show host, she's played both villains and protagonists in more than a dozen productions, and now, years later, she's returned to host a singing competition.

Nostalgia builds in my chest, constricting it. But I'm not sure it's positive. Because it's been over ten years and it looks the same. The poster frames are dusty, like no one has bothered to clean them in years. The carpet is in desperate need of cleaning, coated with white speckles of paint chipped off from the walls, and the lightbulbs keep twitching on and off. The building is deserted. When I arrived, there were only three cars parked outside. I decided to park a block away because my red sedan would be too recognizable if my mother happens to drive by.

I sit on a metal bench out in the hall, next to a glass door that has *Mileidy Romero, Producer* engraved on it, like the young woman at the information desk instructed me to.

"Wait there until they call your name," she said. "La señora Mileidy hasn't arrived yet, but when she does, you're her first appointment."

La señora Mileidy told me to come at nine. It's seven minutes past nine. I don't like having too much free time. Thoughts run rampant when I'm not doing something. This is why I need a job, for the structure, for something to do. That, and for the money.

My mother stares at me from a poster hanging on the wall directly across from my bench. She offers the viewer a coy smile, lifting an eyebrow as she crosses her arms over her chest. The picture must be at least twenty years old. There are no wrinkles on her face, her hair is covered in too-thick highlights, fashioned butterfly style. Above her, in bright bold letters, the words "MÁS POR MENOS" take up half the poster. It was for a game show where people had to use very few words to explain a subject or answer a question. The less words you used, the more points you won. It was canceled after one season.

Seconds tick by on the clock at the end of the hall. I've been staring at the poster for so long, I'm starting to hear my mother's voice inside my head.

I sit up, sharpening my ear. Laughter follows the sound of the elevator doors shutting. Familiar laughter. It's high-pitched, like the cries of the macaws that wake me up every morning.

My mother never just laughs, she cackles; she throws her head back as her entire body shakes. It's very unique.

I hear steps approaching and jump to my feet. She's not supposed to be here, she's supposed to be shooting. I can't let her see me. At least not until I get the job. If I'm going to work at *Talento V*, I want to work there on my terms. If she finds out, she'll do everything in her power to make sure I get it, because despite everything, she's the kind of woman who gets stuff done. I don't want her to intervene. I don't want her to force the producer into letting her sit through my interview with me as she holds my hand.

I'll tell her once I get it. *If* I get it.

Where do I go, where do I go, where do I go?

I start walking, my back to the voices, holding the folder I brought to my chest. I push my hair behind my ear, forcing myself not to look behind, as I rush to where I remember the bathroom is. I turn a corner, only to be met with another giant poster of my mother. I jump, thinking it's her. I wait behind the corner for the voices to disappear, but they don't. In fact, the opposite happens.

"Let me just use the bathroom," my mother's voice says.

No.

I'm at the end of the hallway. If I step out, she'll see me. If I walk into the bathroom, she'll find me. She'll ask what I'm doing here. She'll ask why I didn't tell her, why I didn't include her. She'll say she could've helped me, and I will have to explain that I didn't want her to help me. The thought of having that conversation is like a rock settling in my stomach. Her steps get closer and closer.

Like a movie, a flash of images crosses my mind depicting a little girl, eight or nine, running down these halls on a different floor—maybe the fifth or seventh—deciding the best possible place for a *girl* to hide was the boy's bathroom.

I shut my eyes and take two steps toward the door across from me, ignoring the little black sticker on the door, which is definitely not wearing a dress. I know it's empty. I've been alone on this floor for nearly fifteen minutes and no one has come in or out. I push the door open and shut it behind me, resting my back against it. Not ten seconds later, I hear a different door open and shut on the other side.

"I need to go back to therapy," I mutter to myself, because what the hell was that?

I try to keep calm. Unfortunately, my nervous system doesn't know the difference between being chased by a lion and my mother walking down a hallway. My eyes flutter shut. My mother is the kind of woman who goes to the bathroom after every meal and takes her time to make sure she doesn't have to go again for at least five hours. She'll walk out of there pristine. I should be safe for at least ten minutes.

My head falls back against the door, and I breathe in again, bracing myself to walk out, but the door swings open before I can. The knob jabs into my side, shooting a bolt of pain through my body as the impact sends me flying forward along with my folder and everything in it.

I land on my hands and knees, while sheets of paper scatter around me. Some of them land under a leaking sink and get soaked. *Nooo, my portfolio!*

"What—" a male voice says from above. "OH! I am so sorry—here, let me help you."

"No, please!" My face blazes as I gather my documents, both wet and dry, and stuff them all back inside the folder. The man ignores me and drops to a knee in front of me, holding out some pages with one hand and offering to help me up with the other.

"I'm sorry, I thought this was the men's—" *He's not from here*, my brain immediately registers. The accent is off. He sounds Colombian. Or from Táchira, the state next to the Colombia-Venezuela border. "Do you know you're in the men's bathroom?"

God. Could this get any more embarrassing?

I take the documents without looking at him and push to my feet. He does the same. "Gracias."

"Maria Antonieta Camacho?" a voice calls from the hall.

"Excuse me, I—" I gesture to the door he's still blocking. He jumps out of the way. "Thank you." And I run out of there.

Definitely need to go back to therapy.

As I step back into the hall, I notice a woman waiting for me by the metal bench I was sitting on less than five minutes ago, even though it feels like ten years. She's short and voluptuous, with a puff of white hair crowning her head. She's wearing a long dress that hangs on her body like a nightgown, and no makeup. The contrast between this woman and Eugenia is monumental. This is someone who thinks in numbers, not in words. Practical and sterile, here to do her job and do it efficiently. So is Eugenia, but Eugenia will do it while wearing stilettos, and this woman is wearing animal print flats.

I offer my hand as soon as we're within touching distance. She takes it with a grunt.

"I'm Maria Antonieta, mucho gusto."

"Mileidy Romero," she replies. "Please, come in."

Mileidy Romero's office is old, like the rest of this building. Binders are stacked up in towers behind her desk, labeled with different project names, dated twenty years back, some even older. Her desk is wood and the leather in her chair is slightly cracked. Meanwhile, the chair I sit on has barely any cushion left. It breaks my heart a little and I gulp, trying not to let it show.

"So." She places both hands flat on her desk as she sits. "Tell me why you want to leave your job at *Ellas* magazine to come work in a TV production with no budget for a social media manager."

The question catches me off guard. Every hope I had of landing this job dissolves. I don't want to lie, and she seems to know I'm full of shit before I even get a word out, so I decide to tell her the truth.

"Two reasons, mainly." I clear my throat, fumbling with a chipped edge on my side of the desk. "One, I'm between jobs and I figured a TV production that ends in twelve weeks would be a nice change of scenery, short-term, that would offer me a little cushion while I find something else. Two, I noticed you desperately need engagement in your accounts. It doesn't look intentional, it doesn't look organic, it doesn't show people what the production is about or why it's worth investing their time in it. I can help you give it a fresh look, find what kind of message you want to tell the masses so you can start putting it out there, instead of waiting for the show to be on the air."

Mileidy watches me from her chair, her cloud of hair moving under the A/C. I make myself look her in the eye, not get distracted.

"I like how sharp you are," she tells me, after what feels like an eternity. "You know what you want."

I nod once. "That I do."

"Sí." She purses her lips, then sighs. "Which is why it's a shame having to tell you I can't offer you the job because the position has already been filled and the show can't afford to hire another person."

Whatever drop of hope I might have been harboring flickers.

"I hear you." I square my shoulders the way I've seen Eugenia do when she wants to make sure her voice is heard. "If I may, a successful social media strategy isn't just about posting regularly. It's about resonating with your target audience, it's about building relationships with them, taking people along for the ride. I know how to do that."

Mileidy sits back and her chair groans. "You're a romantic."

"Maybe." Maybe I believe in the power of human connection, or maybe I'm telling her the same words Eugenia has hammered into my brain for years. It doesn't matter. "This isn't about how I feel. From me, you will get a detailed content calendar and regular performance metrics analyses so we know what works and what doesn't work. It's a data-driven approach. But it *is* about how you make your audience feel. They're not thinking about metrics, they're just here for a good time. Let's try it, and if you're not happy with the results, I'll leave."

We stare at each other for what feels like ages, until Mileidy finally sighs and looks away. "I'm sorry."

I want to ask her why she didn't tell me the job was filled, why she had me come all the way here. But I know my place. It's not professional and it's not going to make her change her mind. So I nod and stand, back straight. I extend my hand out to her. She stands too, taking it.

"I understand." I retreat with a step to the side, then one back. "Thank you for your time."

I walk out of her office, holding my head high and never wavering until I'm out of the building, a whole block away, in the safety of my car, and driving to my apartment. Then, I cry the whole way home.

CHAPTER 11

••••••

I GET THE EMAIL AT 5:00 P.M., AFTER I GET OFF THE phone to put the finishing touches on Experiment #4 by confirming a hair salon appointment. I may be searching for a new job, but I still have a relationship to save and an article to write, if I want to get my old job back.

A notification lights up my screen.

My first thought is *Alejandro*—because he's been my first thought since that fateful night at the sushi restaurant. He hasn't contacted me since, hasn't asked if I liked the sushi, much less if I got an allergic reaction from it.

What I don't expect is to find an email from *Talento V.* I've learned to accept noes for what they are. A no is not a maybe. No means no. It's the same email chain from when I first sent my CV, so I can't immediately tell what this is about. But when I open it, there is no greeting, no explanation. Nothing but two lines:

You start tomorrow. Please be at the office no later than 8:00 a.m., sharp.

Mileidy Romero.

I read the words over and over. Behind me, the fridge beeps. I didn't close it. I want to ask what she means by this, even though the line is self-explanatory, but I'm scared she'll realize she made a mistake and didn't mean to send this to me. I'm tempted to ignore my confusion, to show up to VeneTV's offices tomorrow and hope she has no choice but to keep me on. Or . . . I'll embarrass myself further when she asks security to show me out. I decide the best approach is to reply. When she sees it's me, she'll probably know she made a mistake.

Good evening, Mrs. Romero.

I will be there. Thank you for the opportunity.

I watch my email like a hawk, waiting for an explanation or an apology, but nothing appears. My inbox remains empty.

THE MORNING OF my first day starts like any other: with my mother opening and shutting cabinets in my kitchen as she tries to find a plate or a mug or some type of pot I'm sure I don't own. The sweet smell of café con leche floats around my apartment as the blender mixes it all together. She's always added a few drops of vanilla and ensured she makes it with powdered milk so it isn't bland, watered-down coffee, but thick in texture and rich in flavor.

I walk out of my bedroom, almost bewitched by the smell.

"Buenos días," I call, grabbing a banana from the counter as I make my way to the balcony to feed my children. Outside, the sky is already bright blue, even though it's barely seven. No clouds in sight. It's like Caracas knows today is a good day for me. Within seconds of standing here, Marta and Pedro Luis, my usual guests, perch on the railing, ruffling their feathers in anticipation. I carefully lay out half a banana for each and sit on my lounge chair to watch them eat. I love the contrast the yellow in their feathers makes with the sky, and how the bright blue makes them stand out against the background of green that embellishes the city everywhere you look. To me, Caracas always seems brighter and bolder than any other city. It's colorful, alive. Water is clearer and trees are greener and the sky is bluer.

I turn at the sound of the door sliding open. Mamá stands behind me with two steaming mugs in her hand. She offers me one and I readily take it and bring it to my lips. The warmth of the coffee spreads through my body. Another delicious contrast this city offers: a warm beverage against the chilly morning. I inhale deeply, allowing the air to travel through my body, and can't help but smile.

"I have something to tell you." I would hate for her to find out when I walk in the office or when she runs into me in the hall.

"Hm?" Mamá takes a sip of her coffee, leaning closer to the birds with an entranced gleam in her eyes.

"You know how Alejandro and I broke up," I begin.

She straightens, her entire body locking up in what I can only call contained rage. "Ese desgraciado."

I blink, surprised. Calling Alejandro a bastard is actually pretty mild for her.

"Right." I clear my throat. "Bueno, I lost my job because of that situation." I pause, in case she wants to say something, but she doesn't. She simply keeps drinking her coffee. "Anyway, I applied for a job at *Talento V*, to run their social media, and it appears I got it. I start today."

Her eyebrows shoot up as she sets the mug on the railing, startling the macaws. She jumps to hug me, squeezing me so hard I almost spill my coffee. "That sounds splendid!" *Splendid?* "You and me, co-workers, just like I always wanted!" What she always wanted was for us to co-star in a telenovela, but I won't burst her bubble now with technicalities. I wiggle out of her embrace until I'm free again. "I wish you'd told me," she continues. "I would have gone with you to the interview."

Which is precisely why I didn't tell her. This way I know I got the job on my own merit and not for who my mother is. I'm already a disgraced journalist, I don't need to be accused of nepotism as well.

"Oh!" Mamá claps, straightening. "Can we ride together? I'll call the driver and tell him not to pick me up. We're going to have so much fun!"

She runs back inside, I assume to finish getting ready. I check the time on my phone. If I want to make it by eight, I need to leave in ten minutes. She's not going to be ready in ten minutes.

"SO MUCH FUN!" she yells from inside the apartment.

Right. So much fun.

I'M TWENTY MINUTES late to my first day working at *Talento V.* My mother tries to catch up with me, but I keep leaving her behind.

In her follow-up email, Mileidy instructed me to stop by her office as soon as I made it here, so that's where I'm headed.

"Mamita, slow down, you're going to dislocate a hip," Mamá says behind me. "So you're a little late. Just blame it on me, you'll be fine."

How do I make her understand that using her as an excuse for my poor work performance is *exactly* what I don't want to be doing. I'm here to work, I'm not here to have my mommy get me out of trouble with the principal. And it doesn't matter anyway because I don't work for my mother, I work for Mileidy and Mileidy told me to be here at eight.

My mother's breathing is heavy when we stop in front of Mileidy's office. I knock twice. The door opens within seconds. She eyes me first, up and down, with what I can only describe as disdain, then notices the figure standing behind me and rolls her eyes. She turns her back to us and invites us inside with a wave of her hand.

"Welcome aboard, Maria Antonieta," she says. "Viviana, what are you doing here?"

My mother shrugs. "Maria Antonieta is my daughter."

"I don't think you should be here for this," I whisper to her.

She waves me off. "Nonsense. I'm your mother. I can be wherever I want to be."

Sure, maybe when I was underage. I open my mouth to ask her to leave, but she's already sitting.

"Well, daughter or no daughter, she's here to work," Mileidy says. "We had to lay off five people yesterday."

I freeze, my butt hovering over the chair. Surely they're not expecting me to do the work of these five people.

"That's . . . unfortunate."

Mileidy nods. "Very. But you're here now, we'll make it work."

I blink. "Uh—"

"Here's your contract." Mileidy slides a folder toward me.

Hesitant, I reach for it. It's mostly standard—my schedule, etc.—until I reach the payment section. And I choke. Mileidy is saying something to me, but I'm not listening. I'm looking at the numbers. It's ten times what I made at *Ellas*. For twelve weeks? To run their social media? For a TV show that had to lay off five people and couldn't afford to hire me yesterday? That can't be right.

I raise my hand, eyes glued on the paper, counting the zeroes over and over.

Mileidy interrupts herself. "Do you have a question?"

I clear my throat. "Yes. About the payment . . ."

"Are you unsatisfied?" she asks.

Mamá leans over our chairs to read, then pats my knee.

"No!" I blurt out. "I'm satisfied. I'm *very* satisfied but—"

"Then it's settled," Mileidy cuts me off. "Take those papers, sign them, and get them to my assistant as soon as possible so we can get started on training."

That gets my attention. "Training for what?"

Beside me, my mother shifts in her seat. Mileidy assesses me and I have a suspicion she's regretting the decision to hire me.

"Like I told you yesterday, the social media manager position has been taken." Mileidy is speaking slowly, the way people do when they're annoyed to have to repeat themselves. "But we had to lay off five people, so we're short on Production Assistants. This is what you'll be doing. You'll be temporarily assisting one of our judges."

Assistant. Not social media manager. Getting coffee and running errands and being treated like crap for twelve weeks. I really should have listened the first time around.

"Will that be a problem?" Mileidy asks.

Yes. No. I don't know. I need a job, and it will only be for three months. But I'm sure I will be the only twenty-seven-year-old assistant on the entire premises. It feels like a huge step back. That said, the pay . . . I could work this job and then easily be unemployed for six months if I wanted to.

The contract burns in my hand. I'm in this office. I have to decide now. Why it didn't work with the other five people, I might find out soon. But for now, this is the best offer I have. It's the *only* offer I have. And as time passes, I fear I won't get another one.

"No, that won't be a problem."

"Then welcome to *Talento V*." Mileidy stands. Mamá and I follow suit, poised to leave as a loud series of knocks—four to be exact—comes from the door. "Ah, wonderful!" Mileidy says, moving toward the door to open it. "I won't have to fetch you later to make introductions." She steps to the side with a soft "Adelante" that is not meant for us.

A man walks in. Lanky, six feet tall, dark hair and eyes against caramel skin, a five o'clock shadow, and a familiar smile. My eyes widen at the sight of him just a few feet away.

Mileidy places a hand on his shoulder. "This is—"

Simón Arreaza, I think at the same time she says it. Colombian. Twenty-eight years old, lead singer of Caballo de Troya, the composer of my relationship's soundtrack. And somehow, impossibly, here.

Too stunned to speak, I scan the man once more. The tall frame, the soft eyes, the small earring. And then my eyes zero in on his clothes. Particularly his hoodie. And the logo embroidered on it. A horse. Well, a horse head, on the right. A symbol I've seen countless times on Spotify and YouTube and Instagram.

He scans the room, his eyes landing on me first. His eyebrows shoot up in surprise before his gaze quickly moves to my mother. His polite smile grows into a grin as he approaches her to engulf her in a hug. And all I can do is stare.

"And this is Maria Antonieta," Mileidy continues. "Your assistant."

Wait, *his* assistant? *He's* the judge? The thought is enough to snap me out of my daze.

Simón Arreaza from Caballo de Troya offers me his hand. Without thinking, I take a step forward, arm outstretched, perfectly professional and 0 percent fangirl. Except for the fact that I'm shaking Simón Arreaza's hand. He plays the guitar with this hand. His hand is calloused, his grip is strong, all business. It's a nice change from the men who treat my hand like it's breakable. It's not a condescending handshake.

"Mucho gusto," he says in a thick Paisa accent, all the way from Medellín, Colombia.

Wait. I know that voice. I've heard it before, not through my phone or through speakers. I've heard it close, but where—

Oh, God. He's the man from the bathroom. Kill me now. A rush of heat travels through my body, urging me to run away, but I'm glued to the floor, staring at this man I'm so used to seeing ten times smaller on my phone screen. God, he's so much more hermoso in person. And now he's here, his face is within touching distance . . . not that I want to touch his face. And he is also the man who found me hiding from my mother in the men's bathroom. *Agh,* I need someone to knock me out with a frying pan immediately.

He offers me a warm smile, revealing dimples that only add to his already charming exterior. "I'm Simón."

"I know" is what comes out of my mouth. "I'm sorry I didn't recognize you without the rest of the band."

Simón's eyes flash with humor, the corner of his lips twitch.

I know I'm staring, but I can't seem to stop. If I were Mileidy, I'd fire me on the spot. Maybe that's why the other five people didn't work.

He turns to Mileidy with a grin and says, "I like her already."

CHAPTER 12

******

YO: Simón Arreaza is my new boss!
YO: Repito: Simón Arreaza is my new boss
YO: that's classified, by the way

Yes, I signed an NDA not two hours ago. But anyone in my position would have done the same thing.

BLANCA: who?

"Simón Arreaza. From Caballo de Troya," I whisper into my phone, deciding a voice note would work better to convey my current state. "The Colombian band Ale and I love. He's my boss. Okay, not technically my *boss* boss, but I'm assisting him."

BLANCA: ooooohhhhhhh
BLANCA: which one is he? The tortured one or the whorish one?

"Neither. He's one of the lead singers," I say.

I send her a screenshot of the band's Instagram.

YO: he's the boy-next-doorish one
BLANCA: he's cute. Do you think he could be your rebound?
YO: I am not going to sleep with my boss
BLANCA: it's just a thought. You could write a "How to get over your ex fast" article instead. Item #1: have a scandalous fling with your celebrity crush who also happens to be your new boss.

I huff. He's not my celebrity crush. Sure, there was a time when I was twenty-two and single and I'd recently discovered this new band that I liked, and I *might* have had a crush on one of the lead singers and it *might* have been Simón Arreaza. But I am not a twenty-two-year-old single woman anymore. I have Ale. And Simón Arreaza from Caballo de Troya is my boss. Crushing on your boss is highly frowned upon.

YO: I know exactly the kind of article I want to write, thank you

Sitting in my car, waiting to drive the aforementioned boss to his hotel, I reach over the console for my purse. I've been trying to pin down the best experiment to try next. I smooth the list over the steering wheel. I printed it this morning. I've gone through the first two items with little to no results.

The third idea is the easiest: Experiment #3: ***Send him a text that "wasn't for him."***

Tomorrow is Saturday, which is perfect. Ale is free on the weekends. I'll pretend I wanted to text someone else with an *A* name. Another man. Tell him I twisted my ankle and need help getting home. Ale might worry and offer to come assist me instead. We'll start talking, I'll be all damsel in distress, and before you know it, BAM! We're making out on my couch and we're back together because he always said I'm a fantastic kisser.

A knock on my passenger seat window makes me jump.

Simón stands outside my car and waves. I toss both my purse and the list in the back as I unlock the car. They land next to a tower of documents he needs to sign by Monday. Why Mileidy refuses to simply email is something I'm not brave enough to ask.

"Hello!"

Simón Arreaza from Caballo de Troya is getting in my car.

"Hi," I reply, opening the door for him to climb in.

Simón shifts, then shifts again. The man's legs barely fit. I knew he was tall, but Jesus. I don't think I knew what it felt like to look up at someone until six hours ago.

The click of the seat belt helps me focus on the task at hand. He slaps his thighs with both hands then gives me a firm nod.

I nod back, then start the car, but say nothing. The engine whines before roaring to life. I look to Simón, mostly out of embarrassment that my car isn't in better condition. But he doesn't seem to mind.

"Do you think we could roll the windows down?" he asks.

I nod my head. It works for me, I'll save on gas.

"Do you mind if I—" Simón begins, reaching for the stereo.

Two seconds later, Caballo de Troya is blasting from the speakers. Blood rushes to my face as Simón's eyebrows shoot up in surprise, the same way they did when he first saw me in Mileidy's office.

When he turns to look at me, he's grinning. "You actually like our music?"

Like their music? I've followed their career since they started, when not a soul knew who they were. I own every album, a pink hoodie with their logo, and I have notifications on for the band's Instagram. I listen to them in the car, in the shower, when I'm happy, and most recently, when my boyfriend of four years told me he needed a break from me. His music is the soundtrack to my life.

"Don't be embarrassed," he quickly adds. "This is . . ." He can't stop smiling.

"I, uh—" I turn the music off. I can't talk to him and listen to him singing at the same time. "This is not how I planned to confess I'm a huge fan."

Ears blazing and heart pounding, I focus on the road as if I was learning to drive for the first time.

"I hope you weren't planning it for long," he says.

"No, I had no idea you'd be my boss. I only applied because I . . ." I trail off, flicking the turn signal before I turn to the right. I'm sure he doesn't care why I applied and I'm not going to bore him with it. "When you asked for recommendations on what to do in Venezuela, I figured you were planning a tour."

"You saw that?" he asks.

I nod. "I'm the one who said she'd give you a tour of Caracas."

His eyes widen. "Does that offer still stand?"

I smile. "Sure."

I know it's never going to happen. He's here to judge a singing competition alongside other superstars. He's not going to choose to spend time with me. But I am nothing if not polite.

We come to a stop in front of a traffic light. I study his profile. His eyes are genuinely curious, no ill intent behind them as far as I can detect. Unlike Eugenia, whose eyes are always catlike, preying on information she can later use to her advantage. Or my mother, who seems perpetually ready to judge.

"What was your old job?" he asks.

The light turns green. I look away.

"I was a relationship advice columnist for a magazine."

"Wait," he says.

I steal a quick glance his way, trying to maintain a calm façade even as my stomach churns with anxiety. *Please, don't let him have seen the video,* I think. *Please, don't let him know about me from the magazine.*

The curiosity in his eyes changes to softness with a shake of his head. "Never mind. Did you like it?"

I don't push. The fear of hearing, *Hey, you're the girl whose breakup went viral,* is far greater than my need to know what he was about to say.

"I did," I admit, but I'm desperate to change the subject. "Do you need anything before I drop you off at the hotel?"

"Is there a good coffee spot on the way?"

ONE OF MY favorite coffee shops sits comfortably in a corner—a small establishment embedded into a building like a fairy house in a tree. It has a glass door under a red awning, no flashy advertisement outside except for its name—Artesano's. Unremarkable by all accounts, but people still find it. On the drive over, Simón studies our surroundings. The cathedral, tall and proud with its lampposts and iron fences, and the surrounding cobblestone give the impression of having traveled back in time. Above us, wind ruffles the trees' leaves with a soft *swoosh,* while cars honk on the highway. If we don't make this quick, we'll get stuck in traffic.

Luckily, I find a spot nearby and make quick work of a parallel parking job. Something about having your favorite artist in the passenger seat leaves no room for error.

"Wow," Simón says. "Doesn't this place make you want to sit under a tree and people watch?"

"Definitely . . . But not right now," I say, without looking at him. If I pretend he's just another executive I have to get coffee for, maybe I'll survive the day. "I have to get you back to your hotel so you can start signing all those documents."

Simón smiles, pulling the café door open. "I think I like my idea better."

I stand on the sidewalk for one second too long before he gestures for me to go in first.

"Thank you."

The smell of coffee and fresh puff pastry hits me immediately, making my mouth water with anticipation. The familiarity of the establishment welcomes me in—a black countertop and cozy tables, checkerboard tiles, golden light streaming in through the storefront windows. A pop song plays in the background accompanied by the soft tinkling of mugs and saucers and the murmur of friendly conversation. If we had time, we could sit at my usual table closest to the door and watch people pass, watch the streetlights outside sizzle to life one by one, hear the melody of the cathedral's bells.

"Picture it," Simón says, and I'm momentarily confused as to what he's talking about. "Sitting under the shade of a tree, you see two people walking down the street hand in hand. One of them laughs, tugging the other toward a store. The one being dragged toward the store looks over their shoulder, almost in fear. They're afraid of getting caught. It's a secret."

And the thing is, I *can* picture it. Myself, sitting under that tree, writing a piece about this little bit of the city that transports us to a romance lived centuries ago. But I'm a journalist, not a novelist, and ultimately, I care more about the truth.

"*Or*," I offer, "they're afraid of getting assaulted in the middle of the street, because this is still Caracas and we all have PTSD."

Simón laughs, the sound deep and raspy, as we take our place in line. "That too."

"Is that how you write songs?" I ask, looking away. "You watch strangers living their lives and make up stories?"

I sense Simón shrugging. "It's one of the several ways I write songs."

"Interesting," I say as we advance in line. I venture a glance. "Looks like we're spending a couple minutes here. What's *my* story?"

Simón looks away from me to study the counter. "I think I'd rather wait for you to tell me that."

The prospect of being comfortable enough to do that sends a thrill down my spine. This is Simón Arreaza. Almost two weeks ago I was sobbing on my knees, eating Doritos off my apartment floor, while his voice sang about the very heartbreak I was feeling. And now he's standing right in front of me.

"Next," the cashier calls.

I shake my head. The man has known me for a total of six hours. He's still very much in the "idol" category of my brain. He needs to move to the "boss" category. He needs to be another Eugenia.

"What will you have?" I ask.

"Café," he says. "Negro. And a side of whatever you recommend."

I recite the order to the cashier.

"Won't you have anything?" Simón asks.

"That's okay, I'm—"

"Marianto?"

Simón turns around before I do.

My blood rushes all the way to my feet at the sound of that voice. I can't move. Alejandro hated driving downtown because of the traffic; he always complained whenever I asked him to come here with me. He hated how small this coffee shop is, how loud the music is, how crowded it gets at night. This is truly the last place I would have expected to run into him. Yet . . .

I draw in a calming breath before turning around to face him.

Alejandro stands right behind us in line, his eyes scanning Simón, who stands several inches taller than him. I swallow a gasp—there's a woman next to Alejandro. A colleague? They're both in gray scrubs, both looking as sleep-deprived as I am after days of denying myself eight hours of sleep. She's a bleached blonde, judging by the dark roots sprouting from the top of her head. Shorter than him, something I'm not. Curvier than me too. And standing very close to him.

I don't have the higher ground here, and I know it. I'm here with Simón, after all.

But I'm not the one who asked for a break. It's only been eleven days. And this is *my* coffee shop. How dare he bring another woman to *my* coffee shop? Was he expecting to run into me? Make sure I see and get the message? I don't know how many more stabs I can take before I bleed out.

"Ale." The word floats out of my mouth. I hate that my brain didn't use his full name.

His eyes go from Simón to me, then back to Simón.

Simón takes a step forward, offering his hand. "I'm Simón."

Alejandro nods, still confused. "I know. I love your band, man. Nice to meet you."

"Thank you," Simón says.

"Marianto is a huge fan as well, but I'm sure you already know that," Ale adds. A faint note of sarcasm prickles his otherwise chill tone. Simón nods. "So, what are you doing here? Are you on tour?"

Ale's eyes flick to me for half a second. His companion walks around me with a soft "Excuse me," to get to the cashier. Alejandro crosses his arms over his chest, looking more threatening than thrilled to meet the man who inspired him to learn how to play guitar. He ended up quitting after the second lesson.

Simón leans over in my direction. "Can I disclose what I'm doing here?"

I have no idea if he can, but I shake my head.

Simón *tsk*s. "It's still a secret."

Alejandro narrows his eyes, clearly annoyed by the answer. He turns to me and says, "Are you . . . working together or . . . ?"

"It's classified," I say.

"What about Eugenia?" Ale asks.

The barista places a paper cup and a brown paper bag on the counter, and I grab them like they're my lifeline. The last thing I want to do is explain to Ale and his *friend* that I was fired after our breakup went viral.

"Muchas gracias," I tell the barista, then turn back to Simón and hand him his coffee. "We gotta go. It was good to see you, Ale."

As I rush to the door, Simón takes a sip of his coffee and sighs. "Perfect." To Ale and his silent companion, he says, "It was nice to meet you."

I think Ale says something else, but I don't hear it because I'm already pushing the door open and marching toward the car.

No voy a llorar.

Because Camacho women don't cry in front of people. I slam my door with shaking hands after climbing in. Simón's demeanor is slower, calmer. Maybe even a bit hesitant. He places his cup between us on the console while he fumbles with the seat belt. My gaze is fixed ahead, where Ale's car is parked. I can almost smell the leather seats, feel the smooth surface of the glove compartment I opened whenever I wanted a mint. How did we become two people who stand in front of each other and don't know how to act? I miss him. I wish I'd been in the coffee shop with him. I wish I'd been the reason he endured the hassle of driving downtown and dealing with rush hour traffic. It's been eleven days. My eyes sting.

I've been driving in silence for about five minutes when Simón asks:

"Ex-novio?"

I flinch. Alejandro is technically not my ex-boyfriend. He's also not completely my boyfriend. But the truth is too complicated to get into, so I settle for the easier answer, even though it kills me. "Yes."

"You or him?"

"Him."

"Recently?"

I nod. "Almost two weeks ago."

Simón falls silent, takes a sip of coffee. I hit a pothole that has us both jumping.

Eyes ahead, Marianto.

"Sorry."

I steal a glance at him and find him watching me. His eyes are pools of warmth, glistening with a gentleness that mirrors the tiny smile playing on his lips. Heat creeps up my neck and across my cheeks. With clammy hands, I turn my focus back to the road.

"He'll be back," Simón says.

"What?" I mutter.

"Your boyfriend." Oh. Right. "I could tell by the way he was about to jump at my throat back there. When he does, you'll either be the strongest couple on the planet . . . or you'll realize that you don't actually want to be with him anymore."

I don't care for the second scenario, but the first stirs hope in me. This is just a bump in the road. If Simón Arreaza, who made his career writing love songs, sees a semblance of hope, then I can too.

We spend the remaining minutes it takes to get to his hotel in a surprisingly comfortable silence. It's coated in companionship, for lack of a better word. But people don't become friends in a day and a car ride. At the hotel, Simón unbuckles his seat belt, takes his paper bag and empty cup, and climbs out. I wait for him to retrieve his mountain of documents from the backseat before I roll down the window.

He smiles at me from the sidewalk. "Thank you for everything, Maria Antonieta."

"Just doing my job," I reply. And what an odd thing to actually be true. "Hasta el lunes."

He nods, that soft smile still dancing on the corner of his lips. "See you Monday."

THE SILENCE WHEN I'm making my way home is heavy. Without Simón Arreaza sitting next to me, the last twenty-four hours feel like a fever dream. Interviewing, getting rejected, then getting accepted; meeting Simón, taking him to my favorite coffee shop, running into Alejandro . . . I'm convinced I will wake up at any second and this will all be a dream I'm having, induced by listening to Caballo de Troya way too much and by my constant fear that Alejandro will move on.

When I park, I retrieve my phone from the cupholder. If I were Alejandro, and it was *me* who'd seen him with someone else at a coffee shop, I would text.

Actually, I *am* Alejandro. I *should* text, ask who that woman is. Forget sending a fake wrong text. I will send a real, right text. It's what any normal human being would do.

I check my messages. Nothing. No missed calls either. It's like he doesn't care that I was out getting coffee with Simón Arreaza. Hell, I would text just to get the scoop. Not even my pride would keep me from needing to know how that happened.

But I do have one email. From Eugenia:

Maria Antonieta,

How is the project coming along? Have you started?

I'd be more than willing to help you give it the best possible shape. Do you have anything to show me yet?

My stomach churns with anxiety as I stare at the screen. No. I do not. The first experiment was an utter failure. I don't even want to think about the second one. And Alejandro hasn't given me the green light to share how we get back together with the world because he won't even talk to me, much less get back together with me.

Buenas tardes, Eugenia,

It's going great!

I'll send you the first of the experiments next week, once I've finished drafting it.

Crap, crap, crap.

I stare at the words I just typed and hesitate, biting the inside of my cheek before I hit send. It's a promise I'm not sure I can keep. But maybe this is exactly what I need. A deadline. It's not lying, I *could* send her something next week.

I'll brainstorm a bit right here in the parking lot, then go home with clear ideas. I reach for the loose piece of paper, almost instinctively, because I know exactly where I left it. But it's not there. I climb into the backseat, feeling around every inch, under the mats, everywhere. It's not here.

Where is the list—

I freeze. Not two hours ago, I threw the list back here and it landed on top of a tower of other documents, next to my purse. My purse is there, but no list.

My stomach falls to my feet. A wave of nausea washes over my throat.

Oh no. Oh no, no. My eyes fall shut. I can physically feel my blood draining from my face and limbs, a single word bouncing off the walls of my brain: *No, no, no, no, no.*

But it's no use. I know, without a shadow of a doubt, Simón Arreaza has the list.

CHAPTER 13

MY MONDAY STARTS AT FOUR IN THE MORNING, after a full weekend spent preparing for the first day of what will be a weeklong audition process. Running around the theater in semidarkness with other PAs, I realize how small the team is.

"All hands on deck," Mileidy says upon arrival, in that raspy voice of hers.

The judges are scheduled to be here in thirty minutes, and per Mileidy's request, everything has to be spotless.

By the time I'm done unrolling an endless supply of cords, it's six in the morning. I silently move to the catering table and start the coffee. I already left snacks and water bottles in all of the dressing rooms.

As I'm pushing the *start* button on the coffee maker, one of the PAs approaches me, carrying three thick binders. He's thin, with a long nose and slightly crooked teeth. He seems young, probably a couple years younger than me, probably here as an intern. He gives me a tight smile as he sets the stack of binders down on a nearby table.

"What are *those*?" I ask.

The guy looks over his shoulder. "Contestants' info for the judges."

I perk up. "Can I have Simón's?"

Each judge will mentor a team of singers. Irina Montalbán—movie actress and voice-over legend—will mentor teen girls. Federico Gómez—music producer and songwriter—will mentor teen boys. Simón will mentor everyone under thirteen. Wouldn't it be helpful to highlight all the under-thirteen profiles so it's easier for Simón to find them? He could read them prior to meeting the kids, know a little about them before he hears them sing. It's also a good way to stay busy and not think about Simón getting here in—I check my watch—twenty-five minutes. Or that he might have the list. That he might have *read* the list.

"I don't know . . ." the PA says.

"I promise I'll get it to him in time," I vow.

Somewhere behind us, a tray hits the ground with a *clank* and Mileidy is yelling, calling for someone. The PA winces. It must be him. So, his name is Victor.

"Fine," he says, and hands me one of the binders. "Do not lose that. There are like a thousand pages in that and we're already using recycled paper."

"Recycling is good."

Victor ignores me, taking his leave. I carry the binder to the dressing rooms. Armed with a block of green sticky notes, I sit and start flipping pages. The thought of using star-shaped stickers crosses my mind, but that could be a little much. I've only gone through half the profiles when the door opens.

Simón walks in, his nose buried in his phone. He's in beat-up jeans and a navy blue T-shirt. His hair is a little damp, sticking to the back of his neck and leaving a visible watermark on his shirt. With bags under his eyes, he looks less like a rising pop sensation and more . . . normal.

My face instantly warms. Wonderful. Simón scans the room until his eyes land on me. His face lights up, his shoulders relaxing.

"Maria Antonieta, cómo vas?" he says.

"Good," I blurt out. "You?" I push to my feet. "How was your weekend? Do you want coffee? The hair and makeup crew should be here soon, you can sit."

"Good, thanks," he says, following me to the snacks table instead of sitting. "Busy weekend, though."

I'm pouring coffee into a paper cup when a neatly folded square materializes in front of me.

"Odd way to ask for an autograph, but here you go," Simón says.

Slowly, my gaze travels from the cup in my hand to him. Amusement shines bright in his eyes. At my pained expression, Simón smirks. I could officially die.

"Simón, I—"

Behind us, the door flies open. Irina marches in, followed by an entourage of stylists. They all carry suitcases that, when unpacked at Irina's vanity, reveal enough makeup to last a lifetime. Simón and I watch the scene unfold, and when I look back at him, his eyebrows are raised and his lips are pressed together. His beard is longer today. I hadn't noticed. It looks nice.

He shrugs and startles me by taking the cup of coffee from my hands, replacing it with the list before he steps back and moves toward one of the tall chairs in front of a vanity.

I stare after him, the pointy edges of the paper square digging into my palm as I try to regulate my nerves. I didn't know how much I needed him to be okay with this, to not judge me, until I saw his playful gaze. I could pass out from relief.

I start unfolding the list. We can put this whole thing behind us and—

My eyes snap up to where Simón is sitting, watching me through the mirror, biting a corner of his lower lip as he studies my reaction. Because he didn't simply sign the list. He *edited* it.

The Ex-Perimento

1. ~~Evoke a memory~~
   BE BUSY.

2. ~~Be unpredictable (so he knows I'm not a control freak)~~
   BE YOURSELF. HE FELL IN LOVE WITH YOU ONCE, DIDN'T HE?

3. ~~Send him a text that "wasn't for him," so he's thinking about me (repeat as many times as needed).~~
   DO NOT TEXT HIM! STOP TEXTING HIM.

4. ~~Get a makeover so you look the way you did four years ago. He'll remember what he's missing.~~
   SHOW HIM HE'S NOT THE ONLY ONE. MAKE HIM JEALOUS.

5. ~~Send him a bouquet of flowers (manly flowers) so he knows I appreciate him, like he did whenever I helped him through finals.~~
   DO NOT DO THIS, FOR THE LOVE OF GOD.

6. ~~Reconnect with his parents.~~
   TRUST ME WHEN I TELL YOU, HARASSING HIS FAMILY IS NOT GOING TO HELP.

7. ~~Dress to kill and show up somewhere you know he'll be, like you did for your third anniversary.~~
   HAVE A BLAST WITHOUT HIM.

8. ~~*Make him feel needed. Men love to feel needed.*~~

I MEAN, YES. BUT ALSO, NO.

9. ~~*Ask him out on a date to "catch up," then another date, then another date, and before you know it, you're back together again.*~~

TREAT HIM LIKE A FRIEND. DON'T ASK HIM OUT, HE'LL ASK <u>YOU</u> OUT.

ATTE. SIMÓN ARREAZA, LEAD SINGER OF YOUR FAVORITE BAND.

My face grows violently hotter with each item on the list. I must be so red I could stop traffic. *What the hell?*

I turn away, hiding from his knowing smirk. I want to shrink until I disappear.

Not only did he read my list, but he also thinks none of it will work. What does he know? I've known him for, what? Three days? He's met Alejandro *once*. Hell, he's met *me* once. I wrote my list thinking about our past and the reasons Alejandro had for our so-called break. I know these will work because, as Simón so kindly pointed out in his list, Alejandro fell in love with me once. And my list will remind him of that. I fold the piece of paper and put it in my back pocket before leaving the room.

The quiet of the lonely morning has officially broken. PAs run from one end of the studio to another, Mileidy barks order after order, and I'm standing dumbstruck in the middle of it all.

Don't think about it, I say to myself, thinking about it. Back to work.

I make my way from backstage to the auditorium—past thick concrete columns and up a flickering staircase—pushing the doors open to take a peek inside. The faint scent of musty carpet drifts from the open doors. I can hear the clicking of cameras, some hanging from a metal structure while pointed at center stage, and faint background music playing through the speakers. The room is otherwise quiet. Onstage, getting another coat of powder on her face, is my mother. She wears a fitted navy blue dress that comes down to her knees, split at her middle by a beige belt. Her hair is down, a cascade of chocolate brown and champagne highlights.

I make my way down the auditorium stairs. The only binder missing from the judges table is Simón's, so I place it carefully in front of his seat and set down a black gel pen and highlighter.

With that taken care of, now it's my turn to run from one end of the theater to the other. For the next hour, I make sure the contestants all have their badges, bring water to a man who looks a little green, bring my mother a Gatorade so she doesn't pass out because she refused to have breakfast in her dress. By the time I sneak back into the auditorium, Simón is already in his seat at the table. There's a water bottle to the right of the binder, while a large cup of coffee grows cold on the left.

I choose to sit in the very top row, where lighting is poorest, hoping to blend into the shadows.

Simón's attention is split between the binder and his phone. His lips move over the phone as he flips through the pages. Sending a voice message, I assume. He leans closer to the binder and frowns. He sets his phone down and leans over his seat to spy on Irina's pages.

Oh, he must have noticed the bookmarks. I managed to finish with ten minutes to spare.

Simón twists in his seat. I don't know how he knows where I am, but he spots me immediately and smiles. He gives me a thumbs-up before turning back around and slouching over the binder, his phone abandoned.

Even though no one can see me, my chin drops to my chest to hide the smile I'm fighting back.

No, Marianto.

The door to my right opens, light streaming in, as Federico Gómez makes his appearance. He walks in unceremoniously, adjusting his sleeves. When he's almost to the end of the stairs, he looks straight at the camera and waves. Judging by the cameraman's defeated expression, he wasn't supposed to do that. He disappears backstage. Five minutes later, Irina joins Simón at the judges' table. Ten minutes after that, Federico takes his seat beside her.

The sound of shoes clacking on the stage echoes across the auditorium as the first contestant walks in. The spotlight follows a short blonde girl. She's in a skirt, tights, and a crop top. A huge golden sticker depicting a bright "1" is covering her stomach. Elena Pérez, fourteen, according to her profile. The empty stage dwarfs her, her walk to the center unbearably long.

I get my phone ready to record this. I'm thinking it'd be cool to have the first and last person to audition, so I make sure I'm getting the number 1 card hanging from her neck.

After introducing herself, Elena announces she'll be singing "Dynamite" by BTS.

Judging by Irina's and Federico's expressions, they have no idea who BTS is. Nor does my mother.

But Simón smiles and says, "Perfecto."

How is *one* girl going to sing a song by seven men?

Elena begins and *oh* how I wish her song choice was the worst part of her audition, but no. Her singing is. Maybe 10 percent nerves, 90 percent not being able to carry a tune, but her voice is shaky and pitchy and plainly unpleasant to the ear. Not that I'm a great singer; I'm pretty sure I sound worse than she does, but I'm not trying out for a singing competition that will be broadcast on national TV.

Where are her parents? I think, and immediately hate myself for it. Maybe she has supportive parents who didn't want to clip her wings, parents who support her choices even at fourteen. That's not a bad thing. Not every kid needs to hear they're not good at the thing they love. Life will tell them.

Irina raises her hand, stopping Elena abruptly. Elena blinks, trying to see despite the bright lights.

"No," Irina says.

Apparently, today *life* goes by the name of Irina Montalbán.

Elena straightens in place. She's strong. She'll be fine. I'm willing to bet that her parents will be out there ready to console her.

Simón whirls to Irina, wide-eyed.

I dissolve into my seat, lowering my phone. No need to get this on video after all.

CHAPTER 14

TODAY THE JUDGES HAVE A SPECIAL DINNER, SO I'm instructed to go home. I'm glad to have a few hours back to myself today, because I finally have some time to drive my next experiment. I bumped Experiment #6: ***Reconnect with his parents*** to number 4 because today's the only day I can carry it out.

Do you know where my mom could take some Pilates classes while my parents are here? Ale had asked me from the bathroom before his graduation.

And I, dutiful girlfriend that I was, had found a class at a gym in Las Mercedes, pulled some strings, and booked it for half the price. According to my notes, Alejandro's parents are leaving in two days. I had already confirmed a couple days ago that Bárbara would still be attending the Pilates class today. The class starts in ten minutes. I've never done Pilates in my life, but so help me God, I will be on a mat stretching my legs next to that woman because I have to make her love me.

When I make it to the gym, Alejandro's mother is already standing by a pink mat. My hands immediately start sweating at the sight of her. Her dark hair is pulled into a tight ponytail. She's also wearing leggings and a sports bra. Her body is fit.

Like *fit* fit. Like Jennifer Aniston in that Adam Sandler movie where she fakes being his wife. I know she turned sixty-five last year. This is a woman who takes Pilates seriously. I, on the other hand, am a woman who was blessed with a fast metabolism and doesn't really care for the gym.

There is a blue mat next to her, up for grabs. I walk toward it with intention. I don't want to pretend I didn't see her. But I also can't tell her, *Oh, hi, I came here because I knew you'd be here, and I want you to talk your son into getting back together with me.*

Truth be told, I don't want her to talk him into getting back together with me. I want her to like me. Just like I want everyone to like me. I can't marry into a family that hates me. I'll be miserable. I want to go over our differences, smooth things out so when she gets home, she'll tell Alejandro, *Oh, I ran into Marianto today. What a lovely girl.*

I don't think that's asking too much.

With my heart beating in my throat, I approach. "Mrs. Bárbara?"

Alejandro's mother looks up from her phone. She blinks, seeming confused either as to who I am or as to why I'm here. I watch her school her features into a pleasant smile that doesn't reach her eyes.

"Maria Antonieta," she says.

"How have you been?" I go for a hug, but she raises both hands in front of her to stop me. Okay.

"I've been better."

That's it. She doesn't elaborate, doesn't tell me why.

"Oh, are you ill?" I ask.

She shakes her head once. "No."

I blink. She blinks back. I shift my weight from one leg to

the other. Simón's comment on this particular item on the list comes back to haunt me. I hope Ale's mother doesn't feel harassed. For all she knows, I come here regularly. For all she knows, this is a total coincidence.

I try again. "So, how's your—"

She taps her index finger to her lips, then points ahead. "We're starting."

The instructor is setting up the sound system and smiling at her phone. We are not starting.

Bárbara, Ale's mother, turns her back on me, sits on her mat, and starts stretching. The class is an hour long. I can still save this. Her hesitance is understandable. Ale and I are in muddy waters; she doesn't know what's allowed and what isn't. Let's face it, *I* don't know either.

I sit crossed-legged on my mat, facing the mirror. Around me, every single person is stretching. The instructor still hasn't given us any instructions. I watch, horrified, as every single woman here touches their toes, so flexible that their heads reach their shins. It's like they're made of rubber or something. My muscles tense when I try to do the same. The backs of my knees hurt and they refuse to stay flat. The most I can do is touch the tip of my fingers to the middle of my shins. I catch a glimpse of myself in the mirror and quickly straighten. I look like an edgy mannequin. Everyone else looks like a Cirque du Soleil contortionist.

The instructor finally settles on the music . . . and then she leaves. Disappears behind an invisible door. Around me, everyone starts shaping their bodies into some demonic form I'm never going to be able to make. I'm the only one standing, clueless about what to do.

I lean toward Bárbara. "Why isn't the instructor instructing us?"

"This is an advanced class," she explains without looking at me. She's too busy lifting her torso and putting her legs behind her head. "Everything is on the board." The only thing I see on the board is a list of animal names, the first one being "Scorpion." "Which you, of course, know." She side-eyes me from where she's lying on the mat. "Otherwise you wouldn't have shown up. Who shows up to an advanced Pilates class when they've never done Pilates before in their life, right?" The sarcasm in her voice reminds me of Ale. It's amazing that after four years I'm just learning where he got it from.

"Right." Her words immediately put me on edge, a bolt of anxiety shooting directly into my nervous system.

This is my new nightmare. Alejandro's mother appearing at the foot of my bed, legs behind her head, telling me *Who shows up to an advanced Pilates class when they've never done Pilates in their life, right?*

Bárbara's eyes shift away from me, looking at her own knees. A clear dismissal.

Carefully, I lie on the mat, the way she's doing. I steal glances her way every thirty seconds, just to make sure I'm doing this correctly. I'm not sure I'm doing this correctly. Slowly, I start lifting my torso, but I can't support my own weight. My legs, which are still firmly on the ground, begin to shake. This was a mistake. Frankly, I've decided I don't trust anyone who does Pilates because where the hell are your bones? Nope. I'm leaving.

I start to lower the one leg I managed to lift, but a current of pain spreads through my spine. It's so surprising, I let out a gasp. Oh, God. I'm stuck. My heart begins to race.

This isn't happening.

I try again. It hurts again.

"Help," I plead. "Please."

“What was that, dear?” Bárbara asks beside me.

“Help,” I repeat. “I’m stuck.”

No more than a minute later the instructor appears above my head, frowning. She lowers my leg in one swift move without uttering a single word or caring about the blinding pain that shoots from my lower back to my toes.

I curl on my side as I hear her walk away. I’m gasping for air. Out of all the experiments, this was probably the worst. Whatever draft I end up delivering to Eugenia will feature nothing but a long chain of failures.

I push myself up. No one is paying attention to me; they’re all minding their own contortionist business. No one but Bárbara, that is.

“How do you feel?” she asks me. It’s the first time in four years I’ve seen her look at me with something similar to kindness.

I decide to tell the truth. “Foolish.”

She purses her lips, tilting her head. “A word of advice, if I may.” I nod. She reaches between the mats, crossing to mine, and pats my sore leg. “Getting someone to like you shouldn’t be this hard.”

LATER, I’M IN bed, with a bag of ice on my leg.

Experiment #4 (previously #6) was an utter failure, even though it produced a possible entry point into Experiment #8: ***Make him feel needed***. My leg is wounded. I could need him to help me get groceries or something. I’m sure his mother will tell him all about the incident. But I don’t feel like experimenting. I just want to have him with me. I want to cuddle into his side the way I did whenever I got sick, his fingers playing with my hair because he knew it relaxes me. I want to be scolded for drinking some herbal tea instead of going to the drugstore. I want him to roll his eyes at me and make me soup and make sure I get the rest I need. I want to be taken care of. My mother doesn't count. I want Ale.

I get off Instagram and text.

YO: Hola. Are you busy?

And I wait. I know Experiment #3 was supposed to be sending a "fake" text, but I don't have the energy to fake anything. I miss him. I want to talk to him.

An hour passes. Then two. I've been trying to sleep but my body feels electrified with anticipation. It's well past ten. He's probably asleep now. If he hasn't replied, he's not going to. I log back in to Instagram and find his profile again. My heart receives a blow when I see he posted a story. Eighteen minutes ago. He's out with friends I recognize. They're at what appears to be a restaurant. He's slouching on a chair, holding a beer in his right hand. He smiles lazily at the camera. He seems happy. Or lost. I don't know.

A single tear rolls down my cheek, but I quickly wipe it away. How long is it going to take him to miss me? He wanted time. I've given him time. Why does it feel like instead of deciding that he wants me, he's forgetting me?

I pull the list from my purse, study it again. It doesn't look clean and promising anymore. With Simón's handwriting, it looks exactly like the confusing mess the ordeal is turning out to be. I run a finger over Simón's words and wonder, for the first time, if maybe he's right. What could it hurt to try?

CHAPTER 15

******

THE FOLLOWING MONDAY, WE'RE IN STUDIO B, where *Tu Mañana* is produced. A morning show that covers everything from celebrity gossip to the hottest new recipes, it is one of VeneTV's most successful shows. It's only fitting that the stars of *Talento V* make an appearance.

Mamá, Simón, Irina, and Federico stand around the director's chair, listening to instructions. I snap a picture of them and post it to my stories with the hashtag *#bestjobever*. It's far away enough that it won't be a contract breach, but clear enough that Alejandro will be able to recognize them. Let's see if Simón is right. I've stopped texting Alejandro, but it'll take him longer than two days to notice. I also can't show him that there are other people lined up to date me, as there aren't. I can't treat him as a friend, since I'm not talking to him at all. And since being myself is a laughable suggestion, that leaves me with Experiment #7: ***Have a blast without him***.

Am I having a blast? No. I've been up since four. No one can have a blast when they've been up since four, have downed six cups of coffee, and are battling a growing migraine. Judging by our stars' faces, I'm not the only one.

Once the director is finished, our stars scatter around the studio. I follow Simón to the interview set, which is modeled after a very orange living room. He sits on the couch, picks up a black acoustic guitar resting on a stand beside it, and props it on his lap like muscle memory requires it. Behind him, a flat-screen TV shows a video of El Ávila, our emblematic mountain, through a window. Every thirty seconds a blue-and-yellow macaw flies by.

Simón leans to his left, closer to the neck of the guitar, his ear almost pressed against the wood as he begins to tune it.

He looks up when he senses my presence, smiling. His eyes wrinkle at the corners when he smiles. I hadn't noticed that before. They must Photoshop it out of pictures.

"You cut your hair," he points out, a hint of surprise in his tone.

Like that, he's the first and only person to notice. My previously mid-back-length hair now comes to my shoulder blades in beautiful, soft layers, while asymmetrical bangs cover my forehead, ending above my eyebrows. Alejandro would absolutely hate it, which is partly why I did it. I was supposed to get a makeover as one of the experiments. I wanted to look like twenty-three-year-old Marianto to remind him of the good old days, but I was in a fit of rage two days ago after Experiment #3 didn't work and he never replied to my text. Alejandro was the one who insisted I grow it out, so I decided to chop off half of my hair instead.

I force myself to smile back. "I did. Here."

I hand him a water bottle—room temperature because he has to sing today, as Google suggested—which he accepts and immediately takes a sip.

"Gracias," he says, lips glistening. "You look great. It suits you."

Oh? A warm sensation spreads throughout my body and my cheeks flush. His kind eyes twinkle with amusement at my embarrassment. I clear my throat with a nod.

"I should"—I gesture to somewhere behind me, I don't know where—"get back. But, um . . . let me know if you need anything?"

A corner of Simón's mouth twitches upward, his eyebrows pinching together in curiosity. An open book. He looks like he wants to say something else, but I'm already retracing my steps.

I should get back? Where am I supposed to go? I work for him, my whole job is to be where he is.

"Mamita." My mother intercepts me.

"Don't call me 'mamita' in the workplace, please," I say. "It's unbecoming."

She pats my cheeks. "I've called you that since you were a baby, I'm not going to stop now that we're colleagues."

She continues her path to join Simón at the interview set.

Colleagues. We're not colleagues. She's a TV show host and I'm an assistant. I take a deep breath. I remind myself why I took this job in the first place. It's not about my mother, it's about being able to survive while I get back to my real life of an adoring boyfriend, a job with so many perks it's hard to imagine I ever took it for granted, and getting home at exactly 6:00 p.m., Monday through Friday, to an empty apartment.

Is that what you really want? an annoying little voice says. *A life where every day is the same?*

Yes! I scream back. *That's exactly what I want.*

Security. Safety. A solid ground I can stand on, knowing nothing's going to knock me off of it.

Around me, lights dim as the host of *Tu Mañana* takes the stage.

I turn away, deciding to stand by the snack table. Simón will be tired after this; he'll need fuel. Maybe a protein bar and a cup of bitter coffee he pretends to like. I have no idea what flavor of protein bar he might like—apple crumble, lemon pie, peanut butter and chocolate chips?

My phone vibrates in my back pocket. I take it out as I grab one of each bar—Simón will pick whatever he likes best. Or maybe he'll want them all.

I put my phone on my ear, expecting it to be Mileidy because heaven knows the woman can sense when I'm not doing anything.

"Aló?"

Will eating a cupcake get me fired? I skipped breakfast. And the orange buttercream frosting looks delicious.

"Aló, hi," a too-familiar voice says.

I freeze, any thoughts of a cupcake discarded. It must be a butt dial. But if it's a butt dial, why is he saying hello? And if it's not a butt dial, why is he calling me?

Wait. The picture. Did it work?

I can't believe Simón's list actually worked. Looking over my shoulder, I put all the protein bars back on the table and sneak behind a metal ladder. I press my ring finger into my left ear to block any noise from the set.

"Hey," I say, heart racing. "Are you okay?"

Because he must be dying. Why else would Alejandro call me after two weeks if he's not dying?

"Sí, I'm good." Huh. "You?"

Heart going into cardiac arrest, brain launched into turmoil, if you must know. I run my fingers over my chest, trying to soothe my pulse. The true answer to his question would reveal the chaos within me since the "break." And does he really want to know? Do I even want to tell him?

I decide I don't. "Busy."

"With the Caballo de Troya guy," he states. His tone is sharp, his voice tight and strained, and maybe even a bit angry.

Oh my god, I mouth. Is he jealous? Of *Simón*?

My eyes dart to the closest monitor, where I see Simón is laughing at the story of how my mother came to be on the show. His relaxed posture, leaning against the couch, hands behind his back, makes me feel like he's actually in his living room.

I look away quickly, as if afraid Alejandro could see me. "As a matter of fact, yes."

"You know, working for a member of Caballo de Troya feels like the kind of thing you would have shared with me," he says. "I was a little hurt that you didn't."

Hope sparks in my chest. It shouldn't make me glad, hearing I hurt his feelings, but it does. It means he still cares. And if he cares, we can save this. Having a blast without him is proving to be a success.

"I'm sorry, it's a whole legal thing." Not a lie, but it didn't stop me from telling Blanca, so I could have easily told him.

"Oh."

"Um, did you want something or are you saying hi?" I ask. *Please, be saying hi.*

Alejandro clears his throat. I know him so thoroughly, I can perfectly picture him scanning his surroundings, looking for an escape.

"No, I—" He clears his throat again. "I wanted to ask if you remember the moving company I used last year? I'm supposed to be moving next month and I was wondering, since you helped me last time—"

My heart stops. Him moving is not part of the plan. Is he

taking that job near his parents? That's *hours* away from here. He can't move.

"Where are you going?" I ask, voice trembling.

The thought of him leaving Caracas is unbearable. Thinking he's not going to be at my favorite coffee shop again should fill me with relief, but it doesn't. It hurts.

He takes a pause before he replies, unaware of my heart breaking on the other side of the phone. "Barinas," he finally says. My hands stills over my chest.

He's thinking about leaving. And if he's thinking about leaving, then he's *not* thinking about me.

"Do you think you could send me the contact info?" he asks.

Beyond me, and on the monitor, the host turns to Simón with a smile. "We're cutting to commercial in a moment, but please—would you sing a little something before we do?"

Simón grabs the guitar from the stand. "Do you have a favorite?" he asks.

The host waves the question off. "They're all my favorite." Which is code for *I haven't heard any of them*.

The opening notes of the song I've been listening to nearly every day for the past six months fill the studio. To me, they're like a fist closing around my heart.

What wouldn't I give to be loved like that again? Completely, almost maniacally. To feel at home. To have a clear path to happiness the way I make a clear path to everything else. The memories this song brings pile up until they harden into a lump in my throat. Alejandro is in every single one.

Simón's eyes shift and suddenly he's looking directly at the camera, at me. His smile becomes sheepish, as if he knows this might not be the host's favorite song, but is sure it's mine.

"Marianto?" Alejandro says in my ear.

"Sure, I'll send it." Because that's what a friend would do. And Simón says I have to treat him as a friend.

I know that even if I didn't still have the mover's info, I would find it again just because he asked. Because it's him. I would do anything just because it's him.

"Y con ese regalo, we're cutting to commercial. We'll see you in a bit," the host says, grinning so wide her cheeks must hurt. "Don't go anywhere!"

The set, dead quiet one second before, rumbles with movement as soon as the cameras stop rolling. I hang up before Alejandro has a chance to say thank you, then walk back to the snack table and grab a protein bar instead of the damn cupcake. I'll need the energy, if I'm going to do what I think I'm going to do.

CHAPTER 16

••••••

SIMÓN CROSSES HIS ARMS OVER THE TABLE SEPArating us, leaning forward. "Start over."

I frown, looking at his elbows resting on the sticky wood. The smell of sizzling meat and French fries is so overpowering that I can taste the salt on my lips. I should have brought him somewhere nicer. Or at least somewhere we could hear ourselves think. Tayo's Grill is noisy this time of day, with booming music and the clinks and clanks of cutlery against plates.

"Where did I lose you?" I ask, raising my voice over the music. What's so hard to understand? All he has to do is tell me what to do so Alejandro realizes he loves me and does want to marry me before he uproots his entire life and moves six hours away.

Narrowing his eyes, Simón tilts his head to one side and furrows his nose. "The part where you said I can somehow help you get back together with your ex?"

"He's not my ex," I correct. "We're on a break."

"So, you're broken up," he says, like it's two plus two.

"No."

"There is no such thing as a break," Simón adds.

"Yes, there is," I push back. "I'm *in* one right now."

Simón sighs, sitting up. He parts his lips to say something but stops when he notices our waitress approaching with steaming plates of burgers dripping cheese. I'm having a regular bacon cheeseburger. Simón ordered a burger with onions sautéed in rum, and brie instead of cheddar cheese. The waitress places a beer in front of Simón and a Pepsi in front of me, followed by our respective meals.

She smiles at Simón, ignoring me altogether. "Can I get you anything else?"

I dip one of my fries in cheese and pop it into my mouth, savoring the smooth melted cheddar blended with the salty, crunchy potato. This is what I live for.

"We're good for now, thank you," he says, looking at me for confirmation. I nod.

"A la orden," the girl says, batting her eyelashes at him before she leaves.

Simón shoots me a quick eyebrow raise, followed by a contented sigh as he takes a sip of his beer.

"Do you think she knows who you are?" I ask, watching the girl make a beeline back to the counter.

Simón twists on his chair with a small frown, following my gaze. "No. People don't usually recognize us unless we're all together."

His eyes have a glint of mischief when he turns back to me. My face heats at the reminder of our second meeting and what I said. I decide to ignore his jab for both our sakes.

"Does it happen a lot?" I ask. Simón lifts both eyebrows in question. "Getting recognized when you're together?"

He shrugs, picking up his burger. "It happens enough."

Gotta love the humility. Caballo de Troya is an underappreciated gem of a band in the age of reguetón. Soon enough every Spanish-speaking woman under thirty will be falling at their feet. The growth hasn't been fast, but it's been steady. And it's been a real joy to watch.

"Alejandro recognized you," I offer.

"Maybe he's a bigger fan than most," he says.

"And do you think you could help me get back together with your biggest fan?" I venture.

Simón's playfulness melts. "Maria Antonieta—"

My chin dips to my chest as I cast my eyes down to my half-eaten burger. It was a long shot. Not to mention unprofessional. I'm here to make *his* life easier, not the other way around. I take a deep breath, trying to steady myself as I gather my thoughts. I can feel the weight of his attention on me, heavy and warm, and it sends a shiver down my spine.

"I'm sorry." I lift my gaze back to his. "That was out of line. Forget I said anything."

"Hey, it's okay." Simón's expression softens even more, and he reaches out to touch my arm lightly. "I understand wanting to hold on to something good, I do. I'm making a career out of that philosophy—"

I huff. "No kidding. I got a four-year-long relationship because the nerd from med school told me 'Una Vez Más' reminded him of me."

Simón leans back against his chair with a smirk, tilting his head to the side. "'Una Vez Más'? *You might be crazy, you might break my heart, but I'll never know if I don't see you one more time*? That one?" I nod. "And you liked it?"

"Is there something wrong with that?" I ask.

Simón shakes his head. "This whole situation seems very complicated. I don't think I should get involved."

"You got involved when you edited my list," I remind him.

"Well, your list was never going to work." He pops a fry into his mouth.

"You don't know that."

He swallows, then *tsk*s. "I do. I was doing you a favor. It didn't mean I'd coach you through the process."

"No, yeah, I got that," I say, before taking a huge bite of my burger.

He won't help me, but I was silly enough to ask. I'll be lucky if he doesn't go straight to Mileidy and request a whole new assistant. In fact, I should beat him to it and quit.

Silence stretches between us, heavy and awkward. Yup. I'm quitting and I'm moving cities until the show wraps, somewhere I'll never run into him. Maybe that's why Alejandro is moving. He thinks there'll be less chance of us seeing each other if we don't live thirty minutes apart.

Ten seconds later, while I'm still chewing, Simón fixes his eyes on me with a sigh as he runs a hand down his face. I *think* I also hear him groan. "Hypothetically—"

I perk up.

"*Hypothetically*," he repeats, reading the hope that has surely entered my eyes. "If I were to help you, what's in it for me?"

Oh. I hadn't thought this far ahead. It's a valid request. I can't offer him anything in particular, but that doesn't mean I don't have anything to give.

"I could offer you the chance to contribute to something meaningful," I begin slowly, choosing my words carefully, "to someone's life. To my life. You'd be helping someone who needs it and maybe even making a difference in their future." I pause for effect before continuing in an almost breathless manner as the passion of my message begins to take hold of me. "You'd be offering me your friendship and support during a difficult time in my life and showing me that there are still people out there who care about others more than themselves."

My voice softens as I look deep into his eyes, hoping that he'll understand what I'm—

"So, nothing," Simón concludes.

Okay, fine. I know enough about Caballo de Troya to come up with something, even if it's something I'm not sure I can give. The band started five years ago playing in bars all over Colombia. They're talented, which has caught the eye of major artists. Simón and his bandmate Fernando have written for other people, the band has collaborated with renowned artists. That said, I still talk about Caballo de Troya with friends and their go-to reply is, "Who's that?"

I plunge in headfirst. "You're doing *Talento V* for exposure, right? For the band?"

Simón's eyes automatically narrow with suspicion. The man wears his thoughts on his face like sunblock. "Maybe."

Definitely, I think. The band is relatively new. Most bands would have crashed and burned by now. But not my favorite Colombian foursome. That means they're working hard to stay in the industry. *Everything* they do must be for exposure.

"Well, if I succeed in getting back together with Alejandro, I'll be getting a promotion at my old job—"

Simón perks up. "*Ellas* magazine?"

I frown. "How do you know I worked at *Ellas*?"

Simón purses his lips, averting his eyes.

That small moment in my car, a little over a week ago, comes back to my mind with a clash. *You actually like our music?* That's what he asked. *Actually*. Because he knows I used it all the time for *Ellas*' Instagram stories. He *does* know me from the magazine. And if he knows me from the magazine, he probably saw the video.

"How? Why?" I stumble on my own words. How is it possible that I keep embarrassing myself in front of him?

Simón shrugs. "It's a great source of inspiration. Especially your column."

Inspiration. "For . . . ?"

"Songs," he completes.

"Oh my god."

I don't realize I'm laughing until he joins me. I'm half sure it's my anxiety, while he's perpetually amused by my embarrassing myself in front of him.

"So you get inspiration by making up stories about random strangers and by reading my column," I say, just to be sure.

Simón grins, his eyes flashing with undiluted joy.

"I guess you could say we're both fans of each other's work," I conclude.

"Yeah, you could say that." He chuckles with a firm shake of his head. "I didn't realize that was you until you said it in the car. You're a good writer, you know."

I feel my cheeks warm in surprise, painfully aware that a blush is tinting my skin a soft pink. Simón's compliment is unexpected, and it sends a wave of pleasure through me that I didn't even know I was craving.

"Thank you," I say, feeling a little embarrassed and unsure of what to do with the sudden attention. "That means a lot."

Simón's gaze locks on to mine, and for the briefest moment I'm sure he can see all the way into my soul. His eyes sparkle with understanding and admiration.

"Uh, bueno." I look away, clearing my throat. "If you help me and I succeed, I will get promoted to the Arts and Culture Department. I'll be able to write reviews and profiles, among other things. A profile on an up-and-coming hot band is not unheard-of for *Ellas*. I'm sure everyone will be on board. You know how big the magazine is across Latin America. Our target audience is women, which, let's be honest, is also *your* target audience." Simón chuckles at this. "Help me. And once I get my job back, I will write Caballo de Troya a profile so good you'll need to add extra dates to your next tour." Which I happen to know begins at the end of the year because I was already planning to "visit my mother" the same week they're playing in Miami.

"Would you really do that for us?" Simón asks, his voice soft.

"Of course!" I mean, Eugenia would have to green-light it, but yes. "I'll get you on the cover. I'll even get you your own photo shoot, none of that using old pictures you can find on Google." Simón watches me through narrowed yet hopeful eyes. "You want exposure? I'll give you exposure."

Simón sighs, long and low, dropping his chin to his chest. "What does coaching you look like to you?"

I grin. I think I just won. "Well, your list is kind of vague, but effective. What I need is for you to help me find ways to carry it out. How do I have a blast without him? Or how can I be myself if he's not around to see it?" Simón seems unconvinced, watching me through narrow eyes, though not unkindly. His deep brown eyes are soft, almost sad. I shift in my seat. The feeling of being under scrutiny makes me uneasy. "What?"

He shakes his head. "Nada. I'll help you."

I fight the urge to clap and dance right here on this chair. "Yay!"

"But don't blame me if you change your mind about the whole thing halfway through," he adds. "You'll still owe me a profile."

I shake my head, offering him my hand. "I won't."

He accepts my hand and squeezes once before releasing it. "Do you want dessert?"

I start to shake my head. "I don't think I should—"

He pushes to his feet with a sigh. "You want dessert. I'll be right back."

"A brownie sundae, please!" I call after him.

Simón gives me a thumbs-up behind his back. I watch him as he strides out of sight, a gentle draft ruffling the top of his hair. His steps are sure, so confident in his decisions. This is someone who knows what he wants, where he is, what he's doing. Bringing him in is the right call. On the table, next to my empty plate, my phone vibrates. My heart picks up immediately, anticipating Alejandro. It deflates just as quickly.

EUGENIA: How is my article coming together? You said you'd send something this week and I haven't received a single paragraph yet.

I read the text twice before I reply.

YO: The article is going great! I'm making a lot of progress, actually.

For once, it's not a lie.

EUGENIA: I'm tired of waiting. Let's meet at my house. Ask Blanca for my schedule.

My bouncing knee hits the table. Being invited to Eugenia's is a rare occurrence. In five years, she's never asked me to meet her at her house. Meetings were either in her office or speed walking through the halls, sometimes during an accidental ride in the elevator together.

The warm, gooey goodness of the fresh-out-of-the-oven brownie fills our table with its chocolatey aroma when Simón returns. A generous scoop of creamy vanilla ice cream melts slowly on top, dripping off the sides in an indulgent display. Simón smiles down at me, carrying another plate, twin to mine in appearance and content. Eugenia will love this. A romantic Colombian singer-songwriter helping her love guru columnist get her boyfriend back? How can she not?

Who knows, I might even have fun.

CHAPTER 17

DAY ONE OF MY LESSONS. SIMÓN SITS IN FRONT of me after work. There are dark circles under his eyes, which the makeup department always makes sure to correct, but despite him wearing jeans and a perfectly tailored striped baby blue button-down, sleeves rolled up to his elbows, I can see how tired he is.

I took him to the biggest mall in the city: El Sambil, the one in Chacao, since it's close to his hotel and it's not a huge detour from the studio. I brought him to the terrace, where he can choose to eat whatever he wants—Italian food, Middle Eastern food, sushi, ice cream—it's all here, while the starry Caracas sky unfolds above us and the city is on full display as far as the eye can see. Simón's messy hair moves with the wind as he slumps against his chair. He's answering a text from Fernando, Caballo de Troya's other singer. Behind him, Caracas twinkles and blinks, alive. Urban music booms around us, but not enough to drown our conversation. The Ex-Perimento list lies between us on the table. His handwriting stands out more than my computer-generated letters. It's messy and rushed, the way artists' usually is, like if he takes two seconds to care about writing in a straight line, the muse will grow impatient and leave.

Simón puts his phone back on the table, screen facing down. "Sorry about that. Where were we?"

I play with a napkin. I've been ripping it apart and turning it into little balls. "You wanted to know about Ale."

"Yes," he says. "In order to make Alejandro fall in love with you again, I need more information."

Love it. This feels like we're doing something, taking action. Being productive. Like something might come out of it.

"What do you want to know?"

Simón shifts on his chair to sit up and rests his elbows on the table. "What do you like about him?"

That's easy. "I like that he's reliable."

Simón's eyes narrow. "Reliable."

"Yes." He's on time, calls when he says he's going to call, sticks to his routine like his abuela's life depends on it. I tell Simón exactly this. "There are no surprises with him, I always know what to expect."

"So he's predictable," Simón deadpans. "And boring."

"No, he's not boring," I say, defensive. "He's trustworthy."

"A man can be trustworthy without being boring, Maria Antonieta." I ignore the shiver that runs down my spine when he says my full name.

"What's your middle name?" I blurt out. It seems unfair that he knows mine and I don't know his.

Simón's lips twitch upward in that way I notice they always do when he's fighting a smile. "Andrés."

"Well, Simón Andrés—" He stops fighting the smile and grins. It pleases me a little too much, being the one who provoked it. I look away, flushed. "A man can also be interesting without leading the life of a rock star."

He huffs, putting a hand to his chest like I wounded him. "That felt personal."

I shake my head. "It's not. But it *is* another thing I like about him."

"That he has a boring job?" Simón asks.

"That he has a *normal* job," I correct. "I decided a long time ago I never wanted to date someone in the entertainment industry."

"May I ask why?"

I shrug. "I grew up surrounded by that environment. I guess I've had my fill." It's partially true. The other part I keep to myself—that I saw how it destroyed my mother's relationships, both romantic and otherwise. That I'm tired of having to share the people I love with strangers. That when it comes to love, I need someone I can count on. I want my children to have someone they can count on, someone who takes care of them. A parent, not an idol.

Simón nods slowly. "Did you ever consider following in your mother's footsteps?"

I shrug again. For a while, yes. She wanted me to. I was an extra in almost every telenovela she made. I'd go with her to events, fall asleep on velvet chairs in crowded theaters when I couldn't keep my eyes open anymore. But I couldn't be a part of the business I resented for taking her from me. I don't tell Simón this.

"Journalism seemed more suited to me," I tell him instead. "What about you? Did you ever consider a different career?"

"No." He says it fast, automatic. "It has always been music or nothing for me. The closest I've come to considering a different career was becoming a music teacher. But only if everything else fails."

Simón's eyes get lost somewhere behind me, in the sea of

tables, people, and different food stands, but I know he's not thinking about any of that. If he's anything like me, he's thinking about failure. About the current situation, why we need each other. I know we both need this to succeed.

He seems to reach a similar decision. His expression changes; his eyes become more focused when they land back on me.

"So, we've established Alejandro is predictable," he says. I want to fight, but he doesn't give me the room. "Here's the first thing you're going to do, if you want to get him back: You're going to leave him alone."

THE REST OF the week is hell. Turns out Alejandro is much better at leaving me alone than I am at leaving *him* alone. I've fallen into the habit of checking where he is every night through social media, which is a new level of low. But today is different, because I have a legitimate reason.

"Stop texting him."

I jump at Simón's accusation, hiding my phone behind my back. "I wasn't!"

It's a lie. I was. But I have a good excuse: It's his birthday. Twenty-nine. He used to talk about it like he was Schmidt from *New Girl*. Unironically. I *have* to text him on his birthday.

Simón is frowning down at his iPad as he scrolls but stops to raise an eyebrow at me. His liquid brown eyes scan my face, searching for cracks. He doesn't believe me, I know. It doesn't mean I'll admit to breaking the rules. I hold Simón's gaze and feel my chin tilt up. His eyes catch the small movement. A corner of his lips twitch in response. He swallows, his throat bobbing up and down. Why am I looking at his throat?

Stop it.

Simón parts his lips, as if to say something, but the door to our rehearsal room shoots open, making us jump, and a small army of kids ages eight to twelve walks in. Saved by the tiny singers.

The room we were given for coaching sessions is smaller than we'd anticipated, seating only ten children at a time. We've scheduled two sessions today and two tomorrow. We managed to organize ten chairs in two rows of five. Simón had an electric piano brought in, which is sitting in the center of the room, right under an A/C vent. In the back, there are chairs piled up as high as the ceiling, which isn't that high to begin with. The room has no windows, making it feel closed off and isolated. The acoustics are terrible, the sound bouncing harshly off the bare walls. The chill in the air seeps into my bones, as if the room has never felt the warmth of sunlight. It also smells like fresh paint.

"A singer's nightmare," Simón called it.

I try to focus on that instead of the lingering feeling of Simón's eyes moving over my features as if committing them to memory. I point at empty chairs, counting heads as more kids fill the room. I've made sure there's a water bottle under each seat as well as a notebook and a pencil. The disparity in age within this particular group is worrisome. Simón suggested dividing his group by age for coaching sessions, but Mileidy shut it down so fast you'd think he suggested taking the kids clubbing.

"We don't need them becoming friends," she'd said. The result? A sweaty, green-faced ten-year-old girl who can't keep still sitting next to a very cool blue-haired twelve-year-old boy who hasn't stopped riffing since he sat down.

I join Simón in the middle of the room, in front of the electric piano, to meet the first batch of contestants. The lighting here is so terrible that even the latest iPhone wouldn't get a decent picture. The plastic chairs would probably break under enough pressure. And I think the A/C drips, judging by the spot of peeling paint beneath the unit.

"Good morning, everybody, cómo van?" Simón says with a loud clap.

And then Valeria, aka the girl with the green face, lurches forward and throws up all over my shoes. There's a moment of silence before hell explodes. Half the kids are screaming while the other half are laughing. The pungent smell of bile hits me immediately while I stand there trying not to get sick myself. Or think of my shoes. Or the fact that my favorite white jeans are now speckled with a random child's vomit. The little girl's face changes from green to burning red, from illness to shame and heartbreak. I take a few steps forward, reaching out for her, but words die on my lips when she takes off running, slamming the door on the way out. I push my sneakers off, jump over the puddle of vomit, and take off after her.

Behind me, Simón's voice rises over the screaming children, trying to calm them down.

Cold seeps through my socks, freezing my feet. I move down a narrow, poorly lit corridor that once might've filled me with childlike joy, but the girl is nowhere to be seen. Damn, she's fast.

Okay. If I were a ten-year-old girl who'd vomited in front of a famous singer *and* my competition, where would I hide? This particular ten-year-old is built different. If I were her, I would have marched right back the minute I saw the fluorescent lights above me flickering on and off every ten seconds. This floor was taken right out of one of the *Final Destination* movies.

That thought isn't exactly comforting.

"Valeria?" I call.

Alejandro's birthday rushes back to my mind. The experiments have to work because I will *not* spend the rest of my life walking down dark halls, looking for missing children.

Supply closets number one, two, and three are locked. Supply closet number four's floor is covered in tiny black pebbles, which I recognize as mouse poop. But no Valeria. My despair grows with every second I don't find her.

I walk by the bathroom sign depicting a silhouette of a man and halt. Anyone else would think *surely not.* But I did. And I did it again less than a month ago.

God, I hate this job.

I push the door open with my shoulder and immediately hear sniffling. A mirror and sink welcome me in. There are three stalls separated by yellow metal walls, the doors visibly open to all but one.

"Valeria?" I venture.

The sniffing stops.

My knees go weak from relief. Gracias a Dios.

I knock on her stall twice. "Hey, I'm—"

Behind me, the bathroom door swings open, and I'm jarred into stillness.

"There you are. Is it a habit of yours to hide in the men's bathroom?"

My face heats violently at the sound of Simón's voice, recalling our first meeting. Documents raining down around us, me on my knees, him blocking the door.

I ignore him and point to the stall where Valeria is hiding. Simón gazes at me before his eyes widen with understanding. "You found her?" he mouths.

I nod.

"You're a superhero," he says, approaching. "Hey, Valeria, it's Simón. Are you okay in there?"

I don't want to smile, but damn it, his eyes are gleaming and his eyebrows are raised and he looks a bit desperate while trying to fight a smile of his own as he sways on his heels, putting both hands in his pockets.

"No," Valeria says, her voice small but firm.

Looking away, I shake my head and mentally prepare a speech, but a metallic creak silences me before I even open my mouth. The door opens to reveal Valeria, eyeing us as if we're the ones who need a pep talk.

Simón softens beside me and as soon as he sets those liquid brown eyes on her, her chin wobbles and silent tears are running down her face again. She wipes them angrily with her sleeve.

I kneel in front of her, resting my hands on my lap. "Valeria," I whisper softly. She looks up and I can see the tears still glistening in her eyes, but her expression is one of determination. It encourages me to keep going. "We know you're scared right now, but it's going to be all right. It's truly not the end of the world."

She shakes her head.

"No, really, I threw up on a whole row of people once," I tell her. "In a ballet recital. My mother wore white. Her dress never recovered."

Simón and Valeria laugh. That's something.

"Did you go back?" she asks in her little voice.

I shake my head. "I wish I had. My teacher was nice—" I look pointedly at Simón, who is watching me in admiration. I almost wish I hadn't seen it. "And so were the other kids. I was just embarrassed. Now, you only threw up on one person—" I point at myself, drawing a smile out of her. "And I forgive you.

Please, don't let this tiny thing that could have happened to *anyone* stop you from going after your dream."

Valeria nods once. "Okay."

I grin. "Okay."

Simón claps and whoops, making her laugh. She shakes her head as she moves around me to walk out. He offers me his hand and pulls me to my feet.

"Nice job, Maria Antonieta." He says my name like it's a private joke between us. Not bossy, like Mileidy. Not a reprimand, like my mother. Not a punishment, like Alejandro. "Journalist, assistant, and kid whisperer. I think I almost have you figured out."

I give him a short, humorless laugh. "Feel free to tell me what you find. I might need it."

He shakes his head slowly. "You don't need me to tell you who you are."

Maybe not. But I still want to know what I seem like to him, what he sees when he looks at me.

We stare at each other for a second, two, before I cave and my eyes drift toward the urinals, meeting my gaze in the mirror. My thoughts travel back to our first meeting, in a similar bathroom, where I was the one hiding. What did he think of me then versus now? My neck is flushed under my wool sweater, locks of hair curling around my ears as my bangs fall unceremoniously over my forehead. I push the loose hair behind my ear.

"Um, I'll—" I point to the door and practically run out of there.

In the hall, I lean against a wall and try to steady myself, ignoring the pounding of my heart. I count to thirty, then force myself to walk calmly, as if there's nothing wrong, but I can feel my cheeks burning with embarrassment.

God, how starved am I for attention that Simón being grateful I helped him is enough to send me into cardiac arrest? He's grateful. And he's an artist, so he has to be dramatic about it. It's not a big deal.

As I'm walking back to the room, my phone vibrates in my pocket. *Please, let it be Alejandro.* I need it to be Alejandro. Alejandro will put my head back where it belongs. But of course, it's not. It's an email from a newsletter I can't remember signing up for. If I were sticking to my list, I'd show up at his birthday party today. I'd go buy a red dress and a new pair of boots and I would show up there looking every bit the important doctor's wife. But I'm not following my list anymore. I'm following Simón's. And Simón's list is designed for me to lose control over everything and lose my sanity in the process.

"Hey, what—"

I jump at the sound of his voice behind me. He eyes the phone in my hand and the empty chat I'd been staring at. The chat I hadn't even realized I'd opened. I lock my phone and put it away.

He bites the inside of his cheek, eyebrows close together. "I have to ask. What's so important that it can't wait for the end of the day?"

"It's his birthday," I explain, pathetically. I wasn't thinking about Ale's birthday just now. It was more about how . . . Ale isn't Simón. And I need Ale. "He'd never buy that I forgot his birthday."

"He wanted space, Marianto." That's the first time he's ever called me Marianto. "Give it to him."

I say the first thing I can think of: "He didn't invite me."

I sound pathetic. Yes, I want Ale to invite me, I want him to miss me, I want him to call and beg me to spend his birthday with him. But at the same time, Simón called me Marianto. Like we're friends. Not just boss and employee, or crazy-woman-who-dragged-me-into-this-mess and relationship coach. Friends. For some reason that thought overpowers the thought of Alejandro. And I don't know what that reason is.

"Would you invite your ex to your birthday?" he asks, unaware of the chaos that is my mind.

Focus on Ale.

"He's not—"

Simón sighs, raising both hands as if I were the police. "Fine. Perdón. We want you to succeed. If you want an invitation to his party, I'll get you an invitation."

"What?"

Suddenly, his phone is in his hands and his face is right next to mine with the biggest smile I've seen on him since we met.

"Say 'whiskey.'"

Instinctively, I smile just in time.

I watch, mouth open in horror, as he logs into Caballo de Troya's Instagram account and posts the picture on his feed, captioned "Ride or Die." I feel my eyes widen. The feed is important. The feed is permanent.

"Done." He gives his phone a little shake. "Viviana told me we're going to karaoke tonight. If you want to try having a blast without him, you know where we'll be."

Simón gives me a tight smile before walking around me and disappearing behind the corner.

I guess we're done leaving Ale alone and we've moved on to a different type of experiment. What I don't understand is why Simón seems angry about it.

CHAPTER 18

"ARE YOU SURE YOU DON'T WANT TO COME, MAmita?" my mother asks me, standing by the door in her sequin jumpsuit and tall boots.

I'm on my couch, in my comfiest pj's, balancing a bowl of cereal on my lap while scrolling through old *Caso Cerrado* clips on my phone.

"I'm sure."

It's nearly 8:00 p.m. No one is getting me out of this house after 8:00 p.m., certainly not to a karaoke party my mother organized as a bonding experience for *Talento V*'s stars.

"It won't be the same without you," she says, pouting. "Who's going to drive me home?"

"You'll find a ride."

My mother sighs. "Bueno, I won't insist. Enjoy your night."

"Thank you," I reply, bringing a spoonful of cornflakes up to my mouth.

She blows me a kiss from the doorway before walking out.

There's only one party I wanted to go to tonight and it's obvious I'm not going. Spending the night watching la Doctora Polo dealing with a woman who is sure her husband is also her long-lost brother is the next best thing. I bring another spoonful of cereal to my mouth, morbidly enjoying the screaming woman on my phone, until the video stalls, replaced by a familiar name flashing on the screen.

Alejandro. Calling. Like I wanted him to. And I'm in my pajamas, eating cereal.

Irrelevant. He can't see me. But that does nothing to calm my racing heart, to help me push air into my lungs. The anxious part of my brain whispers, *He'll know.* Hands shaking, I sit up and set the bowl down on the coffee table before I finally pick up.

"Aló?"

"Marianto, hi," he says.

His voice is a time machine. My chest tightens at the way he says my name, like it's a welcome surprise. Soft in my ears, in stark contrast with the urban beat I catch in the background. He could be sitting right next to me, talking about his day. He could be pushing a stray lock of hair behind my ear. He could be leaning over to kiss me. It physically hurts that it isn't the case. And I have to pretend I don't care about those things anymore. Like it was nothing, like we were nothing. How can someone feel so distant yet so familiar at the same time?

"Feliz cumpleaños," I say.

Ale chuckles on the other side. "I thought you forgot."

I wince. "Of course not. I was just busy. Are you having a good time?"

Without me? I want to add. Is he having an amazing birthday *without me*?

"Yeah, I am," he says. "Sounds like you're having fun as well."

Fun? I frown. I'm spending my night watching *Caso Cerrado* and eating stale cereal. This is the opposite of fun. "I don't know about that."

"Please, you're famous!" Ale laughs, but it's bitter. "Which surprised me, considering you always said the one thing you *didn't* want to be was famous."

"I don't know what you're talking about," I say, a little harsher than I meant to.

"Marianto." He says it like *C'mon*. "The picture."

The picture . . . Simón's picture? My first instinct is to laugh, but I'm too stunned to do it. I can't help feeling pathetic.

"Is *that* why you're calling me?" I ask. "You're jealous of Simón?"

But deep down I know. Because I know Alejandro. And apparently so does Simón. Honestly, I should be happy that the experiments are working. That *he* called, that his jealousy means he still cares. Instead, I'm annoyed.

"No!" Alejandro snickers, the way he always does when he's lying. "I wanted to invite you over. You did help plan the party, after all. You should get to enjoy it too."

I helped plan it? That's an understatement. I booked the venue, the DJ, ordered the cake and the catering. I spent hours on Pinterest saving decoration ideas. I still have a board named "Alejandro's 29th." Simón's words rush back to memory. *You want an invitation, I'll get you an invitation.* I remember that night at the mall, talking at the terrace, Simón concluding Alejandro is predictable.

"I want to see you. Talk."

I believe him. So far, Simón's list has been working perfectly. If I want it to keep working, I need to stick to it.

"I can't tonight." I grimace, like it's physically painful. I don't know who's more surprised, Alejandro or me. "I have plans with my mom."

The line goes silent for one, two, three seconds. Over the background music I hear someone laughing and calling his name.

"You should get back to your party," I say.

"Okay." He pauses.

My eyes flutter closed. "Bueno, have fun."

"You too."

I hang up before I regret it. Then I get up from the couch. I have to go have a blast without my boyfriend. But first, moral support:

YO: I need you to meet me at Cusika in thirty minutes.
BLANCA: already here!
BLANCA: your mom invited me.

SALSA IS PLAYING loud enough to make me wince every two beats. I recognize my mother's energetic yet slightly pitchy voice in Marc Anthony's song and am immediately reminded of the time she tried (and failed) to have a career in music. Moments like these are when I wish I were as brave as her. The reality is that if I'd been the one to crash and burn, I would never touch a microphone again, the same way I never went back to ballet. Sometimes, it's like we're different species. I made my peace with that a long time ago. But damn, if only I'd gotten her courage instead of her nose.

The air is thick with smoke and floor cleaner. The bar itself is not big, which makes it easier for me to bump into one sweaty body after another. There might only be fifty friends and crew members here, but it feels like two hundred. The room is filled with small round tables and benches crammed inside. At the far back, there's a cement platform that serves as a stage, where I can see my mother having the time of her life.

As if by instinct, she spots me in the crowd and yelps, waving frantically. A dozen heads follow the trajectory of her excitement toward me. I purse my lips and wave back.

Ducking my head, I walk toward the center of the bar, where I spot Blanca. She looks impeccable, her hair tied behind her back, bringing out her sharp yet delicate features. She grins down at her boyfriend, Gustavo, sitting on his lap with an arm draped around his shoulders.

"Hey," I say.

Blanca turns her blinding grin to me. "Hiiiii!" she sings. "You're here!"

"Yup." I nod. There's a red drink in a tall martini glass in front of her. "Is that yours?"

"Yes?" Blanca says. "It's a cosmopo—"

Carrie Bradshaw's classic. Very on-brand. I don't usually drink, but tonight it feels appropriate and necessary. I grab it and inhale it. Bottoms up.

"Whoa!" Blanca pushes to her feet so fast I wonder if she got dizzy.

I hardly feel the burning sensation as the alcohol goes down my throat. The vodka hides under a fruity, citrusy flavor that *really* works for me. Blanca takes the glass away.

"That was good, I want another one," I say, suddenly enthusiastic.

Suspicion flashes through her eyes. "Spill the tea, Marianto."

I slump on one of the tall chairs, defeated. "He invited me to his birthday party."

Even Gustavo knows what this is doing to me, if his wide eyes are any indication. "I'll get you that drink," he says, then bolts before I can thank him.

Blanca gently places a hand on my back, drawing little circles with her thumb. "Isn't inviting you a good thing?"

I huff, slumping on the chair Gustavo was occupying. "He only did it because he's jealous."

Her eyes widen, hungry for chisme. "Of who?"

"Mm." I don't want to say it. So, I open Instagram, find Caballo de Troya's profile, and show her instead.

Her eyes bulge. "*Oh!* Man, I gotta start following these guys, I'm missing so many of the juicy bits."

I roll my eyes, groaning. "There are absolutely no juicy bits."

Blanca pulls me closer to her, laughing. "I'm glad you didn't go," she says. "And that you're here with us instead. Heaven knows we're more fun than Alejandro and his snobby doctor friends."

Predictable and boring. If Simón was right about the predictable part, then maybe Alejandro *is* boring and I've been laughing at bad jokes for the last four years.

I'm about to defend Alejandro for the millionth time when Gustavo comes back holding two identical drinks, one for each of us. I grab mine, ready to drink the whole thing in one go.

"Marianto—" Blanca begins, but something over my shoulder catches her attention.

"Buenas noches," a thick Colombian accent comes from behind me.

I choke on my drink, jumping to my feet. I wipe my damp lips with my thumb before turning around to face Simón. "Hi!"

Am I drunk already?

As if reading my mind, Simón eyes the glass in my hand before his gaze slowly moves back up to my face. "You're here."

I nod a hundred times in ten seconds. "I am."

Simón takes a step closer to me, so I can hear him over my

mother's second song of the night since I arrived. He smells like the leather jacket he's wearing, crisp yet soft and well-worn. The faintest hint of cologne, but not too strong.

He leans into me, bringing his lips close to my ear so he doesn't have to yell. His hand closes around my elbow. His touch is soft, feather-like. Not to grip me but to ground me, or himself. To give me attention. My heart goes *boom, boom, boom*, syncing to the music.

"So, I take it he didn't—" he begins, breaking the spell.

"Oh, no, he did," I yell, stepping back. "About an hour ago."

Surprise flashes in Simón's eyes, tipping his head to one side as his hand releases my elbow. With his other hand, he's swinging a beer bottle between his fingers. "And you're here."

I shrug one shoulder. "I'm having a blast without him."

Simón grins. "Is it weird that I'm proud of you?"

"Too soon to tell," I say, ignoring the little flutter in my chest at the word "proud." His eyes flash under the dancing lights in the club. He looks too pleased with himself. "This is my friend Blanca."

Blanca takes the cue and steps between us, taking his hand. "Blanca, nice to meet you. This is my boyfriend, Gustavo." Gustavo nods in acknowledgment.

"This is Simón." As if they didn't know that already.

Blanca nods. "From Talón de Aquiles."

I sit back down as my mother's song comes to an end and she jumps offstage with a loud *Whoop!*

"Caballo de Troya," I correct.

Blanca winks sneakily as Simón takes the chair closest to mine, laughing. "Talón de Aquiles would have been a better name anyway."

"A CANTAR!" My mother's booming voice startles us. She

puts an arm around my shoulders and squeezes me against her. "MI REINA! A CANTAR!"

Uh . . . no. "How many drinks have you had? It's not even midnight yet."

"Oh, hush," she says. "We're having fun!"

I eye my cosmopolitan and push it away. I don't want to have as much fun as she seems to be having. My mother, sensing she's not going to make me get up from this chair, moves on to another table. A minute later, she's getting onstage again with a man I recognize as her favorite designer. The familiar merengue beat of "A Dormir Juntitos" fills the venue.

Blanca jumps to her feet, raising her half-empty glass. "HELL YEAH, VIVIANA!" She grabs Gustavo by the arm and pulls him to his feet as well. "Come on, let's dance."

"I like your mom a lot," Simón says when they're gone. "She reminds me of mine."

I watch Mamá dance chest to chest with her singing partner, swaying together while people cheer around us.

"Is your mom loud and extravagant too?" I ask.

She's always been this way. She's a force of nature, the brightest light in any room. At least one person falls in love with her everywhere she goes. She believes in following your heart, which is why she's had five husbands. François has been her most lasting marriage, going on six years now. Her shortest marriage was to my favorite husband, Arturo Goncalves, a gay fashion designer. It lasted two weeks. He secretly sends me dresses to wear on my birthday and on New Year's Eve.

Simón smiles, looking down. "No. The opposite. But she's very caring. *And* this happens to be her go-to karaoke song."

I laugh. "What is it about Eddy Herrera and Liz? This song came out like twenty years ago."

Simón grins. "It's a classic. Who doesn't love sleeping together and erasing what is dampening their love?"

I laugh harder. And then I have a horrible thought. "Oh my god, is that what I'm doing?"

Simón frowns. "What?"

"With the list!" I remind him. "Am I begging Alejandro to . . . dormir juntitos . . . again?"

Simón watches me for what feels like forever before he bursts out laughing. His face transforms. His eyes are crinkled, his cheekbones high, his whole face exuding joy.

"Don't make fun of me," I say, but I'm smiling. I can't help it. He seems delighted. "It's a real question. I've always thought that song was a little desperate. And Alejandro hates merengue."

"I'm not making fun of you!" He shakes his head. "I'm just . . . fascinated. By the way your mind works."

I give a little tap to my temple. "This mind?"

He nods. "That mind."

"This mind that runs on cortisol and caffeine?"

Simón shrugs one shoulder, leaning back on his chair. "I mean, don't all our minds run on cortisol and caffeine?"

My mother's song ends. Or perhaps I stopped listening to it. Meanwhile, Simón and I stare at each other. The neon lights of the bar bathe the side of his face, making his beard appear more red than brown. He's truly so handsome, which shouldn't be a surprise. But his presence, the way he takes up space, it's like the universe would gladly rearrange itself to make room for him in a way it's never done for me. The way he reaches for his beer, finishing it in one gulp before leaning forward, elbows on the table, traces of an easy smile still on his lips, makes him seem at home. There's no way his mind runs on cortisol too.

"Do you miss being home?" I ask, because I can't keep dissecting him like this. It's . . . a lot.

Simón shrugs. Then nods. Then shrugs again. "It comes and goes. I'm used to it."

"Being used to it doesn't mean you can't miss home," I say.

"Then, yes," he decides. "I *am* used to being away, but the truth is this is the first time I've ever traveled for work without the band. We have this . . . routine, I guess? We take any moment we get to unwind." He laughs, remembering. "It's like traveling with five-year-olds. We come up with stupid games to pass the time, to take our minds off how stressed we are. I think tonight's the closest I've gotten to loosening up since I got off the plane—did you know we grew up together?"

I nod. The other members of Caballo de Troya are two of his best friends and his younger sister. His sister is my age. And he's known the other two since preschool. They're more a family than a band. Maybe that's why they've managed to stick together despite how hard it can be to break into the industry.

Simón smiles. "Oh, you're a *real* fan."

"Did you think I was making it up to impress you?" I ask, drawing a chuckle out of him.

"Yeah, I thought Alejandro was a paid actor in the coffee shop," he says.

I hide my face behind a curtain of hair, laughing. He joins, staring right at me, his expression open and inviting. The room is suddenly suffused with warmth, like a cozy quilt wrapping us both in a comforting embrace. I'm not sure anymore whether it's him or the cosmopolitan, but even the cigarette smell floating our way takes a backseat.

With a sigh, I pat his arm twice, then pull my hand back as if he'd burned me. "I'm sorry you're missing home."

"Thank you," he says. "It's not so bad, Caracas reminds me a lot of Medellín."

I want to ask what exactly reminds him of Medellín—the traffic? The endless motorcycles? The organized crime? But a pair of arms circle my shoulders from the back, almost choking me. "I signed you up to go next!" Blanca yells in my ear.

I shift out of her embrace, twisting on my chair until we're face-to-face. "You *what*?"

CHAPTER 19

"TRUST ME, YOU NEED THIS," BLANCA SAYS, USHering me to my feet.

I look to Simón for support but don't find the kind I hope for. Instead, he sports an unfaltering, smug smile. He raises both eyebrows at me, a dare if I've ever seen one. It's not going to work. I have spent my entire adult life going against my mother's wishes of seeing me up on a stage. Is it because I'm terrified? Yes. But a pair of challenging brown eyes isn't going to change that.

"Okay, I'll go first," he says, pushing to his feet as he grabs my drink and takes a sip. Then he marches toward the short stage before we have a chance to say anything. My eyes are glued to the glass. We practically kissed.

Blanca screams, "Selfie!" and leans closer to me, making me jump. I smile despite myself. I'd sooner die than let someone post a bad picture of me.

Simón takes the mic from the sound guy and takes his place onstage. The spotlight shines down on him, illuminating his chiseled features and framing him in a halo of golden light. His hair is dark and artfully messy under his baseball cap. He smiles at the crowd. He's wearing black jeans and a white T-shirt under his black leather jacket, the epitome of a rock star. Watching him, I fidget with my hands and don't register I'm biting my lower lip until it starts to hurt. I let the fangirl inside of me take a peek through my eyes. The second she's out, my heart picks up, my shoulders relax. Excitement runs through my veins, and I can't help the giggle that bubbles out of me as I push to my feet. This might never happen again and, damn it, I'm going to enjoy it.

Familiar notes float to us as Simón squares his shoulders. The soft yet infectious sound of cumbia takes over my senses and I'm swaying without meaning to. Blanca gasps as she realizes which song he's about to sing. She beats me by half a second.

"No," I mutter. There's no way he's singing "Como la Flor" by Selena. But the eruption of cheers from every table at the bar confirms that he is, in fact, going to sing Selena for us. He could have sung anything, he could have played the cool guy, could have played the rock star, could have shown off with a song more suited to his voice. Hell, he could have picked something by Caballo de Troya and drawn attention to the band. But no, he chose the most iconic karaoke song in Latin America. He chose something everyone knows, no matter how old they are, something we can all sing along to. Somewhere in the crowd, I can distinguish the high-pitched screech coming out of my mother's mouth right this second.

"This is for you, Viviana!" Simón says, pointing at her.

More cheering. I laugh, feeding off the audience's energy. Simón knows how to command a room. Not two seconds pass before people are on their feet, phones at the ready, recording him or using them as flashlights as they dance. Blanca is on her feet, throwing an arm over my shoulder and belting out the song along with everyone else. The atmosphere is intoxicating. Some glorious combination of the song, the crowd, and him. I'm grinning so hard my cheeks hurt, my heart is so full it could burst, and Blanca records the whole thing.

Too soon, the song is over. The energy in the room dies down little by little, the rustling of people walking around or sitting back down ringing in my ears. Simón jumps off the stage, grinning larger than I've ever seen. There's a light to him I hadn't seen before today, an aura of giddiness and passion, a kind of wildness. The full force of who he is hits me like a ton of bricks. He utterly transforms when he's happy. I want him to go again. I want to see it again.

He stops in front of me and sighs, the smile still firm on his face. "Your turn."

My smile falls. "Do you really expect me to follow that?" Not only because he has the voice of an angel and I . . . don't, but because no one can top that. They should call the whole karaoke night off. "I'm not you, dude. I can't do that."

Simón's smile softens, as well as his eyes. "All right. Do you mind?" he says, hands hovering over my short excuse of a ponytail.

I shake my head. He takes a step closer to me. I stifle a gasp, grateful for the dim lights and the shadows of the surrounding people as they move around us to get to their tables or to the bar. I don't know what I would do if he called me out on the color surely creeping up my face. And he would. I have no proof, but I also have no doubts.

Gently, he frees my hair from the ponytail, smoothing it as it grazes my shoulders. The soft pressure of his hands on me, the warmth exuding from his skin, both soothes me and sends my heart into a gallop. Simón takes off his baseball cap and places it over my head. I stand still, looking up in shock. I adjust it, smoothing the tips of my hair immediately after. With that, a corner of his smile twitches. He's standing so close, I'm pretty sure it could be considered a contract breach. He smells like cigarette smoke—*everything smells like cigarette smoke*—Irish Spring, and cedarwood. And now that smell is on my head. My stomach plummets at the intensity of this moment. The crowd disappears. Blanca and her boyfriend too. Somewhere in the bar, my mother cheers as the man behind the karaoke calls my name, but none of it matters. Stepping back, he reaches for something in his wallet. He takes my hand and places something flat and pointy on my palm. I look down to find a white guitar pick with the Caballo de Troya logo on it.

My eyes dart back up to Simón. He scans my face, his gaze lingering on my lips half a second longer.

An image—almost like a memory—of his hands traveling up to my neck and pulling me toward him flashes in front of my eyes. So real I almost feel the weight of his lips, of his body on mine. So real it's almost like that's what we *should* be doing.

Wait, what am *I* doing?

I stagger back, startled by the vision.

"There," he says, closing my fingers over my palm to trap the pick inside my fist. "You're me now." He gestures toward the stage with his head. "Vas."

And the way he's looking at me, eyebrows raised, with . . . *faith* . . .

I need to get away from him and if this is the only way, so be it. I grab my forgotten cosmopolitan and finish it in one gulp.

Voy.

Shaking my arms, I march toward the sound guy. He hands me the iPad and I scroll down the pages until I find it.

My index finger lands hard on the title. "That one."

He hands me the mic. I walk onstage, shoulders back, chin up, the way Simón did. The song begins. I try to count the beats with my shoe. The room is holding its breath. It's gonna suck. It's gonna suck so bad, but I'm up here, and I'm not ashamed to admit that pride is the only thing getting me through.

I mumble the first verse. Down in the crowd people look unimpressed, but when my eyes land on Simón, he's grinning. Grinning and nodding, encouraging me. The track builds the closer we get to the chorus. I think about Alejandro moving to Barinas. I think about Eugenia firing me. I think about Alejandro calling me because he was jealous. And then I think about Valeria going back to fight for what she wanted, and how *I* was the one who helped her do that. And I know I can yell the hell out of this and live to tell the story. I turn Simón's guitar pick around between my fingers, hoping his talent will rub off on me. Knowing it won't. Not caring either way. The chorus hits and I scream into the mic, "SINCE YOU'VE BEEN GOOOONE!"

The crowd erupts into cheers, jumping to their feet. It's exhilarating. Simón, Blanca, and Gustavo all have their arms around one another's shoulders and are jumping, singing along.

The lights flash in and out, casting a dreamlike haze over the bar. I feel like I'm living in some kind of beautiful fantasy, and as I continue to belt out the lyrics, my heart soars with each word. The excitement is tangible. The crowd is screaming along, clapping their hands and singing at the top of their lungs. The energy is palpable. I can see everyone's faces lit up with joy; it's like they all know this moment will never come again. For those few minutes, we're all connected through the music.

My eyes close as my entire body is taken over by the music. Nothing really matters anymore except the rhythm of the beat and the lyrics spilling from my tongue. I sound horrible, but, for the first time in a long, long time, I don't care about making a fool of myself.

When I open my eyes, my eyes land on Simón again and I think, *No wonder he chose to do this for a living.* I should tell him that. I decide that I will. But when the song ends and I return to my table, he's gone.

Blanca smirks, shaking her head at her drink. "He went out to take a call."

I sit, grabbing a tequeño from the center of the table. Thank God someone thought to order food. I bite into the doughy, cheesy, deep-fried goodness and slump against a chair, forcing myself not to look behind me toward the exit.

"I like him," Blanca adds, and gone is the lighthearted Blanca I know and love. Her voice is stone-cold sober, serious, uttering words she never once used regarding Alejandro.

My eyes snap back up to meet hers. "Yeah, he's nice."

I know that's not what she meant. And she knows I know. But the implications of such a statement said in such a tone are not something I can think about when I'm tipsy and high on adrenaline and still wearing a baseball cap that smells like him. That's a problem for future Marianto.

CHAPTER 20

MAYBE IT WASN'T THE BEST IDEA TO TAKE UP DRINKing the night before my meeting with Eugenia.

Pressing a hand to my temple, as if that would help with the traces of the migraine I was nursing earlier, I drag my feet to Eugenia's front door and I try not to trip on the thick glass steps leading up to her porch. Her house is all hard edges, sharp corners—floor-to-ceiling windows reflect the setting sun behind me, pink-orange clouds and everything. It's like a house wrapped in a painting of the late afternoon sky. If the sight didn't feel like being stabbed with a screwdriver in both eyes, I might be able to appreciate how truly beautiful it is. Behind the darkest sunglasses I could find in my mother's possession, everything is tinted a sepia brown.

At least I'm not throwing up anymore.

"I suppose I should be relieved that you weren't lying when you told me you weren't out drinking with your friends as a kid," my mother said this morning while she was holding my hair. I'd grunted in response, wishing I was dead.

Now I hug my iPad closer, adjusting my purse's strap on my shoulder before I ring the doorbell. The sound is muffled, but it's not a regular *ding-dong*. It's a melody. I swear it goes on for a full minute before the door silently swings open, revealing a housekeeper and a grinning golden retriever at her feet.

"Hello." I smile, fighting the urge to drop to my knees and play with the dog. "I have an appointment with Mrs. Fajardo. Is she home?"

"Maria Antonieta Camacho?" the woman asks. I nod. "Follow me."

Inside, the temperature is cool. The smell of fresh leather and pine cleaner permeates every corner of the house. If having your life together had a smell, it would be this.

Happy paws clack on the granite floor in rhythm with my ankle boots as the dog walks in slow circles around me. I fight back a sneeze. We walk in silence through the foyer, by a small living room area, then through the kitchen and finally to the terrace. The housekeeper puts an arm out before I walk straight through a set of glass doors.

"Sorry," I mumble.

She smiles, sliding the doors open. "Don't be. I take it as a compliment."

I walk out to a gorgeous backyard. Surrounded by chirping birds and flowers of a thousand different colors, Eugenia stands from her seat at a chic outdoor dining table. Behind her, a waterfall splashes into a pool made of turquoise tile. A sturdy four-seat wooden table rests between us on a wood-plank patio.

"Maria Antonieta, welcome," Eugenia says. "I'm terribly sorry you had to come all this way, but nothing is getting me out of my house on a Saturday."

"It's fine," I say. "I'm happy to be here. You have a beautiful home, by the way. Very Zen."

Eugenia smiles. With her whole face. Her eyebrows move and everything.

"Thank you. I was going for Zen," she says. "Make sure you have a place to unwind at the end of the day, Maria Antonieta. It'll prevent you from having early wrinkles."

Plastic surgery will also do that.

She gestures at the empty chair to her left. "Please, sit."

I obey, placing my things on the table one by one—phone first, then my iPad, which I align with the edge of the table, and finally my purse next to it in a perfect straight line. Eugenia watches me in silence. As I'm lowering my body onto the chair, my phone lights up. Both my attention and Eugenia's go to it.

SIMÓN: hey. How are you feeling?

I turn the screen off. It lights up again.

SIMÓN: [video]
SIMÓN: [photo]
SIMÓN: [photo]
SIMÓN: let me know if you want these burned or framed

"Do you need to address that?" Eugenia asks, still standing, gesturing at my phone with a perfectly manicured hand.

My cheeks burn hot as I activate sleep mode. "Nope. It's nothing important."

Eugenia eyes me as she sits, intertwining her fingers. "So," she says. "It's been a month. What have you achieved?"

Just like that, this beautiful garden turns into her sterile office, as if the flowers wilted and a previously cloudless sky suddenly turned gray.

"Well—" I begin.

She narrows her eyes, leaning in my direction. "You *have* achieved something, haven't you? It wasn't long ago when you were working under my tutelage, I'm sure you still remember how little I enjoy wasting my personal time."

"No!" I blurt out. "Of course we're not wasting time, I have achieved so many things. I just . . . I have this . . ." I run both hands down my jeans to calm my nerves. "When you read what I've written so far, it might not look like what we originally discussed."

Her eyes sharpen. "What will it look like?"

"It might look like I'm not doing this alone," I venture.

The look she's giving me is menacing. And yes, that is the kindest term I could use. My shoulders hunch forward as I try to make myself small, try to hide from whatever she's about to say.

After an eternity of silence, she says, "What are you talking about?" I part my lips to speak but she stops me. "And *please*, may the next thing that comes out of your mouth make some sense."

"I found a coach. An expert, if you will."

"A coach?" Eugenia repeats. "Who?"

"His name is Simón Arreaza, he's Colombian. A singer. We work together," I explain.

"Would I know him?" she asks.

"He's the lead singer of Caballo de Troya."

"The band you keep pushing on our audience?" My eyes bulge. Eugenia crosses her arms and leans back on her chair. "You work together? How did that happen? And how did he get involved?"

I lay down the truth about why I needed help from Simón and everything leading up to it—the failed experiments, the edited list, the surprising progress ever since he started helping me. I mean, Alejandro called me last night, for God's sake. A month ago, it was like I didn't exist. And now . . .

She listens to every word with a frown until I'm finished. I leave out nothing, except the tiny detail of what I promised Simón in return for helping me. While I'm talking, the housekeeper comes back with two glasses of what I *hope* is just iced tea and a display of cheeses, crackers, and dips.

"Let me see if I understand," she says, lifting the glass to her lips. "You're working at VeneTV's biggest production since your mother was the face of the Christmas specials. There, you met the lead singer of this little band, and now he's helping you get back together with Alejandro. Did I miss anything?"

I shake my head slowly, grabbing a cracker and laying a piece of gouda cheese on top. "That's exactly it."

She snaps her fingers, straightening up. "What does this boy look like again?"

"Simón?"

Eugenia rolls her eyes. "*Yes*, Simón."

I fish my phone out of my purse and go through my gallery until I find the picture Simón took of us yesterday. Hand shaking, I slide it toward Eugenia. Her eyebrows go up in surprise as she leans over the table to peek.

"He actually took that to make Alejandro jealous," I say.

She looks up. "Did it work?"

"Mm. He called me later that night."

A beat of silence passes between us as Eugenia seems to ponder. Around us, the sun slowly disappears behind her artificial waterfall. Across the pool, the water turns to glitter.

Eugenia returns my phone. "All right. Write about it."

"About . . ."

"The coach, the list, the whole thing. Experiment #1: ***Get a coach***, then you take it from there."

"What about what I've already written?"

"We're trying a different angle now," she says. "No one wants to read about your failures. Start with the story of how you got a coach, then move on to the first successful experiment."

"Okay."

"I expect to see it in my inbox on Thursday."

BY THE TIME I make it out of Eugenia's house, a cloudless night has fallen over Caracas, with a full moon so bright it might as well be a streetlight. I look up, counting stars in order to calm my racing heart as an orchestra of cicadas and little garden frogs accompany me to my car. Telling Simón that Eugenia wants me to include him in the article shouldn't be hard. He wants exposure. That's . . . one way to get it. I could expand on the band, why they're relevant in the grand scope of my relationship. But this is not the article I wanted to write on Caballo de Troya.

I'm sixty-five stars into my counting and halfway to my car when my phone buzzes in my hand.

Simón, I think. He texted me earlier. I haven't replied.

I stop in the middle of the sidewalk to pull it out of my back pocket, stressed once more, and . . .

Oh. My heart sinks in disappointment. Alejandro.

I mean, *Oh! Alejandro!*

His contact photo stares back at me, smiling green eyes boring into mine, asking why I'm not picking up. Asking why I'm not excited that he's calling. Why I'm disappointed that it's not someone else.

The phone stops buzzing, the screen darkens. Then it immediately starts up again. I stare at the screen, at Alejandro, lounging on a chair by a pool, hands behind his neck. I took that picture. I love that picture. This is what I want. Not twenty minutes ago I was meeting with my former boss to discuss how successful the plan is turning out to be. Success equals Alejandro loving me again, marrying me, having three kids and a dog with me. Feelings are temporary. Feelings are chemical responses to stimulation. Decisions are eternal. And I've decided that I want to get Alejandro back.

So I pick up, even though what I really want is to get home, take a long shower, and sleep for a week.

"Heeey," he says with a laugh, and the familiarity of the sound is an anchor in the turmoil that's become my life. It's exactly what I need. I immediately forget that, a second ago, I wasn't even sure if I wanted to talk to him.

"Hi, Ale," I reply. "How was your birthday?"

"Not as fun without you," he says, and my heart squeezes. "I'm sorry I didn't get back to you sooner, it was crazy at the hospital today."

Get back to . . .

"What?"

"Your text," he explains. "From last night?"

I halt in the middle of the street.

Nooooooo!

"Oh." I fumble with my phone, put it on speaker, and begin searching for my text chain with Alejandro. "Don't worry about it."

"No, I thought it was funny," he says.

What the hell did I do last night?

"Anyway." He clears his throat. "I was wondering if maybe you'd like to have dinner? Catch up?"

I stop looking for the text and stand up straighter. I expect the elation to bloom but instead there's a void inside me. A rushing car nearly blinds me with its headlights, but I'm too numb to feel it. "You want to have dinner with me?"

Alejandro chuckles. "Of course."

"Why?"

"I . . . guess I miss you."

"Oh." I swallow.

Be happy about it, I command my heart. But the part that used to beat faster in anticipation of seeing him is quiet. My mind is spinning—Eugenia's house is still behind me, I'm still standing in the middle of the sidewalk. I concocted this entire plan because I want Alejandro back. I try to focus on that truth, but my migraine is threatening to return, I'm thirty minutes from home, I have unread messages from Simón, and I simply can't think straight.

Eugenia's voice crawls into my brain saying, *Good job, darling.* This is what I want. So why am I hesitating?

"Listen, I'm about to drive home," I say. "Is it okay if I call you back?"

Alejandro is silent for a second. "Sure," he says at last.

"Thank you."

I hang up.

Questions flood my head on the drive home—*Should I tell Simón that Alejandro wants to have dinner? Does Ale want to get back together? Would quitting* Talento V *mean not seeing Simón anymore? But that's what we want, isn't it? It is. Right? Yes.*

With each question, an imaginary fist squeezes my chest a little tighter.

As I ride the elevator up to my apartment, I wipe my sweaty hands on my jeans. I try not to focus on the metallic whirring, normal for this ancient machine. Instead, I focus on the lit-up buttons, signaling which floor I'm crossing. As I step farther back into the corner, the cold surface of the mirror soothes my electrified skin. I shut my eyes, breathing in. Then open them immediately when the elevator stops and a young mom steps in, a baby pressed to her hip.

I smile. "Good evening." No reason to burden her with my emotional breakdown.

She smiles back.

Calm down, I think. All I did was ask Ale if I could call him back. People do it all the time. He's not angry. He's probably already forgotten about it.

The elevator dings and opens on my floor.

"Good night," I say, then step out, grateful for the open space.

This is ridiculous. I'll call Ale, we'll talk, and then I'll decide if I want to go to dinner with him tomorrow. But Simón *is* my coach, so I should let him know. Right? I should let him know. What if he tells me not to go? What if I hate him for it? Or, worse, what if I think he's right?

Maybe hating Simón is exactly what I need right now.

I sit on the stairs by my apartment door and pull out my phone. I go through my chats until I find Simón . . . and his five unread texts. I don't watch the video out of self-preservation. There's nothing I can do about the pictures. In the first one, Blanca and I are on either side of Simón, laughing with our heads thrown back, a red glow behind us. Simón smiles directly at the camera, his eyes bright. I'm wearing his hat, my hair cascading out of it. We all look happy. In the other, it's the two of us. We were sitting close together, talking about my mother plucking the microphone out of someone's hands because they were singing her only hit wrong. Blanca yelled "PICTURE!" We looked up, half smiling because we were laughing. Blanca refused to show me the result.

I read Simón's last text.

SIMÓN: let me know if you want these burned or framed.

And then I read it again. And again.

Framed. I want them framed. One on my nightstand, the other on my living room table. I know exactly what kinds of frames I would use, exactly where they'd go, exactly which trinkets they would look good next to. I can't ignore the sting in my chest when I think about it. Or the quickening beat of my heart, or the heat on my face, or the sudden burst of anxiety as my brain weighs the implications.

I leave Simón's texts unanswered and go to a different, more familiar chat.

YO: dinner tomorrow night?

I hit send before I regret it. This is the path I chose. This is what I've been working toward. This is the future I had planned out. My eyes zero in on the text right above this one, from last night, thirteen minutes before midnight.

YO: yellow for the riches, blue for the Caribbean sea, red for the blood spilled

I frown. Why the hell was I explaining to Alejandro what each color in our flag represents at 11:47 p.m.?!

ALE: tomorrow night doesn't work for me, I'm working the night shift at the clinic until Thursday. Friday?

And a second later:

SIMÓN: are you feeling better?

I send the same reply to both of them.

YO: yes.

Simón replies first.

SIMÓN: I'm proud of you for what you did last night
SIMÓN: you seemed to be having fun

That's the thing. I did have fun. After I got there, after Blanca and Gustavo understood how I felt about Ale's birthday, after I had that conversation with Simón, after singing . . . I couldn't remember why I was sad in the first place. I couldn't remember that it was all supposed to be for show. I liked that I stepped out of my comfort zone, that I didn't take myself too seriously for three minutes. I liked that I was offered the room to do it while still feeling safe. I don't know if I would have been able to do it if Alejandro had been there.

YO: I was
YO: it's the most fun I've had in a while

And isn't that sad? Living a perfectly planned out life, thinking I was content, when it turns out I was just bored. Maybe Alejandro is right in some of the things he said. Maybe I *am* controlling and I need to loosen up a little. It's not the karaoke and the drinking that made the night fun, though.

That's not what I'm missing. It's freedom, I think. Allowing myself to be messy from time to time.

SIMÓN: this week's homework is easy.
SIMÓN: all I need you to do is hold on to that memory and not feel guilty about it.
SIMÓN: you're allowed to be happy, even when you're sad

The step I'm sitting on grows cold as a draft of cold night air snakes through the window. On the floor above mine, a dog barks. I hate that Simón can see me so thoroughly, that he knows I would feel guilty about having fun without Alejandro if I sat with my thoughts long enough. Well, he can ask me not to feel guilty all he wants. That doesn't mean I know how.

Groaning, I stomp into my apartment and lock myself in my bedroom, hell-bent on focusing on the one thing I can control: me. I have an article to write and damn it, I'm going to write it.

CHAPTER 21

I NERVOUSLY FIDGET IN MY SEAT, HANDS GRIPping the edge of a pillow as I watch Blanca balance my laptop on her legs, reading an article I spent all Sunday drafting.

My mother is out. I left Simón at his hotel an hour ago and picked up Blanca for a girl's night right after. By girl's night, I mean forcing her to critique my work and rewarding her with a pepperoni pizza and a rewatch of *You've Got Mail.*

Mouthing the words as she scrolls down the pages, I wait for the verdict. I've read it so many times I have it memorized:

Experiment #1: Hire a coach.

Status: Ongoing.

When singer/songwriter Simón Arreaza told me my plan of action was doomed to fail, I didn't believe him. But his methods proved me wrong, so I decided the smart thing to do was bring him along for the ride. After all, two brains are better than one.

So far, no complaints. My partner in crime is wise, patient, and most importantly? A man. Which, as much as it pains me to say, is perhaps the key to the success of this entire experiment. No one knows the mind of a man better than another man. So if you're planning to embark on a similar journey, I suggest recruiting your best male friend and make your breakup his business. Even when he claims he wants no part of it, he's probably lying . . .

Experiment #2: Don't text/call.

Status: Ongoing.

According to my coach, you should do this until your target reaches out to you, and then for a while after that. Apparently, this will make him miss you (emphasis on "apparently"). He can't miss you if you're always there, reminding him of why he broke up with you. So, be absent.

I have been following this rule for the past two weeks. Here are the results:

Number of times he's called: 2

Number of times I've called: 0

Not that I'm keeping score . . .

Experiment #3: Treat him like a friend.

Status: Completed. Successful.

Okay, I will be the first to admit this one is a little harder, but the results are AH-MAY-ZING. By following this experiment I've gotten him to break his no contact rule, which is what we want.

There's a delicate balance on how to carry this out. You can't simply send him memes with the excuse of friendship. You need to wait for the perfect moment, or it won't work . . .

Experiment #4: Have a blast without him.

Status: Completed. Successful.

Warning: Having too much of a blast can be dangerous. Make sure you're with a trusted group of friends or family and above all that you're truly having fun.

My coach—

"Okay, I can't read any more." Blanca slides the laptop off her legs. "I get that Simón is like your love guru, but there's entirely too much of him in this."

Frowning, I grab the laptop from where she discarded it and skim the document. "I think there's a good amount of Simón content. It obviously needs expanding, but I'm just trying to paint the picture of what it could be. Eugenia said I should talk about him."

"Expanding?" Blanca stares blankly at me, as if my words weren't making sense. "You mention him more than you mention Alejandro."

How is that *too much Simón*? He's the one giving me advice. Alejandro is the one trying to kick me out of his life. One is obviously going to be more present than the other.

"Well, he's my coach," I remind her, like she needs it. "Again, Eugenia said I should include him. And Simón wants exposure. This will expose him."

"Sweetie, people are going to ship you with your 'coach.'" Blanca makes air quotes at that last word. "Also, what would Alejandro think? Have you stopped to ask yourself how he would react to this article?"

"He'll never see it. In all the years that we've been together, Alejandro has never read any of my work. He thinks it's too cheesy."

Blanca shoots me a doubtful look.

"Do you not remember how the internet works? Besides, I don't think this is the kind of exposure either of them want."

My heart falls to my stomach, my hands growing cold. Oh, I can picture it. The comments, the ship names, the videos displaying evidence of Simón and me dating. The complete invasion of our privacy. Not that there's anything for us to be private about. Suddenly, the room is too hot.

"I—"

My leather couch creaks as Blanca pushes to her feet, a satisfied smirk playing on her lips. She collects both our empty glasses and gracefully carries them into the kitchen.

"You know, when you asked me over to read the article, I figured you had *a lot* more done," she says, poking her head out from the kitchen. The sharp whistle of my coffee maker reaches me at the same time the smell does. "What with all the time you two have been spending together."

"Is that jealousy I sense in your voice?" I ask, glad for the change of subject.

Blanca makes her way back, carrying two steaming mugs, one in each hand, as she snorts. "Hell no. Better him than me." I take my favorite Mickey Mouse mug from her. "I just thought, you know, that you were on top of things."

Notes of cocoa and wildflowers waft inside my nose as I take the first sip. My body temperature rises as freshly brewed coffee enters my bloodstream. Heavenly beverage. Pizza should be here in about ten minutes. If I want her to read my other project, the time is now.

With a few clicks, the document is open before me.

Caballo de Troya (Profile)

Picture this: It's twenty years ago and bands play real instruments. "La Camisa Negra" by Juanes is playing on the radio as you make your way to Los Cayos with your family. Your mother is not yelling at you to turn off that god-awful music. Your father is not reminiscing about the good old days when music was more than just noise.

In an age when the charts are dominated by urban music, I'd like to offer an alternative for the brave and the willing . . .

I bring the mug to my mouth again, stalling, but my hands are shaking so much I'm spilling some down my chin. It's fine. It's exactly the kind of piece I've been dreaming of writing my whole professional career. The kind of piece I've never had the chance to write. The first thing I've written that isn't a restaurant review or relationship advice.

I offer her the laptop again. "I've been working on something else." Blanca frowns, looking down at the screen. "When I asked Simón for help, I offered him a profile on Caballo de Troya in exchange, when I get the promotion. I figured I should—"

Blanca lifts a hand. "Shh."

I obey. The only sound in the apartment is my upstairs neighbor's A/C dripping water onto my balcony. Blanca's eyes move swiftly across the screen. I don't think she notices, but as she reads, she leans forward more and more, until her nose is almost pressed to the screen.

My leg bounces up and down as I wait, but she's taking forever.

"It's not finished or anything. I still need to meet the rest of the band and interview them, but—"

"Marianto." I shut up, meeting her eyes over the computer, my heart beating faster with each second. I wait for her verdict. "This is really good."

I exhale, relieved. "Is it?"

Blanca nods. "Why don't you take this somewhere else? I heard Eugenia talking about a new magazine, it's called *Ethos*. Apparently, they're growing superfast, like they could give *Ellas* a run for their money. It's all anyone's talking about."

I shake my head. "Eugenia will see the potential in the band, she'll want it. They're a hidden gem."

And me being back at *Ellas*, getting a promotion . . . it's almost a done deal. If I started sending this out to magazines, I'd look like a groupie trying to make her favorite band happen, not someone who has grown up in the entertainment industry and could have a critical eye for new talent.

At least Eugenia already knows that side of me. And even if I *were* to leave, I still need a good reference from her. As proven by the previous interview process I went through, no one is going to take me seriously without one.

"It worries me how much you idolize Eugenia," Blanca says. "She already hired a new Ella."

"What?" My voice comes out pathetically soft.

"She started this morning," Blanca says.

I sit a little straighter. "It makes sense to hire a new Ella if I'm not coming back to my old job, though."

Blanca sighs. "Stop defending her. You may not see it right now, but this is the best thing that could have happened to you."

"I—"

"The profile is good," she continues. "You should focus on *that* and drop the whole experiment thing entirely. You deserve better than jealous phone calls and little airhead articles teaching women how to go back to the trash men they think they love."

Knowing Blanca, she didn't intend for her words to hit an invisible wound, but they do. Sharp little needles that poke at the bubbles I'd blown in front of my doubts, in front of the nagging voice saying this—the experiments, Alejandro wanting me back, writing about how a near-perfect stranger is helping me put my heart back together—isn't what I initially imagined. I'm getting good at ignoring it. I almost did. But I can always count on Blanca to see right through my smoke screens.

Her gaze softens and she sighs. "I'm sorry." She's not. "If you want my opinion on the experiments . . . cut Simón out of it. Unless you want to retitle it 'How I Fell in Love with the Man Helping Me Get Back Together with My Ex.'"

My eyes snap up to meet hers. I'm stunned at the words. It's one thing to objectively say people are going to ship me with him. Fine. That, I can see. And yes, Simón is ridiculously attractive, with messy hair, his signature hoodie, and his Paisa accent. Have I fantasized about him kissing me? Yes, once. But love? "I don't know what you're talking about."

"Sure," she says, pushing off the couch to grab my laptop. "Would you at least send an application to *Ethos*? You applied to all those other magazines and didn't hear back, right? It can't hurt."

"Fine." If it'll get her to stop talking about Simón.

I get a notification for our food delivery, and she volunteers to go get it while I read through the application instructions on the website. I hate that every line of the job description is like I'm being called home—*looking to highlight the cultural scene of Latin America, looking for sharp, fresh, up-and-coming talent . . .*

I don't want to hope. I do anyway.

CHAPTER 22

"THAT'S A WRAP!" MILEIDY ANNOUNCES, AND THE crew lets out a collective sigh. Fluorescent lights suddenly sizzle to life as the neon-colored lights onstage die down circuit by circuit. My mother, who'd been standing tall and proud in a sequin pantsuit, slouches. She pushes a loose wave of caramel hair out of her face as she exits the stage.

My throbbing feet and pulsing lower back are begging for a chair. My body is knotted up in aching muscles from standing all day; I can't help but slouch. When I get home, I'm going to take the longest, hottest shower in the history of showers. I'm going to order pizza, and I'm going to eat it in bed rewatching *New Girl*. I almost start drooling at the thought.

Fingers snap in front of my face twice, bringing me back to the imperfect world I actually live in. I blink, tracing the hand all the way back to Simón. A bemused smile dances on his lips, matching the flash of delight in his eyes. He's changed out of his shooting outfit and is back in the Caballo de Troya hoodie he's been wearing to work every day of this week. He pushes his sleeves up to his elbows, right one first, revealing the watch he wears literally every day.

I swallow hard.

"Are you okay?" His eyes scan my face in a series of micro-movements—forehead, eyes, nose, lips, and back up. He has the you-have-my-full-attention/I'm-only-looking-at-you thing down pat.

I clear my throat. "Mm-hm."

Simón leans against the table covered corner to corner in radios and microphones, casually crossing his arms in a motion that he *must* know makes the muscles on his forearms flex.

"What do you need?" I ask, rearranging the radios into perfectly symmetrical lines to have something to do.

"You."

I knock one of the radios down and the rest follow, falling like dominoes. "Me?"

I curl and uncurl my fingers as I take a step away from the table and clap my hands together so they stop moving. *Holy crap, relax.*

Simón pushes off the wall, amusement glinting in his eyes. I don't want to know what he sees written on my face, which is flaming. I miss my long hair and the protection it used to provide for me in these situations. Now I can only hope he thinks it's about knocking over the radios and not about the way his grin has my stomach fluttering out of control.

"Viviana arranged for some of us to go to dinner," he explains. "She asked me to get you."

Oh. I sigh, relieved. Okay. "Um, sure, let me just—"

"Maria Antonieta."

I whirl to the voice that will surely be plaguing my nightmares tonight. Mileidy looks younger under the fluorescent lights of the loft. Not a surprise, considering she's probably absorbed what's left of my good years. She hugs a binder to her chest, shifting her weight from one leg to the other, in the exact opposite way *I* hug binders to my chest and shift my weight from one leg to the other. Almost in boredom instead of anxiety. It screams, *I have better things to do.*

"I need you back in the office." There it is. "Apparently there's been some mistake with the scripts, and I need someone to proofread and reprint in time for tomorrow's shoot."

She must be joking. It's almost nine. Proofreading, not to mention revising and reprinting, will take me all night. Why do we even print stuff anymore? iPads exist. Hell, I bet she could smuggle a couple hundred of those cheap tablets the government gives to public schools into the office. Everyone ends up selling them anyway.

"Can't I proofread the scripts at home and print in the morning?" I ask instead.

"No." She doesn't even pretend to consider it. "Too many variables. You could die tonight." *What?* "Or traffic could slow you down tomorrow morning. Don't leave for tomorrow what you can do today."

I fight the urge to check my watch. *Today* has like three hours left. And this isn't something I can do in three hours. It's too much work. I'll have to spend the entire night at the office. By myself. My only company the flickering fluorescent lights.

I take a step closer to her. "Mileidy, is that really necessary?" I don't understand why she's doing this. We're all exhausted within an inch of our lives.

"Yes," she says, then turns to me with a barely there smile. "I knew we could count on you."

She leaves before I can protest again. Simón is staring at Mileidy's retreating figure in disbelief. His apparent outrage warms my heart to the point of tears. But I will not cry in front of my boss. I am a competent employee, and I do not burden my employers with personal problems . . . that much. I am receiving a salary for this job, and this job is financing the roof I sleep under, the cereal I inhale every morning, and the article that will ultimately get me my old life back. I square my shoulders (even though it hurts), swallow the lump in my throat, and blink away the sting in my eyes.

I hate this job. But screaming it at the top of my lungs isn't going to help my case. And I signed a contract that binds me until the end of the shoot. I remember the job application I sent last night, the one I've been trying not to think about because if I got it . . .

I sigh, rearranging the falling radios.

"Marianto." Simón shifts so he's facing me with his whole body.

Right then, one of Irina's assistants walks up to him and wraps an arm around his elbow. Simón freezes at the contact, and I feel my eyebrows rising, my expression changing. Um, what the hell? Why is this tall woman, gorgeous from every angle, touching Simón like they're . . . not even friends, like they're *together*, like she does it all the time? I scan her. I'd bet my future wedding she'll be on Miss Venezuela next year. Simón, to his credit, looks slightly panicked but he also isn't moving away from her, so he can't be *that* uncomfortable.

"We're all about to leave," she informs him. "Are you coming?"

Simón, eyes on me, untangles himself from her grip. The man is a mind reader. "No. I'll stay."

A sick little sense of satisfaction sparks in my chest, making me stand up straighter. Wait. Am I jealous? My cheeks flush. The embarrassment I feel is instant. Humans are horrible creatures.

"Oh." She rubs the back of her neck. "I thought we were all cleared."

Simón *tsks*. "Not all of us. Maria Antonieta and I need to go back to the office."

Irina's assistant eyes me and snickers. "Well, she can always ask her mother to talk to Mileidy. Isn't that how she got the job in the first place?"

I take one step forward. "Excuse me?"

She shrugs one shoulder, feigning innocence. "Couldn't hurt."

Before I can say anything else, she turns on her stilettos and leaves.

My eyes snap up to Simón. "You don't have to stay with me."

"And what do you suggest I do instead?" he asks. "Go eat a fancy, paid-for dinner with a pleasant group of peers? You insult me."

I gather my belongings and head toward the door. This is exactly why I could never follow in my mother's footsteps. It doesn't matter where I am, if she's also there, if she knows the producer or director or anyone in a position of authority, then my presence is automatically linked to her intervention. There would be no merit, no achievements of my own.

Simón catches my elbow, pulling me back. "Come on, don't listen to her."

"You do know we won't meet them after, right?" I say.

Simón's gaze softens. "Sí." He adjusts the strap on his back with one swift movement. "Let's go. You'll finish faster if we do it together."

Okay. It's math. 2 + 2 = 4. If Simón helps me, I'll finish faster. But still . . .

"Only if you let me buy you dinner."

Simón grins. "*Only* if I can choose the menu."

I laugh. "Deal."

MIDNIGHT FINDS US on the floor. The office is deserted except for the security guard posted at the front gate. And probably a ghost or two. The only lights on in the entire building are the ones on this floor and the stairs. We've set up camp in the only office with a panoramic view of Caracas. Thousands of lights twinkle out the window. It's like Christmas. Come sunrise, we'll see nothing but poor neighborhoods with mud and brick houses, old buildings with faded paint and mold stains. But at night, Caracas puts on her best clothes.

A little ball of neon pink paper hits me on the cheek. I look away from the window with a gasp to find Simón laughing as he covers his mouth with one hand.

"I'm sorry," he says, backing himself closer to the wall on the opposite side of the office.

We've been playing this game for at least an hour. The goal is to see how far we can throw a paper ball made of Post-its. Once either of us hits the mark, we answer a question or move farther away. So far I've learned Simón hates to cook and that he's the only person in his family that doesn't have a college degree.

"Montserrat, my sister, decided to get a degree too," he told me. "And she's also in the band, so I have no excuse."

"Why didn't you get a degree?" I asked.

He shrugged. "I always knew what I wanted to do. I didn't need a degree, I just needed to do it. It doesn't mean I don't take it seriously."

"That's very artsy of you," I said.

He yawned, throwing his head back. "You say that like it's a bad thing."

I shook my head. "It's not." And, surprisingly, I meant it.

"What do you want to know?" I ask him now.

Simón puffs his cheeks, looking up, pretending to think. His legs are stretched out, he's leaning back on his elbows. Exhaustion oozes from him, but to his credit, he's a good actor. I almost believe that he actually wants to be here with me instead of sleeping peacefully in his bed.

"A ver." He taps his chin with his index finger. I bite the corner of my lower lip, amused. "What's the real reason you swore off dating someone from the entertainment industry?"

"I told you the reason." It was when we were at the mall, and he asked what I liked about Ale. It feels forever ago.

"Not all of it," he retorts.

Pushing his hair back with one hand as he holds himself up with the other, he seems energized. His T-shirt slides up on one side, revealing a thin strip of tan skin. My eyes follow the movement of the fabric, until he absentmindedly pulls it back into place. Eyes on his torso, I ball a green Post-it, puncturing my hand in the process. *Look up*, I command. I look up.

Simón is staring at me, waiting. I swallow. My throat is dry.

"My mother," I finally say. "Growing up, she wasn't around much. I'm not the kind of woman to play it cool and pretend I'm looking to go with the flow. I want marriage, I want children. I want security, someone I can trust to be there for me when I need him. And I don't want to subject any future children I might have to the same life I had."

"You know that could happen to anyone, in any field of work, don't you?"

I nod. I do. But it happened to me in *this* field of work. If I can lower my chances of coming second to someone's career, I will.

I don't want to play this game anymore. I throw my little green ball and it travels in an arc between us. It lands about two feet shy of where he is. Game over. We look up from the ball at the same time.

I scramble to my feet. "That was fun."

Simón stands up too. "It was. Should we go?"

"Simón, I can't leave." I gesture at the mess we've left in our wake. Scripts piled up, ready for delivery, plus more to print; discarded foam containers and plastic cutlery from our dinner; about a thousand paper balls tracing a path from me to him. If Mileidy comes to the office tomorrow and finds this mess, she'll have my head. "But *you* can. You should leave. I'll stay here. Forever and ever and—"

Simón crosses the space between us in two strides. "I'm not going to leave you here alone."

He grabs a chair from the desk we've been using all night, turns it around before sitting with arms crossed over the backrest. Oh, for the love of God.

"That's not fair," I say. Out loud.

Simón frowns. "What's not fair?"

You, sitting in front of me like that, looking at me like that, offering to stay with me like that.

I clear my throat. "You shouldn't have to endure this with me."

He huffs, drumming the fingers of his right hand on the back of his left. "What's not fair is you having to go through dozens of scripts for no reason."

"The reason is that Mileidy told me to." I shake the list of edits she had a PA give me for emphasis.

I squat and start picking up the balls. No way in hell am I exploring this place at the witching hour in search of a broom. Simón somehow manages to roll his eyes out loud as he pushes from the chair and joins me on the floor, so close our noses would touch if I lost my footing.

"What if I tell you we need to go?" he asks, and I feel the warmth of his breath against my cheek. I meet his eyes. They're the color of cedarwood, framed by long lashes that could catch snowflakes if given the chance. Why am I thinking about snowflakes on eyelashes? "What if I need you to drive me back to the hotel?" he continues. "Who would you obey then?"

I can't hold his piercing gaze. Not when his hair is sticking up in all directions after he ran his hand through it one too many times, not when his hoodie is rolled up to his elbows and he's wearing ripped jeans and exhaustion like he was born for it.

"Mileidy."

Simón huffs, rolling his eyes. "Sure."

The word has a low timbre, a rasp. And a hint of disbelief. With a second, final glance my way, he shakes his head, smiling, as he piles up neon paper balls in his hands.

I force myself to remember Alejandro.

Alejandro also smiles. Alejandro also says *sure*—mostly in a condescending way, but still. Alejandro is also male. *Focus.*

"So, um." I stand up, adjusting my clothes, and take two steps away from him for good measure. "What's next in the plan? I can hardly show Alejandro I'm having a blast when the only thing I do is watch kids sing for money and get you coffee."

Simón's eyes shoot up. "We can always show him he's not the only one in line for your heart. That's item number four on my list, if memory serves. Sit back down."

"What?"

Simón drops to the floor and immediately crosses his legs. "Floor, Maria Antonieta," he says, patting the space next to him.

For what feels like forever, I stand beside him, looking around. I don't know who I'm expecting to find; we're the only ones here. Judging by the bright red numbers on the clock over the door reading 12:32 a.m., we'll continue to be the only ones here for a while. But this tiny action, sitting by Simón on the cold floor of this deserted office, is the kind of thing I would never do under normal circumstances. The Marianto I am at my core doesn't sit on the floor beside hot singers. The Marianto I know myself to be wouldn't have allowed Simón to stay behind in the first place. He should be resting. I should be working. But the me that's here tonight, looking down at him as he looks up with a daring glint in his tired eyes, wants to let go for once. To not do what's expected even when no one is watching.

I sit on the floor. Cross my legs. Silence the voice of my first-grade gym instructor saying I shouldn't cross my legs. Simón cocks his head to one side, grinning, as he appraises me. One second passes . . . two . . . three . . .

Simón sighs, shaking his head once.

"So . . ." I venture. "How do we do this?"

"Right," Simón says. "First, we need something that's undeniably yours. Something someone else probably doesn't have."

That's easy. "This bracelet?"

I shake my wrist the way I often do when I'm too anxious. Charms *ding-ding* together, and my chest loosens a little. I've had it since I was fifteen. My mother gave it to me. She's been adding a new charm to it every year since then. The first one was a lipstick. Now it has several books, a globe, a telescope, and a few pearls. It's such a part of me now that I never think about it, the same way I don't think about breathing, or the same way I never think about dropping several pens in my purse before going out.

Simón studies my bracelet like the storyteller he is. I don't know how I know, but he's trying to figure out the best way to ask for the tale behind it. Unfortunately for him, that book has closed.

"That and my fixation for hibiscus tea every Wednesday," I add.

Simón checks his watch. "It's Wednesday."

"Oh, it's already on the way."

He chuckles. "Why Wednesdays?"

I fumble with the lipstick charm on my bracelet. "At *Ellas*, Wednesdays were Fitness Day. I had to post health content, diet food. Couldn't post about coffee and cookies. Instead, I posted about salads and tea." Simón gives me a thumbs-down. I laugh. "I know. Hibiscus tea is the only tea I liked, so it became like my signature drink. After a while, I didn't even have to pay for it anymore. We drove so many people to the café under our office, they owed *us* money." I sigh, wishing I could have a cold brew of hibiscus tea right now. "There were a lot of perks to that job."

"Is that why you want it back?" Simón asks, nudging my knee with his. "The perks?"

Some days, yes. But not always. "Mostly I miss knowing I was good at something, and people *knew* I was good at it. I don't want to start over somewhere new."

Simón nods, *hm*-ing. "Is that why you want Alejandro back too? Because you're afraid of starting over with someone new?"

My head snaps toward him. I'm gaping, I know I am. I can't help it. The tightness in my chest comes back full force, two fists squeezing my lungs, while a secret third hand punches me in the gut. Simón doesn't look away. The opposite, actually. He scans every inch of my face, giving each feature individual attention. He studies each eyelash and eye freckle. The air is charged. He swallows. I follow the movement of his throat bobbing. This is Simón in HD and in private. No photo or video does him justice.

I look away first. "Who said I was afraid?"

He doesn't move. His eyes burning the side of my face almost feel like a challenge. "Aren't you?"

My throat goes tight. Maybe it's sitting on the floor next to the man who wrote lines like *Tell me how you like your coffee in the morning, your bedtime routine each night, what does the weekend look like, if it's you and I*; maybe it's the fact that his relentless questions feel like he's genuinely interested in me, which I haven't felt in . . . forever, now that I think about it. Whatever it is, I want to tell the truth. And I hate that. I hate that it's him who gets to pull it out of me, that things with him always get out of control. Not in a crazy, I'm-going-to-find-my-bra-hanging-from-a-ceiling-fan-tomorrow-morning kind of way. More like an I-can't-get-you-to-follow-the-script kind of way. In a you're-always-challenging-me kind of way, and the competitive, straight-A asshole in me does not want to back out. So, I don't.

"What about you?"

Simón chuckles. "What about me?"

"What are *you* afraid of?"

Simón gives me an infuriatingly knowing smile. "Do you really want to know, or is this your way of putting me back in my place?"

I want to laugh. Of course he knows my question for what it is. Of course he sees right through it, through me. It's like he was born with a Maria Antonieta manual that he wasn't able to open until now. It's unnerving.

I shrug instead. "Answer it anyway."

Simón sighs. "Bueno. I guess I'm afraid of failure." He pauses, fidgeting with the hem of his jeans. "As cliché as that might sound."

"Failure of what?"

He huffs. "Anything? Everything." His voice is thick, speaking faster as the words rush out of his lips. "I'm scared of failing so spectacularly I'll resent music for the rest of my life. I've sacrificed so much for it—time, a billion different job opportunities. Love." He swallows. "I'm afraid I'll wake up one day and realize it was all for nothing. That I've been feeding myself, my family, and my friends lies upon lies. That I could have fewer gray hairs at twenty-eight or sleep more than five hours a night . . . that I could have been happier sooner, doing something else. If that makes sense."

I don't realize it, but I've been inching closer to him as he speaks. When he's finished, my hand is resting on his knee. I don't move it. He turns to me, eyes a little lost, breathing unevenly.

"It does," I say.

Simón nods, lowering his head as he blinks. When he looks at me again, his expression is determined. His smile is back, but it's not as wide or genuine as before I challenged him to bare his soul to me on the office floor. And before I can decide against it, I reach out and grab his hand. Surprise flashes across his features. It takes a second before his fingers close around mine, warming every inch of skin he's touching.

I focus on that and not on the fact that I'm holding Simón's hand.

"You'll be okay," I whisper. "I'm going to make sure of it."

"So will you." Simón squeezes my hand softly. "And so will I."

I don't know how long we stay like that. Could be seconds. Could be hours. He lets go first, placing my hand over my own knee, as the brief moment of true friendship melts into oblivion. His phone materializes in his hand; he angles it toward the desk we'd been occupying hours ago, foam containers from our dinner still scattered all over its surface. What's the creative process behind this particular shot? I have no idea, but twenty seconds later his phone is back in his pocket, and I have yet to approve the picture.

Simón turns to me with a playful smirk. "He'll call."

I almost blurt out a *Who?* But then I remember. The experiments. Making Alejandro think he's not the only one in line.

Simón is my coach. I should tell him Alejandro already called. I should tell him about dinner on Friday. I should ask for his advice.

I don't.

"There's only one problem with your plan," I say. "He *is* the only one in line."

If he's even that. Simón pushes to his feet, then offers me a hand to help me back up. I take it.

"That's for him to decide," he says, pulling me up. I almost crash against his chest. He looks at me like he wouldn't have minded one bit. "But just to be sure: Tomorrow, have a blast without him."

I take a step back, then another for good measure, dusting my pants off.

"And do what exactly?"

Simón shrugs. "You still owe me a hypothetical tour of Caracas."

My heart races a little faster at the implication. I feel my cheeks grow warmer with each second. The corners of Simón's lips twitch. If he doesn't find it anxiety-inducing to spend more time together, just the two of us, there's no reason I should.

"Of course." I try not to choke on the words. "Sounds good."

For all our sakes, I hope this one works.

CHAPTER 23

••••••

GIVING SIMÓN A GRAND TOUR OF CARACAS IS UNrealistic. We got off work at 4:30 p.m. today. A tour would require a lot more planning and a lot more time. So I settled for the next best thing: seeing the entire city at the same time.

Simón waits for me at the entrance to the cableway that will take us to the highest point in the city: El Ávila.

When I join him after buying the tickets, he smiles and says, “There is a cableway in Bogotá too. It takes us to Monserrate. My sister, Montserrat, is named after it.”

“Why?” I ask him as we follow the line to our cable car.

“It’s where our parents met,” he says.

The line moves fast. People don’t usually go up around this time. It’s almost five and the cableway only takes people up until six but brings people back down until ten.

“Who are you named after?” I ask, just to keep the conversation going. I try not to check what time it is again. My mission is subject to the trajectory of the sun. As soon as we make it up there, we’ll have to start the walk up to Hotel Humboldt. The journey up the mountain takes approximately fifteen minutes, the walk would be another ten.

"My father," he answers. "His name is Andrés Simón."

I stop walking and appraise him. "You're kidding."

Simón chuckles, shaking his head. "I wish. I'm afraid creativity in my family started with my sister and me."

The gondola operator ahead does a quick head count and motions eight of us forward, guiding us to cram into a cable car.

Simón gestures for me to go first, then settles into the seat beside me. Our shoulders, thighs, and legs gently press together. The proximity makes every thought in my head dissolve. When he says, "They weren't very creative," it takes me about ten seconds to remember what we were talking about. I force out a laugh. I scan the group of people sharing this experience with us and quickly realize we're the only two who are not a couple. The rest of them are either holding hands or touching in a way that suggests they're very comfortable with each other. The couple directly across from us share a quick peck and a grin.

"The landscape is beautiful," I tell Simón, and immediately want to kick myself. He turns to me. I remain facing forward. If I faced him, our noses would touch.

"I believe you," he says, his voice a low rumble, meant only for my ears.

As we start moving up the mountain and away from the city, the buildings look tiny, like pieces of a puzzle that fit perfectly into the landscape. The vegetation surrounding the mountain seems to whisper old stories, and the sea of houses and streets stretches as far as the eye can see, framed by the blue sky and the clouds that seem so close I can touch them.

Going up El Ávila is something every person visiting Caracas for the first time needs to do. If I can't give Simón a full tour of the city, then I have to make sure he doesn't leave without seeing this. If all he does after today is shuffle between the studio and his hotel and never sees anything else, then his visit would still be worth it. I wish I could take him to other places too—a hike to the top instead of taking the cableway, showing him the wildflowers and the animals, having him drink water directly from a stream, but there isn't enough time. If I had my way, I would take him to every park, every restaurant, every museum. I would take him to watch a musical at the Teresa Carreño Theater, to art shows, book fairs, film festivals. Caracas is a city brimming with art and culture, with brave people willing to experience it all. It's also dangerous and unpredictable, the way all big cities are.

At the top, we get off the cable car and the first thing I notice is how many people are still up here. The song "tranqui, te puedes enamorar" by Alleh and Yorghaki is playing somewhere in the distance. Colorful lights dance over the ice rink as families and couples skate. Smoke floats from different food vendors and the smell of grilled food coats the crisp mountain air.

We step into the cold. Today, the clouds are low, dressing everything in a thin white cloak. A giant Venezuelan flag waves in the wind, making a slapping sound. I inhale deeply.

"Hot chocolate?" I offer.

Simón nods. "I would love that." When he speaks, fog comes out of his mouth. His cheeks are rosy, like the mountain spirits kissed him.

I check to make sure we're good on time, get two cups of hot chocolate, and begin the trek uphill along the paved path.

Simón takes small sips from his cup, scanning our surroundings. His eyes get lost on the tall trees growing at each side of the path, the birds perched on the branches, the children squealing and running while blowing soap bubbles at one another. Then his attention jumps to a group of people laughing while sharing a cachapa con queso on a bench.

"People come up here to be happy," I tell him.

His gaze shifts to me. "Hm?"

"We come up here to be happy," I repeat. "Whenever I feel like I need to touch grass, this is where I come. It's always here when I need it."

"It's beautiful," he says. "I like that you have somewhere you can go."

I take a little sip of my chocolate. "Where do you go when you need a refresh? What is your safe haven?"

"I don't have a place I go to," he says. "I'm not always home. Sometimes I'm in a city I've never been to before, sometimes I'm in a city I don't particularly like. I think I have people." He pauses, flattening his cup before throwing it in the nearest trash can. "Yeah, I have people I go to when I need to feel better. My friends, my sister. You."

You.

Heat creeps up my cheeks despite the cold. "I don't think I've done a good job of that."

Simón smirks. "No, trust me. You help."

Finally, after a few minutes of ascent, we reach the hotel. Just in time.

"We're here," I tell him.

As the sun begins its slow descent, the sky transforms into a palette of colors that looks like something out of a dream. I lead Simón to a wooden bench, the cool breeze caressing my face and the soft murmur of the leaves accompanying the silence. The city of Caracas stretches out at our feet, its buildings and streets engulfed in a golden light that seems to merge with the flaming sky.

In the distance, the clouds are tinged with shades of pink and orange, as if the sky itself is burning in a final act of beauty before nightfall. My heart relaxes. The view is so breathtaking it seems as if the world has stopped just for us to experience this magic.

In the silence, our gazes meet. Here, in this corner of the world, there is only us. The sun bathing every surface it can touch also falls upon us. Simón is transformed into a creature made of gold. My brain replays his voice and that one word, *you*.

Simón's hand finds mine before he shifts his attention back to the sunset falling over the city. "Gracias."

I swallow hard, feeling the weight of his hand in mine. There are people around us taking pictures, talking, basking in the moment the same way we are, but somehow all that feels like another world entirely. In this moment, I feel lighter than I've felt in weeks. And it occurs to me it's not just the power this mountain always has on me, but who I'm sharing it with.

"Simón?" I venture, my voice so small to my own ears I fear he might not have heard it. But he does.

"Mm?" His Adam's apple bobs with the sound. The tips of his eyelashes shine gold, as does his brown hair, tousled by the wind. From this close, he doesn't look like someone I would just recognize on the street. He looks like someone I could trust—a warm face and kind eyes lost on the horizon in wonder. A friend.

"You help too," I confess.

CHAPTER 24

••••••

THIRTY CONTESTANTS ARE LEAVING THE SHOW today. Ten per team. It's chaos. The dressing room is hot and stuffy. As people rush past, they bump or brush against one another, adding to the frantic energy. A mix of sweat and body odor hangs heavily in the air, mingling with the scent of hair spray and perfume. It's a reminder of the intense physical and emotional effort put into the show. The sound of screaming mothers makes me feel right at home. It reminds me so much of my macaws, I'm fighting the urge to feed them little cubes of papaya.

Simón watches from a corner, horrified. The show has sent people home before, but this is different. These are *his* kids. He coached them, gave them singing and performing lessons. He spent time with them and got to know them. And now he has to tell them they're not good enough. The other two coaches are unbothered.

"That's the job," Irina claimed. "If these kids expect to make it, they better get used to rejection."

Simón masks his discomfort as he's standing across the room from me. He looks every bit the part of a proud coach;

every day we've worked together I've watched Simón be nothing but the most encouraging coach to these kids. The adult in the room. Today, surrounded by ten potential dreams about to be shattered, it occurs to me how young we really are. How young he really is. How not too long ago, he was begging someone else for a chance. Older, sure. Wiser, maybe. But still, just a person with a dream.

I move toward him, like a pin to a magnet. Stepping over a puddle of vomit, zigzagging between pale children and angry parents, pretending my job isn't my job. Pretending I'm here for support. As his friend. I tap his shoulder. He turns to me, eyes wide. Last night rushes through my mind and I feel a sudden wave of affection for him, remembering. The two of us sitting together, hands clasped, shoulders touching . . .

We can be friends. We *are* friends. The vow doesn't have to be only about our careers. It can be about *us* too.

"Hi." I drop my voice so only he can hear. Not that it'd be hard with all the screaming. "Shouldn't you be out there?"

Simón nods, his arms crossed tightly in front of him. His attention moves back to the kids, his brows furrowed and forehead creased in frustration. Then he sighs. I can't help but feel a twinge of worry for him.

"I can't do it," he says, shaking his head almost in defeat.

My heart aches at the sight of him like this. "Simón—"

"I'm serious," he cuts me off. "I know who's leaving and I can't do it."

The urge to reach up and touch him, hold his hand in support the way we did sitting on the office floor, is like a pulsing wound. Hard to ignore. Demanding to be soothed. But I can't.

"There's nothing you could have done to make them all win," I say instead. "You know that, don't you?"

"But couldn't I just . . . pretend to be dead? Like a possum? Until this is over?"

I laugh, despite myself. "You're making them nervous. Why don't you join Irina and Federico outside?" He hesitates. His expression is pained. I give up and touch his shoulder, squeezing softly. "They'll be fine."

Simón's gaze darts to the spot where I'm touching him, so fast I could easily convince myself I imagined it, then moves back up to meet my eyes. He gulps, then gives me a tight smile before he steps back and leaves.

I command my face not to warm, not to give me away. But before he walks through the door, Simón looks over his shoulder at me and smiles, genuinely this time. My heart beats so fast it could leap out of my chest as I stand there, watching the door fall shut behind him in slow motion. Bells ring in my ears. Warning bells? Maybe. But I don't have time to linger on them, or on the instant void in the room now that he's left.

I shake my head once and swallow the rush of conflicting feelings back down. I clap my hands twice, the way my history teacher used to when we were being particularly loud. "Listen up!"

Twenty pairs of eyes turn in my direction. "Who wants to make Mr. Arreaza a card?" Twenty sets of hands shoot up.

THE DAY ENDED quietly. No confetti cannons, no hugs, entirely too many tears. Children cried, parents cried . . . I cried. Simón, usually ready to make conversation with anyone about anything, went silent after Mileidy announced we'd wrapped. He stood alone by the door, nose deep in his phone. He seemed exhausted, worn. The circles under his eyes were visible even through makeup.

Mileidy had made reservations for the cast, producers, and directors to go to dinner together. No assistants. It was the best news I'd heard all week. I was already anticipating the silence that awaited me in my apartment, knowing my mother would be gone for hours; I could feel the cotton pj's I was going to wear. The things I'd started to dream about since I started this job were pathetic. But, right then, all I could think about was my bed and a huge arepa con queso for dinner, watching *Pride and Prejudice* (2005, duh), and how I'd go to bed and sleep in past 5:00 a.m. because Mileidy gave us Friday off.

And then, a single sentence burst my bubble:

"Are we ready to leave?" Simón asked beside me. I didn't even hear him approach.

"You're not going to dinner?"

"No," he said. "Ready when you are."

So now Simón and I are standing in front of his hotel's restaurant's closed doors. There is a sign on the glass surface, right above the door handle, claiming the restaurant is open until nine. I check my watch. It's 9:34 p.m. They can't be serious. What kind of hotel restaurant closes at nine? There must be people still eating there. The stove must still be hot. I knock on the glass.

Simón clears his throat. When I look up at him, he's pointing at the small letters under the closing sign.

ROOM SERVICE UNTIL 11:00 P.M.

"Your room or mine?" Simón asks.

Warmth instantly creeps up my neck. Even if I had a room here, I wouldn't let him in it. Although I don't trust myself enough to not conjure a dream version of him in my bedroom at home or keep my mind from making up stories where he's not Simón Arreaza, lead singer of my favorite band, and I'm not . . . me.

I better go, is what I should say. Or any number of similar things—*It's late, you're probably tired, you should get some rest. I can't be alone with you, it doesn't go with the plan. Nothing is going according to plan.*

But my stomach growls, I'm starving. And it's Simón. And, lately, I can't say no to either of those things.

He watches me expectantly. His expression is not pinched with worry or fear. There are bags under his eyes and redness around his irises. And patience. Like he knows what I'm going to say, he's simply waiting for me to say it:

"Yours."

It's one word. Small. Five letters. An answer within an answer to a question within a question:

Will you stay?

Yes.

Simón grins, his eyes twinkling like Christmas lights. I swallow a gasp. Immediately, I turn my back on him and march down the hall.

Alexa, play "Bad Idea" by Ian McConnell.

We ride the elevator in silence. Walk down the hall in silence. It's only when he slides his key card into the lock and opens the door that he says, "Do you mind if I take a quick shower?" gesturing to the bathroom, directly to our right.

I shake my head. "Go ahead." If I spent my day shattering other people's dreams, I'd want to shower as soon as possible too.

He disappears behind the bathroom door. Two seconds later, I hear water running, so I wander deeper into the room. It's cozy, clean. The bed is made to perfection; the corners of the mattress almost look sharp. But it doesn't smell like cleaning products or chemicals. It smells like cologne, like Simón.

"Don't wait for me to call the restaurant, you must be starving!" I jump at the sound of his voice from the bathroom.

"Okay. What are you having?"

"Something light," he replies.

Club sandwich for both of us then. I order our dinner and as soon as I hang up the phone, I have nothing to do for the first time all day. I sit at the round table next to the phone and rest my head back against the wall.

Behind me, in the bathroom, Simón hums. The sound, enhanced by the bathroom echo, is soothing. Almost celestial. I can't make out the song, but I close my eyes and let myself enjoy it while nobody is watching.

How often do you get a private humming concert from your favorite singer? I have better odds of getting hit by lightning.

Without permission, my mind wanders to a place where this is my everyday life—*magical hotel lobbies, late nights ordering room service while someone I care about hums in the shower. Then we eat, and whine to each other about how tired we are but end up laughing about it anyway. He could tuck a loose strand of hair behind my ear, or move his fingers down my jaw until he's cupping my neck, or pull me in for a kiss. I could run my hands through his wet hair. He could smile against my lips, and I—*

"Todo bien?"

My eyes snap open, face blazing. It's probably tomato red right now. I swallow through a lump in my throat and nod, sitting up.

"Food's not here yet?" he asks.

I shake my head, unable to meet his eyes. "They said fifteen minutes."

"Ah."

He doesn't sit across from me at the table. Instead, he moves around the room in sweatpants and a worn-down Hard Rock Cafe T-shirt that is a little big on him around the neck. His hair is brushed back behind him, soaking the shirt where it drips. He bends over the bed to pick something up. When he straightens, he's holding a guitar.

My entire body flushes. Oh, God. Oh no. I can't have that picture in my mind. He's hot enough and kind enough and funny enough. I don't need to add *played me a private concert in his hotel room* to that list. I need to think of something. Fast. But he's already sitting on the bed, across from me. He places the guitar on his lap, its curve resting on his left leg, which he lifts up slightly; his hands move up and down the neck of the guitar, his long fingers caressing the string with a featherlight touch. My throat is suddenly dry. I cough.

He immediately looks up. "Are you okay?"

"Mm-hm." I nod. "I just . . . I—" Then I remember. "I have something for you."

The card we made him is nothing fancy, just twenty different ways of saying thank you. It took me nearly an hour to get everyone's name on it. Most of the children's handwriting is unreadable, but the sentiment is there. I snatch the piece of paper from my bag and stretch my hand to him. If remembering how stressful it was to make it doesn't cool me down, nothing will.

Simón grins, gratitude written all over his face. Instead of cooling down, my heart swells, proud I did something to make him happy. I'm afraid my pulse might be visible through my chest, like a cartoon.

"Thank you," he whispers. His eyes move over it in random circles, like he doesn't know where to look.

I shrug because I don't trust myself to speak. Maybe I should have just let him serenade me.

His smile widens, looking up. At me. "Marianto, I—"

Someone knocks on the door, interrupting him. The food. We ordered food. Fifteen minutes ago, approximately. And now it's here. He pushes to his feet without finishing the sentence. But do I even want to know what he was about to say? It's probably better if we don't blur any more lines.

Shifting on my chair for something to do, I give up and grab my phone right when it vibrates with an incoming text from—I check—Alejandro. Of course. Who else?

For someone who wasn't sure he wanted to be with me, he seems pretty adamant about demanding my attention. Below Ale's, there are five unread texts from my mother demanding to know where I am, plus one from Eugenia asking where the next batch of experiments is. I'll get to those later.

ALE: I'm watching You've Got Mail and it's not nearly as fun without you swooning over Tom Hanks

You've Got Mail is my favorite Meg Ryan movie. I used to make him watch it all the time, at least once a month, usually around the time I had my period. He complained every single time but still sat on the couch and watched it with me. Once a month. For four years.

I don't get how you can watch this over and over, he'd say. *There are a million other cliché romance movies to choose from. If I have to be bored for two hours straight, at least bore me with something new.*

But now he's watching it. By choice. The gesture is meant to be moving, I'm sure of this. It says (or at least I think it says),

Look! I miss you so much I'm watching your favorite movie. And if he'd done this two weeks ago, I would have cried at the mere fact that he did something he used to hate just because it reminded him of me. It's progress. I should be happy.

Simón makes his way back to the room, and I place my phone screen-down on the table. I don't know what Ale expects me to reply. *I miss you too*? I'm not even sure if that's the case anymore. I guess part of me still does, but there's a bigger part—albeit a more confused part—that doesn't have time to miss him. The same part that's sitting in Simón's hotel room, waiting to have a platonic dinner with him. And replying that I do miss him or any of the things I know he's fishing for feels like a mistake.

The truth is . . . I don't know if I wish I was there with him.

No. I *don't* wish I was there with him. And I haven't felt that way for . . . a few days now. A week? More? I've been so distracted by my job and Simón that I haven't had time to miss Alejandro. Regret hits me square in the chest but I have nothing to regret. Do I? He wanted time. I gave him time. It's been over a month. A lot can happen in a month, and I did what he wanted. I didn't want "a break." I wanted to get married. And now I—

"Remember when you offered to help me succeed in my music career?" Simón asks, carrying a tray into the room.

"Vaguely," I reply, but I'm not paying attention.

Simón sets the tray down on the table, then taps his chin with a finger. Twice.

"That's funny," he says. "Do you remember asking for my help to get your ex—"

"Yeah, yeah!" I throw both hands up. "I remember."

I swallow hard. My ingenious plan to get Alejandro back is the last thing I want to be thinking about.

Simón grins, sitting on the bed. "Excellent. I need to cash in."

"The profile isn't ready."

Simón waves me off before he places the guitar on his lap again. The movement seems second nature for him.

"We'll worry about that later. Could you please listen to something I'm working on?" he says. "While you eat."

Simón dips his chin ever so slightly, giving me a hopeful look through long eyelashes. His eyebrows lift and draw closer. His expression is painfully pleading.

I know if I said no, he wouldn't force me to listen to him. But he bought me dinner. And rain is starting to patter against the window. And my sandwich is getting cold. And I don't want to leave yet, even though I should. So, I nod.

Simón grins before he strums softly on his guitar. Soft, intricate combinations of notes float out of it, bouncing off his fingertips. I imagine them like soap bubbles in the wind, bursting when they touch me. I don't know much about guitar playing or the technical aspect of making music, but it's my job to know about feelings and how to evoke them through words. And this feels right. And unfair.

Suddenly I'm angry. At Alejandro. At Simón. At myself for not leaving when I had the chance, for saying yes when I should have said no, for dragging Simón into my mess and losing focus on the plan.

My head is in tangles. Simón is looking at me with intent, with purpose. What would I do now if I was certain I didn't have a boyfriend? Would I shorten the distance between us and make the thoughts I've been having about Simón a reality? Unlikely. But the confusion I've been subjected to for the past few weeks renders me unable to even consider it. Because before

Simón showed up, I had never once wondered if I was settling. I never wondered if I could do better than Ale, if there even was better. Now life is shouting a big *Wake up!* in the form of Simón Arreaza. And for some reason, that feels like treason. Against Alejandro. Against the person I was over a month ago. Against the Maria Antonieta I am at my deepest core—someone who plans and sticks to those plans, who honors her word, who is not surprised by life.

I didn't plan on Simón. I didn't count him as one of the variables. I was so busy worrying about what would happen if Alejandro met someone else during our "break," I didn't have time to plan for what I would do if that scenario happened to me.

Simón plays the final notes of his song, ending the whole show with a very excited, "Well?"

I nod ten times in two seconds. "Mm-hm. Love."

It? Him? I don't know.

But I know I can't act on it. It wouldn't be professional. That has to be my new plan. Be professional. No matter what. And one more thing:

Tomorrow—Tell Alejandro I'm the one who needs time now. Wherever that leaves me with Eugenia, the experiments, the article . . . I'll find a way to resolve it. I always do. But I can't keep lying to myself. Because I think I'm falling in love with Simón Arreaza.

CHAPTER 25

••••••

ALEJANDRO IS SUPPOSED TO PICK ME UP FOR DINner in—I check my watch—fifteen minutes ago.

I'm waiting for him on my couch, pulling at a loose thread in the sleeve of the black cotton dress I decided to wear. I'm rewatching season 2 of *Friends*, but I'm thinking I should change it to season 5, which is my favorite. Chandler and Joey left Ross's baby on a bus and they're running after it. Behind me, my mother is banging cabinets in an attempt to search for heaven knows what.

"I can't find anything in this house," she mutters, loud enough for me to hear.

I check my watch again. Alejandro is twenty minutes late.

I grab the remote and turn the TV off, pushing to my feet. Waiting for him when he's late gives me too much room to think. My head has been in turmoil since last night. Thoughts of what seeing Alejandro again might be like are overpowered by memories of Simón last night—sitting in front of me, completely oblivious as my heart beat frantically at the realization that I'm developing feelings for him.

There. I said it. I have romantic feelings for the coach I recruited to help me get back together with the ex-boyfriend I'm meeting tonight. The coach who also happens to be a rising star, and who is going back home to his glamourous life in less than a month.

Mamá curses colorfully, a steel bowl clattering on the floor. I'm left with no choice but to walk into the kitchen.

"What are you doing?"

"What does it look like I'm doing? I was looking for a bowl to make the arepas." She bends over to pick up the one she dropped. "But who keeps the bowls with the pots and pans?"

I move around her to get to the fridge. "Lots of people."

"Será," she says, but sounds unconvinced.

I pull the fridge door open and grab my water bottle *and* the corn flour before she starts tearing my kitchen apart looking for it.

"*Where* is the Harina P.A.N.?" my mother asks behind me.

I turn around and hand her the corn flour.

She looks from my hands to my face, then back to my hands before taking it.

"Fridge," she says. "Who keeps the Harina P.A.N. in the fridge?"

I'm starting to repeat that lots of people keep stuff where *I* keep stuff, but the buzz of the doorbell silences me.

Oh my god. I'm going to puke right here. A wave of nausea rises up my throat and I gulp down the entire bottle of water to help my stomach settle.

Mamá looks at me and smirks, her eyes shining with mischief. "I wonder who that is."

I frown, backing out of the kitchen as I point a finger at my mother. "Pórtate bien."

She slaps the finger away. "I always behave."

I snort, halfway to the door.

"Mamita, I'm but a poor old woman," she says, following me. "Do you think I'm going to pretend to take out the trash and slash his tires so he can't take you anywhere?"

I turn and give her a pointed look. Surely, she wouldn't do it twice.

"That wasn't me," she says, but the evil smirk she's trying to hide says otherwise.

Rolling my eyes, I fight a smile as I pull the door open before Alejandro rings the bell again. He's not fond of waiting. Ironic, considering he's over thirty minutes late now.

But it's not Ale.

My breath catches at the sight of the person—or rather *people*—standing at my doorstep. Simón and Blanca stand side by side at my front door, my neighbor's little dog barking at their footsteps from inside his apartment. Behind them, the elevator doors shut with a loud *clank* and the stairs' fluorescent lightbulb flickers on and off and on again.

A gasp escapes me. What is Simón doing at my door? "Wha—"

"Ay, llegaron!"

I whirl toward my mother and shoot her a questioning gaze. Is Simón her guest? At my own place?

"Hi."

My chest both hurts and tickles at the word slipping through his lips. God, that voice. Raspy, deep, playful.

"Hi," I finally say. Simón's lips slowly curve into a smile, eyes fixed on me. "Come in."

"My talented guests, welcome," Mamá says, arms wide.

Simón and Blanca follow my mother in. "Blanca, what do you think about becoming a podcast producer?"

"I think I have no idea how to do that but . . ." Blanca's voice drifts as they disappear behind the kitchen wall.

Simón stays behind, hands deep in his jean pockets. "You look nice."

Self-consciously, I look down at my outfit, running both hands down my clothes to flatten invisible wrinkles. "Gracias," I tell him. "I'm having dinner with Ale."

I should have told him sooner. I should have included him. Maybe he would have celebrated. Maybe he would have helped me make sense of my feelings the last few days. But then I would have had to explain said feelings, and that is simply not going to happen.

Simón nods. "I know. Viviana told me. I hope you have a lovely night."

"Thank you," I say again. He responds with a small smile, then takes a step toward the kitchen. My hand shoots forward, closes around his arm. Simón looks back at me, then down to where I'm touching him. "Uh . . ." I don't know why I did that. I just don't want him to leave me here alone. "Do you have any last-minute advice?"

Simón chuckles, scratching the back of his neck. "You know, I can't think of anything."

"Okay." He tries to leave again, and again I stop him. "Don't you want to come with me and sit in the corner with sunglasses? Maybe a hat? And then you can tell me what to do?"

Simón laughs at this, shaking his head. "Not even a little." He takes a step in my direction and my body tenses. He places both hands on my shoulders and squeezes. His touch is reassuring, comforting. I fear when he walks away, the shape of his hands will be engraved on my skin. I don't look at him. If I do, I won't want to go. If he tries to leave again, I will let him.

"Hey." He tilts my chin up with a hand while the other slips down my arm. His touch is soft and I have no option but to meet his gaze. "Just be yourself. If it's not enough for him, I promise it will be enough for somebody else."

He drops his hand to grab mine, gives it a soft squeeze, and steps back. This time, with a lump in my throat, I let him go.

THINGS ALEJANDRO HAS done since we sat down: Compliment my outfit. Take two—two!—phone calls. Ask how big of a diva Simón is.

Things he hasn't done? Apologize for being late.

The soundtrack to my evening is as follows: a cacophony of scraping chairs mixed with the rustling of people trying to navigate the narrow space between tables, paired with the sound of silverware on porcelain.

In another life, this would be the highlight of my day. I wouldn't care that the restaurant is too small, too loud, too crowded. Alejandro would be all I'd care about. Even now, he's still one of the most beautiful people I've ever laid eyes on. My chest constricts at the sight of him sitting across from me. A wave of nostalgia hits me, taking me back to being a broke twenty-three-year-old who fell in love with Alejandro and his Greek-god looks, halfway through our first date.

But he isn't that person anymore. Right now, this Alejandro yawns, looking up at the TV hanging from the wall above my head. It's on mute, replaying a soccer game he most likely watched live, yet he's paying no attention to me. I clear my throat and Ale lowers his gaze from the TV to me, smiling.

"So," he says. "How's the new job?"

"Demanding," I answer. "Listen, can we—" I begin, but a waitress materializes next to us, notepad in hand.

"Are we ready to order?" she asks.

"Not quite," I say at the same time Ale says, "Yes."

We stare at each other for what feels like an eternity while the waitress, who clearly wishes she'd been sent to a different table, watches.

"I guess we're not ready yet," Alejandro finally says, adding an apologetic smile for good measure.

That simple change in his features infuriates me. I'm most likely reading too much into it, but it feels like he's apologizing on *my* behalf, because *I'm* not ready to order, like I'm making her life hard or something.

"Can we . . . ?" Alejandro says once she's gone.

I sigh. "Can we skip the small talk? I think we're past it."

He half frowns, half smiles. "You haven't even asked how I'm doing."

I stare at him without blinking, refusing to give in to his attempts at playfulness. But as his smile widens and he raises both eyebrows, I can tell that he's being sincere. A part of me wants to know how he truly is, but another part is too stubborn to give in so easily.

"We were together for four years," I remind him. "If you were miserable, I'd be able to tell."

Ale laughs under his breath, giving a single shake of his head. "That's fair." And he doesn't say anything else. Instead, he fixes his green eyes on me, almost pleading. He wants me to ask anyway. And I bite.

"How have you been, Ale?"

He grins, but where it once made me feel giddy and triumphant, it now leaves me feeling . . . manipulated. It turns my stomach, eviscerates my appetite.

"I'm really well," he says, his tone almost affectionate. "I mean, at first it was . . ." He pauses.

I wait. If he's expecting me to fill in the blank, he's dead wrong. I want to hear this. *What's it been like for you, Ale?* I want to know.

"Challenging," he finishes.

Challenging? So did he miss me as much as I missed him? Did he create an elaborate plan to get me back the way that I did? From where I stand, his life didn't take a turn for the worse after dumping me. In the meantime, it's been challenging for *me*. I thought he was proposing, and I got dumped instead. I lost my job because of it. I lost everything in the span of twenty-four hours, and until I dragged Simón into my messy attempt to get him back, Alejandro didn't seem to care about any of it.

The words are on the verge of spilling out but instead I sigh and grab my glass of water and gulp some of it down.

"I missed you," he adds. "All the time. I still do."

Ale and I stare at each other for a heartbeat. I try to bask in the softness in his eyes and the words I've been begging for since that night, at a different restaurant. But I can't. I can't recognize the man I loved in him. I don't know if what I'm seeing is honesty or more manipulation.

"So, what now?" I ask.

Ale frowns. "What do you mean?"

"Ale, if we base our entire relationship on missing each other, we'll only work when we're apart," I tell him. "What do you want to do now?"

Alejandro stills in his seat. He casts his eyes down, unable to say the words to my face. I know what's coming. I didn't see it the first time around, but I see it now.

"I'm not ready to let you go, Marianto," he says.

My stomach turns. And not in a good way. Those words

were not what I was expecting. But he said them. He said exactly what I wanted him to say. I've been dreaming about this. But now, I try to find the desperate feelings that had me vowing this was the man I wanted to marry; I try to reach for them in the bottom of my heart, and my hand comes out empty.

"Ale, I—"

But he's not done. "I'm just not . . . ready to think about marriage either—"

I shake my head, hoping he'll stop. I'm not ready to think about marriage either. For the first time since this started, we're on the same page. But my heart is hammering against my chest, and I can't think clearly. I don't want to hurt Ale. The thought immediately brings tears to my eyes, but I can't—

"—I'm only *starting* to find myself," he continues. "And I know you, you think you're so sure of everything, but you're not. You have to work on yourself too. You can be very . . ." He looks like he's choking on his own words. Like he's holding something back. "Controlling."

"Controlling?" I repeat.

"Marianto." He says it like *C'mon*, the way he always does, like I'm being purposefully obtuse. The confusion I was feeling dissipates under blazing anger at this man, who I wanted to spend the rest of my life with, inviting me to dinner to remind me why he broke up with me. One moment saying he missed me, the next telling me that he thinks I should change. He doesn't stop there: "You've controlled this entire conversation. You didn't even let us eat before you started ambushing me with questions."

"We came here to *talk*, didn't we?"

"Right." He nods. "And now you're getting angry because I was honest with you about where I stand."

"I thought you were moving to Barinas," I say.

Ale shrugs, nonchalant. "I'm willing to reconsider."

"Why?" It comes out harder than I intended.

I don't even know why I'm so angry. Maybe it's because he's always told me where he stood when it came to me, and I chose not to believe him. Or maybe it's because I dragged Simón into it and now I might be in love with him. And maybe it's because my feelings for Alejandro aren't clear and, even now, I'm not brave enough to say it. Instead, I lash out at him for telling me the truth to my face. I do have stuff to figure out. But he chose the most hurtful way to let me know.

Ale throws his head back and sighs, but it might as well be a grunt. "I think we can get back together, just . . . with no plans. Let's see where it goes this time. It'll be good for us. You see it, right?"

That question. That's the question that makes me see red. He's only *starting* to find himself. He wants to see *where this goes*. And *I'm* starting to realize that maybe this is not what I want after all.

"I'm sorry, I don't."

To hell with the article. To hell with the last few months. To hell with everything. Love isn't supposed to feel like this. It's not supposed to make me feel insecure. Love is supposed to be an anchor, to make me feel safe and sound and protected. That's what I've always wanted. Someone I can trust, someone I can rely on. Alejandro is not my anchor anymore, he's the storm.

And yet, as I see his confused expression, I can't help but feel conflicted. A part of me still cares about him, despite everything. But another part wants to scream and push him away.

"What are you saying?" he asks.

"I'm saying I don't want to get back together." I expect the words to shatter me, to break me further, but they don't. As soon as they're out of my lips, a huge weight is lifted off my shoulders. It's true, I don't want to get back together.

"Marianto—"

"You obviously have things to figure out. And, as you kindly pointed out, so do I." I swallow. "It's best if we do it on our own. No ambiguity." Alejandro blinks, speechless. "Consider yourself free, okay?"

I down the rest of my drink, snatch my bag off the table, and march out of the restaurant into the chilly night.

Anxiety is like a superpower. When I left my apartment, I didn't know how tonight was going to end, so I predicted every possible outcome and prepared myself accordingly. I think, on some level, even me finalizing the breakup was something I could see happening. What I didn't prepare myself for is the relief I feel as I leave the restaurant, glad I'm finally going home.

CHAPTER 26

I SNEAK INTO MY APARTMENT WELL PAST MIDNIGHT. I went to the twenty-four-hour McDonald's in Las Mercedes for dinner and sat by the window on the second floor, watching the cars drive by. After one of the workers came around my table to ask if I'd like anything else for the third time, I decided it was time to go. Now, my bare feet freeze as I tiptoe to my bedroom. Slowly, I open the door and slide in before shutting it behind me. Once I'm safe inside, my body relaxes. I flip the light switch on and—

"Qué pasa?" my mom asks from under the sheets—*my* sheets—before she pokes her head out.

I yelp and back away until I'm pressed flat against my door, whimpering like a wounded dog, rubbing my chest in an attempt to put my heart back where it belongs.

"What are you doing here?!"

My mother looks at me through narrowed eyes, scowling. "Sleeping, pues."

OH! That explains it! Never mind that I gave her a room of her own to avoid this exact situation.

"Madre, why are you in my room?" I ask.

"Because Simón is in mine." She utters those words like it's obvious.

My heart stops. I heard her wrong. I must have heard her wrong because I *think* she said Simón is here? As in, sleeping *here*? Inside the apartment I live in?

"What?"

Mamá sits up, annoyed. Well, that makes two of us. "Qué?"

"Did you say Simón is here?"

"Sí."

Sí. My left eye twitches. "Why?"

She shrugs one shoulder, with feigned innocence. "Because it was too late for him to go home."

I rub the space between my eyebrows with my middle finger. Too late for him to go home? What is he, according to my mom, six? Instead of, I don't know, a grown-ass man? I could scream. I want to scream. But apparently Simón is asleep in the next room.

I march to the bed and rip a pillow from under her head, startling her. "Pero bueno, Maria Antonieta, qué te pasa?"

I ignore her.

After grabbing a spare blanket from the closet, I move to the living room, flipping the lights off on my way out. The couch creaks when I sit, loud in my ears now that I know Simón is here. I listen for Mamá's footsteps, sure she's going to come and beg me to take the bed or talk things out, but she doesn't. She's probably going to wake up tomorrow thinking it was a dream.

Moonlight streams in through the windows, bathing the living room in a glow brightened by the streetlight outside the building.

Quietly, I slide down on the couch until I'm fully on my

back. The ceiling fan I never turn on stares back at me and I imagine it turning on its own.

I'm 50 percent sure this apartment is haunted. That's why I have a mini fridge in my bedroom. I don't even come out for water after ten. I'm fairly certain that, even if the fan *did* start turning on its own, I wouldn't go back to my room. That's how angry I am. I sigh, sinking deeper into the couch. The events of the night play in my head like a movie in a torture chamber. Alejandro and I broke up. *Really* broke up this time. I should be sad, but I'm not. I should be waiting for him to text me, asking me to reconsider, begging to take me back, but I left my phone in my purse, and for the first time in years I'm in no rush to get it back. Tonight, I threw the life I always thought I wanted overboard along with the opportunity to get my job back. The old me would be screaming, crying, throwing up. The new me—and how new is she anyway?—is . . . okay. Out of all the things that happened tonight, this is the most surprising. I'm okay. The world didn't end, and it won't end tomorrow either.

After God knows how many minutes staring at the ceiling, my eyelids grow heavier and heavier, until I can't keep them open anymore. I'm almost asleep when my eyes snap back open. A doorknob rattles. I think. Or did I dream it? No, there it is. I push myself up on my elbows as the squeaky sound of a door opening reaches me. Took my mother long enough. I wouldn't put it past her to have waited just so she could enact revenge on me for waking her up.

I start to sit, bracing for the conversation I'm about to have, but quickly duck back down. It's not my mother.

It's Simón.

Shirtless.

I gulp down a breath so fast I nearly choke on it.

He's shirtless. Walking down *my* hallway, toward *my* bathroom. He rubs sleep off his face with one hand, pushes his hair back with the other. It's the sexiest movement I've ever seen a man do. Men rubbing sleep off their faces while pushing their hair back is now my specific type.

Heat creeps up my cheeks first, spreading to the rest of my body just as fast. Thank God Simón doesn't seem to know where the light switch is.

The light pooling into my apartment reaches him when he gets to the bathroom door, turning his pale skin silver. Simón is . . . human. No six-pack or shoulders you could build a house on. Defined? Yes. A musician's arms—lean and strong, yet soft. The torso of someone who doesn't spend every waking moment in the gym but has an active life. He has a tattoo by his rib cage, but I can't make out what it is. His boxers' waistband peeks out from his jeans, which hang low on his waist. It's like he was pulled out of a photo shoot for *Rolling Stone Colombia*.

I shouldn't be looking at him like this, but I can't help it. I'm frozen. My brain burns the image of him here, in my apartment, surrounded by things that make up my entire life, to use for future reference.

Simón struggles with the door. It has a trick my mother must have failed to teach him. I hope he doesn't have to go too bad. I would sooner let him pee on himself than reveal my presence.

"Cómo se abría esta vaina?" he says, leaning to get a closer look at the door.

I wince. He has to give it a little kick at the bottom right corner because it sticks.

Five seconds. I'm going to give him five seconds to figure it out and if he doesn't, I'll help.

The door opens, thank God, and Simón sighs with triumph, while I collapse on the couch from relief. The bathroom door clicks shut.

I stare at the ceiling, then turn my head in the direction of the hallway. In reality, my eyes land on the leather surface of the couch, but my brain is still on Simón, longing. This is ridiculous. I should be mourning the four-year relationship I ended less than twelve hours ago, *not* wishing I was deep into a decades-long marriage with the man currently using my bathroom. I've known him for, what? Two months? Wishing I could have walked up to him and kicked the damn bathroom door while running a hand down his bare back is unacceptable. I don't know what happened to my brain when I met Simón. People do not behave this way. *I* don't behave this way.

Too soon, the bathroom door opens again. This time, I lie as still as a statue until I'm sure he's back in the spare bedroom.

Diooooos. I press my wrists to my eyes. If this place wasn't haunted before, it is now. I'll live with the ghosts of a thousand what-ifs my imagination will conjure every time I sit on this couch, walk down that hall, kick the bottom right corner of that door.

I wish this thing was simple attraction. It's so much easier to get over someone if you merely want to sleep with them. But how do you get over someone who makes you believe in eternity? Not in the *I'll be with you forever* kind of way. In the *there was a beginning, and in the beginning, there was you and there was me and the world has only gone on this long so you and I could finally meet* kind of way.

I let my eyes flutter closed. Tomorrow will be better.

I hope I'm too tired to dream; I don't trust my brain not to give me impossible scenarios. There is an 80 percent chance I'll never sleep again after tonight.

"Come on, brain," I whisper. "Shut up and shut down."

Not even a second later, the atmosphere in the living room changes. I feel him before I see him. Please, let it be a ghost.

Simón clears his throat. I pretend I'm asleep. Maybe he'll go away.

"I know you're pretending to be asleep, but you're not breathing," he whispers, right next to my ear.

I open my eyes with a jolt at the sound of his sleepy voice so close. He smiles, kneeling next to me, the corners of his eyes wrinkling.

"Hey. Go sleep on the bed. I'll take the couch."

I wrap myself with the duvet. "I'm fine here. Go back to sleep."

Instead of obeying, Simón sits on the opposite end of the couch. I notice he's carrying the pillow and blanket I bought for the guest bedroom forever ago.

"Simón." I try to channel an ounce of authority while whispering and being covered up to my neck with a duvet. "Go to bed."

"I am," he says, settling into his corner.

He closes his eyes. I press my lips together to keep from smiling.

"Simón."

"Shh. I'm trying to sleep. Big day tomorrow," he says.

"What are you doing tomorrow?" I ask, my voice so low it barely qualifies as a whisper.

He has tomorrow off. If it's a big day, I should know. Shouldn't I? Unless it's something private. Like a date. He's going on a date. And that's fine. I just broke up with my boyfriend of four years. Simón can go on a date.

He abandons his act, sitting up. "I'm buying a suit to wear to your impending nuptials. What color should I get?"

"The men in my Pinterest board are wearing burgundy," I say.

Simón *tsks*. "I don't look good in burgundy."

I fake a frustrated sigh. "I guess black will do. Do you know what you're singing at my wedding?"

Simón chuckles. "Do you have money to pay me to sing at your wedding?"

"As a matter of fact, I do."

A grand total of zero dollars, as there will not be a wedding.

"Right, I forgot you're a personal assistant to a mildly successful singer," he says with a smirk.

"You're very successful, Simón," I say.

Simón's smirk melts into a soft smile. "If you say so."

He closes his eyes again, resting his head on the side of the couch. With his throat exposed, I see his Adam's apple bob. Outside, the streetlight flickers. He's falling asleep. He can't fall asleep. If he wakes up with a stiff neck, Mileidy will have *my* neck.

"Simón?"

"Mm?" I can see the muscles of his jaw twitch with the sound.

Go to sleep, I should say. I should assure him that I'm fine sleeping here, that I prefer it to my own bed, that there's nothing like it. But then he'll go. And I'll be alone.

"Did you have fun tonight?" I ask instead.

"I did," he breathes. "Up until Viviana kidnapped me, that is."

I laugh, muffling the sound with my duvet. I hug my knees to my chest as Simón opens one eye to look at me.

"Did *you* have fun?" he asks.

Fun is not the word I would use to describe tonight. It was certainly eventful. Infuriating. Cold. But not fun. Not until now anyway, which I can't admit to him.

"We broke up."

Simón stills. I don't know how it's possible for someone who is not moving to *not* move more, but he manages.

"So that was fun," I add.

Silence stretches between us; the only sound is the rustling of the leather as he shifts, sitting back up. I swallow hard. Simón simply stares at me while I try to fix my eyes on any shadowed silhouette that isn't him. The confession leaves me feeling exposed. A little embarrassed. Here I am, sitting in the dark with the man I recruited to help me get back together with the boyfriend I broke up with hours ago. Here I am, admitting I failed.

"Don't worry, I still owe you a profile," I say, because the silence is unbearable.

Simón leans forward, eyes wide. "Marianto, I don't care about that."

Then he's a better human than I am. He practically told me I would change my mind, and I did. I would be rubbing it in my face if I were him. I would be livid someone made me waste my time helping them only to throw it all away. I could have said yes to Alejandro. Hell, I *should* have said yes. We would have been back together. Eugenia wouldn't have known the difference. I would have gotten the promotion, an ending for my article, albeit an anticlimactic one, but still. I would have gotten a foot in the door to give Simón what I promised him. If he knew, he *would* care. I screwed things up for both of us.

"Are you okay?" Simón asks.

I hug the duvet tighter. "Well, I was the one who ended it, so I better be."

"You can be sad about it even when you feel you did the right thing," he says. "When I broke up with my last girlfriend, I was devastated."

"What happened?" I whisper.

He shrugs. "She hated that I was in a band."

"She dumped you because of the band?"

"She asked me to choose."

Oh. "And you chose the band."

Simón nods once, slowly.

Silence hangs heavy in the air. The only sound is the gentle rustling of sheets as we shift in the dark. Somewhere in my apartment a cricket is chirping while I try to unpack what Simón just said.

"In her defense, long distance is the only way to have a relationship with me, which is hard enough." His statement is a needle to the small bubble of fantasies I'd been having. "Throw in the lack of a reliable schedule, the fact that our careers are taking off so we're spending less time at home . . . It's not for everyone. It wasn't fair to force her into accepting a lifestyle she didn't want."

The words wrap around my heart, squeezing until it hurts. It's good that we're having this conversation. It'll help me keep my wits about me. I came second to my mother's career my whole life. She missed important events, milestones. She was never available. Too busy shooting a telenovela, or closing a deal, or eloping with her co-star. Simón's career is his priority. Breaking up with Alejandro doesn't change that. I won't put myself in a position where I have to compete for his attention. Whenever he starts to look like a possibility for me, I'll remember this conversation and how he told me, with his own lips, that he's exactly what I've always said I don't want. Even if I don't know exactly what that is anymore. This way, maybe we can be friends.

"Did you . . . consider it?" I ask. "Quitting the band?"

"I did," he admits. "I loved her. We'd been together for over a year. I had a ring." A ring. For someone. After barely a year. I swallow hard. "I almost quit. And then Juanes wanted us to open for him."

"That was two years ago," I say, because I can't talk about how he was ready to marry someone after a year, and it wasn't the right person. Meanwhile, I spent four years with Ale, and he was never sure he wanted me for forever.

Simón laughs. "The guys wanted to kill me." He pushes his hair back, a front-row version of the motion he did by the bathroom door. His eyelids are heavy with exhaustion. "I swore I'd keep writing for them. They didn't want me to write, they wanted us to live our dream together. And when I went to her house to tell her that Juanes wanted us to open his tour, she wasn't happy for me. She got angry. And that's when I knew." He shrugs. "If we stayed together, one of us would always resent the other. Love is not enough. People want to believe it is, but it's not. Your passions, your dreams, your goals . . . all of that matters. Geography matters too. Time. It's two lives, and all their parts, joined together. For us, there wasn't even room for compromise. She hated the part of me I loved the most." Simón swallows. I want to reach out, touch him, comfort him for having to go through what he did. I wish I could say I can't imagine loving someone enough to want to marry them and have them not return the feeling, but I can. My heart breaks for him. "It was the easiest decision I've ever made. I'm still sure I made the right choice. But it hurt."

He yawns, settling deeper into his corner of the couch. I watch him in silence as he blinks lazily, breaking the quiet of the night with a low, tired moan that I feel in every fiber of my body. He truly is beautiful in his lanky, relaxed state. He's beautiful in his kindness, in his generosity. In his friendship too. That's where he's the most beautiful. In the support and help he's offered me throughout the short time we've known each other. Which is why I ask:

"Do you think I made a mis—"

"No." Simón answers before the question is fully out. His voice is firm, no room for debate. It makes my eyes sting.

"Even if I don't get the promotion?" I whisper.

He pins me with a look from where he sits on his end of the couch. "Even if you write an article dragging Caballo de Troya through the mud and publish it in *The New York Times*, I will still be glad you broke up with Alejandro."

"Why?" I ask.

Simón yawns, looking away. "Because I'm selfish."

My heart races as soon as the words are out of his mouth. What is he saying? That he *wants* me to be single? Even if I don't hold up my end of the deal?

"Marianto?"

I snap back into focus. "Yes?"

"I'm not moving from this couch, so we'll be sharing it unless you take the bed," Simón says, unselfishly unselfish.

With an eye roll I'm not sure he can see, I push to my feet. "Fine. But you'll regret this in the morning."

Simón shakes his head as he stretches both long legs on the couch. He doesn't even fit on it. "I won't regret any of it."

I smile to myself on my way to the room, looking over my shoulder to find his eyes on me. "Hey." I clear my throat. "I hope you know you deserve someone who loves all of you."

He gives me a small smile. "So do you," he says. "Good night, Maria Antonieta."

"Good night, Simón Andrés."

CHAPTER 27

••••••

WHEN MONDAY ROLLS AROUND, I CAN ONLY THINK about one thing: I'm not going to finish that article. And consequently, I'm not going to get my job back, and I'm not going to write Caballo de Troya a profile. And I need to tell Eugenia.

I shake my hands, pacing in front of the building where the magazine's offices are located. Above me, the trees move with the wind and release little droplets of water from last night's rain. Two men chat and push past me. One of them throws me an annoyed look over his shoulder.

It's seven thirty. I know Eugenia is already in her office. I have to be at the studio in an hour. If I'm going to do this, I have to do it now.

I march up the steps leading to the door. Walking these halls is second nature to me. I go straight for the elevator, the way I used to. I wave a hello to my favorite barista on the way. I march out on the *Ellas* floor and Blanca immediately looks up. I expect the familiar pastels to make me feel right at home too, but they don't. They seem just as foreign as VeneTV. Known, but not mine. Which is weird, because if there was a place I considered another home, it was this one.

Blanca stands, leaning over her desk, wide-eyed. "What are you doing here?"

"I need to talk to—"

The rhythmic clicking of heels on ceramic makes me stop. I know that sound. I trained myself to recognize that sound for five years straight.

"Maria Antonieta," Eugenia's sharp voice says behind me. "Do we have an appointment I don't know about?"

Slowly, I turn to face her. A pressure settles on my chest, making me almost dizzy with nerves. "Eugenia. Uh, no. But could I speak to you anyway?"

Eugenia crosses her arms, then shrugs one shoulder. "Sure."

But she doesn't move. Doesn't ask me to follow her. Nothing. She stands in the middle of the reception and stares. Today, she's wearing a black leather coat as if it were a dress. Her hair is pulled back so tight she might as well have gotten Botox. She looks a little like Cruella de Vil.

"Well?" she presses.

I'm not sure how to start the conversation. With my conflicting feelings? With Simón? I have no idea, so I blurt out the first thing I can think of:

"Alejandro and I broke up." But it sounds more like *AlejandroandIbrokeup*.

"Oh?" Eugenia arches an eyebrow.

I gulp. "And that means I can't finish the article."

"*Oh.*" Eugenia presses her lips into a thin line, nodding slowly. Somewhere in the reception area, a clock ticks. I could hear a fly if there was one.

My hands shake as I stand under Eugenia's scrutiny. Her face betrays nothing. Her eyes travel up and down my body, followed by a click of her tongue.

"This could have been an email," she says, then steps around me toward her office.

AT WORK, I'M trying to stay busy. I couldn't beg Eugenia to hear me out without risking being late. I force myself to keep that conversation out of my head and focus on the tasks at hand. I've categorized Simón as one of today's tasks. I speak to him only when strictly necessary, keeping things professional. If he notices, he doesn't let it show. The alternative is remembering him shirtless in my apartment and that will not make for a very productive day.

The remaining contestants are more nervous after watching half their friends leave the show at once. No one is sure they will make it to the next round, but each kid has to come in with some family members for interviews and promotional videos.

I'm standing in a corner watching Mamá interview a young father. The room is dark except for an LED screen depicting a poster of the show. His daughter, a fifteen-year-old girl, sits beside him, misty-eyed, as the man tells a story of how she started singing with her mother, who passed away two years ago, when she was three.

My mother, to her credit, keeps her composure throughout the interview. As soon as they leave, she excuses herself and marches to the bathroom, but I notice the red in her eyes. Camacho women don't cry in public.

AN EMAIL ARRIVES after lunch.

Simón is giving a pep talk to his team. Ten pairs of eyes look up at him through unshed tears. Tomorrow they will become half as many. Out of all the talented children we've met throughout the last two months, only five will move forward to the live shows. His voice is strong, commanding. But I have no idea what he's saying because of The Email.

From: admin@ethospub.org
Subject: Re: Ethos application

Dear Maria Antonieta,

It's a pleasure to be in touch. My name is Xiomara Isea. As you know, Ethos *is an emerging platform and we are especially keen on hiring emerging talent.*

We were very impressed with your application. There are several roles we think you would be a good fit for, and we would like to meet with you as soon as possible. If you are still interested, we would love to speak to you.

Are you available to schedule an interview for this afternoon at 4:00 p.m.? We understand this is last minute, but we are looking to fill these positions soon. If this time does not work for you, please reply to this email with your availability.

We're looking forward to hearing back from you.

All best,
Xiomara

I read and reread the words. Because it says I got an interview for . . . several positions?

Applying to *Ethos* was the definition of me shooting my shot. After not hearing back from any of the other places I applied to, I figured even hoping would be pointless. But here it is. An email. From Xiomara Isea. At *Ethos*.

"You okay?" Simón asks behind me. I didn't notice when he stopped talking to the kids. Or when he approached me. I turn to him, still speechless.

Whatever he sees on my face makes him take a peek at my phone. At first, he frowns. Then he grins. "Congratulations!"

I shake my head. "It's just an interview."

"Your face says it's not just an interview."

"I don't even think I can make it," I confess. "It's at 4:00 today."

Simón checks the watch on his wrist. "It's 1:00 p.m."

"The first leg of the show wraps tomorrow. There's a lot to do."

"Marianto." Simón grabs me by the shoulders. I'm keenly aware of the curious eyes watching us from different corners of the room. He either doesn't notice or doesn't care. "Don't worry about work, we'll figure something out. Tell them you'll do the interview."

His deep brown eyes bore into mine, almost pleading, like he knows how important, how enormous this is for me. Not only the job interview, but where it comes from. Not just the email, but what it represents. His gaze pleads like he was there that night, watching me send out the application.

Simón squeezes my shoulders once. I take it as my sign to step out of his grip and look away.

"Okay," I say.

To: admin@ethospub.org
Subject: Re: Ethos application

Good afternoon, Xiomara,

Thank you for the opportunity. I am still interested. 4:00 p.m. works.

Thank you in advance.

From: admin@ethospub.org
Subject: Re: Ethos application

Perfect! I will send over a Zoom link shortly.

Talk soon,
Xiomara

Simón is beaming at me when the door to our rehearsal room flies open and Mileidy comes streaming in, looking directly at me.

"Maria Antonieta, make sure the parents of the finalists get this form tomorrow." She hands me a stack of papers. "They need to sign it, otherwise the show won't cover their expenses when we leave for Margarita."

"Sure." I nod.

Simón steps between us, putting an arm around her shoulders and leading her to the opposite end of the room. "Mileidy, I have an appointment I can't miss at 3:00 p.m. and I need Maria Antonieta to assist me," Simón tells her. "It's for publicity."

Mileidy grunts her agreement, walking out of his semi-embrace to bark commands at some other unfortunate PA.

Simón turns to me with a grin before softly slapping the back of my shoulder. "Back to work."

"Why did you say three?" I ask, following him. "The interview is at four."

"Maybe I want to spend a little time with you without being surrounded by a dozen harmonizing children," he says. My cheeks instantly warm. I feel my eyes go round as my heart pounds against my rib cage. "Or maybe I want you to have a little time to prepare." He shrugs. "We may never know."

FINALLY, MY MOTHER taking over my apartment is paying off. Her podcast station will be my interview set this afternoon. With a hand perched on the curve of my waist, I look over my shoulder toward the door. Simón leans against it, arms crossed, assessing the space.

"Maybe if you moved the desk to one side?" he offers. "Here, let me."

And then the man rearranges my furniture.

"You really don't have to do that," I say. He ignores me until the desk is exactly how he envisioned it, which does work so much better. "Gracias."

"It's nothing," he replies. "Are you all set?" I nod. "Great. I'll just . . . wait in the living room."

My heart skips. The thought of not doing this interview alone is like drinking café con leche on a particularly cold morning. Knowing I'll find someone outside my door when this is over, someone who is rooting for me, who would probably comfort me if it goes south . . . I haven't felt the need for that kind of support in years, and though I really don't want to be alone . . .

"You don't have to stay, Simón. It's okay," I force myself to say. Because that is what I *should* say.

Simón stares at me for a second . . . two . . . until I have to look away. I can't function under the weight of his scrutiny.

Out of the corner of my eye, I notice he's nodding. "Okay."

I put all my strength into not deflating, not showing how disappointing it is that he's leaving.

"Could I stay anyway?" he asks. I look up, slowly. He blinks rapidly. "Let me rephrase that: I would like to stay. I want to stay."

I want you to stay too. I think the words, but I don't say them. It's crossing a line I don't dare approach. After all, he's leaving. He wants to stay today, maybe because he needs to see this through, maybe because he's *that* nice, who knows? But in five days, he's still leaving. I know because I booked the ticket to Bogotá. I know what day and what time he's leaving, I know through which gate, on which flight. Getting attached is a mistake. I know it is. But I still nod again. Twice now.

Simón smiles, then checks his watch. "Good luck."

With that, he steps out, closing the door behind me. It's just me and the rest of my life in the room now.

Okay, Marianto, relájate.

The screen, black until a second ago, displays a woman. Her skin dark with rich chocolate tones, her hair in a loose Afro pulled back by a colorful headband that matches the flower print on her bright pink blouse, her makeup photoshoot worthy—nude lips, neon eye shadow, not a wrinkle in her foundation. This is a woman who knows who she is and doesn't spend eighteen hours a day worrying about getting older and not amounting to anything. Of course, she looks like the exact person I would kill to work with. I already feel like I want to be her when I grow up.

"Maria Antonieta." She says my name with a grin. "I'm Xiomara, we spoke over email."

"Hi," I say. "It's so nice to meet you officially."

Xiomara waves my comment off. "Please, this isn't a meeting. Save those words for when you and I sit across from each other to have coffee."

Oh. Does that mean I have the job?

I almost ask. But I'm not here to interview her, I'm here to be interviewed. And to get a job in my dream field, a job I applied for on my own merits. A job I'd be good at.

"Are you ready?" Xiomara asks.

I run both hands down my pants and nod. No need to show my nerves. If I'm not ready, we're already here. It doesn't make a difference. She doesn't need to know.

"Perfect." Her smile widens. "Let's begin."

THE INTERVIEW ENDS and Xiomara leaves the call with a promise to reach out when they've made a decision. I slump in my chair, staring at myself in the virtual meeting room. My face is stunned but my eyes are bright. Slowly, a grin unfolds across my cheeks and the anxiety in my chest loosens, replaced by this intense feeling of elation. Hope. I haven't felt truly hopeful in months. I have only seen little glimpses of light, most of them caused by Simón, but now . . .

Editor. That's what she said. It's the longest shot in the history of long shots, but damn. I want it. Entertainment Editor. A dream. And I didn't have to beg for it. Or offer my private life in exchange for it.

I push to my feet, yank the door open, and march down the hallway.

Simón stands when he hears me coming. There's a question at the tip of his tongue that I don't let him ask. I fling my arms around his neck and pull him down toward me in what has to be the most unprofessional hug in the history of hugs. The soft "whoa" that scrapes the side of my face as it slips out of his mouth confirms it. His arms close around my waist, loosely. He doesn't press me to him, he doesn't take more than I'm offering. I'm so full of gratitude to him for being exactly what I need, exactly when I need it. Again and again, over the past two months. An idol, an accomplice, a friend.

"Thank you so much," I whisper, my voice tight.

His grip tightens, just a little. "You're welcome so much."

And next thing I know, I'm blurring another line.

I take a step back and ask, "Do you like cake?"

CHAPTER 28

I SCOOP MORE TRES LECHES ONTO MY SPOON. The smell of cake permeates the air, filling every corner of the coffee shop while soft instrumental music plays from invisible speakers. The clinking of golden spoons against porcelain plates and the low hums of friendly conversation add to the Zen aesthetic I'm perpetually seeking. The fact that the tres leches is to die for is a bonus. I mean, sponge cake, soaked in a mix of condensed milk, evaporated milk, and cream topped with the fluffiest meringue and salted caramel? What's not to love?

As I bring the spoon to my mouth, I freeze midair when I catch Simón's gaze from across the table. A lopsided grin is born on his face the second our eyes meet, but he's sitting too straight. His hands are hiding under the table while his coffee grows cold between us.

"What?" I ask.

He shrugs with one shoulder, picking his mug up. "Nada."

That's not an answer but I don't push it. Instead, I slowly eat the bite of cake I left hanging, then set the spoon down on the plate with a soft *clink*. For a second, we're staring at each other, electricity building over the table separating us. If I squint, I think I can almost see the sparks.

"This is really good." Simón breaks the silence. He gestures at his own dessert—passion fruit cake—with the spoon.

I nod, a little too eagerly. "Right? Thought you should try it. You know, before you leave."

A corner of his mouth twitches. "I'm glad I did."

"Yeah." I clear my throat. "I mean, I owe you. For helping me with the interview."

In that precise moment the instrumental song that's been playing on a loop since we sat ends. People stop eating. And Simón's eyes find mine. The smile playing on his face becomes a thin line when he presses his lips together, nodding slowly.

"Is that the only reason you invited me?" he asks. "Because you thought you owed me?"

Yes.

No.

I don't know. What am I supposed to say?

"I invited you because I wanted cake," I lie. "And I thought you might want cake too."

The words taste bitter on my tongue, wrong. But admitting I invited him because I want to spend more time with him before he leaves, admitting I'm growing covetous of the scarce moments I have left with him before I have to grow up and return to reality? Not happening.

"Are you sure it has nothing to do with the interview you're refusing to talk about?" he says.

Thank God his usual perceptiveness is failing him today. But I take the change of direction like the blessing it is.

"I'm not refusing to talk about it," I say.

"Bueno, how did it go?" he asks.

Breathing in, I let the words take shape on my tongue before I breathe them out. "I don't know."

Simón frowns. "Cómo así?"

I shrug. "I answered all her questions, she answered all of mine, she said she'll be in touch, we said goodbye, and that was it. Could go either way."

"But did you like her?" he presses. "Do you want to work for them? Did she seem as bad as Mileidy?"

I fight a chuckle. She's still my boss and I'm still her employee. "Mileidy is not—"

Simón silences me with a look.

"Okay, she's not great but—"

Simón leans back on the chair, rolling his eyes. "You're too nice. It's hard to watch."

"I am not!"

"You are." He nods, drinking the last of his cold coffee. "I love that about you."

Our eyes lock.

"Uh, I . . ."

"Anyway, the interview? Did you like them?" He blurts the words out.

"Yes," I answer, too quickly. "I lov—I mean, I liked them. A reasonable amount. They seem . . ."

Not for the first time, I study Simón—the curve of his lips visible despite the beard, the waves of hair that frame his face. I remember all the expressions those features have offered me: more smiles than I can count, the confused frowns, the shocked, wide eyes, the laughter, the twitch of his lips when singing . . . and I wish I could have met him at a different point in my life. I wish I could have met him five years ago, before he was him and I was me.

I clear my throat. "They seem perfect."

Simón's expression softens.

"I'm sure they like you a reasonable amount too," he says. "And that they also think you're the closest thing to a perfect woman they're ever going to find."

I don't think we're talking about the interview anymore.

I cast my eyes down, shoving the rest of the cake into my mouth, just to have something to do. This is dangerous. I'm torturing my own heart. It doesn't matter that I obviously have feelings for Simón. It can't. And even if it did, how would it work? He spends half the year touring, the other half he spends doing I don't even know what. I don't need that. I don't *want* that. Not after growing up with my mother. I want something tangible, someone I can call in the middle of the night and know he can show up at my door if I need him. He's not that. I should know better. Hell, I do know better.

But after our plates are empty and the bill has been paid and he says, "Would you like to walk around?"

I say, "Sure."

And hours later, when we're watching the sun go down at Plaza Francia, macaws flying over our heads, and my cheeks hurting from laughing so much, and he asks, "Are you hungry?"

I say, "Yes."

And after we're finished eating, I offer him a ride back to his hotel because it's dark, and he lingers a little too long in the car before he asks, "Would you like to come sit by the pool?"

I say, "Why not?"

Even though there are so many reasons why not.

I'm welcomed by the soft hum of the water moving in the wind. A blue glow stretches over the tiles around the pool. Out here it is silent except for the water, the crickets, and the distant sound of cars passing on the highway.

I rub my arms up and down, trying to warm myself as I

walk toward one of the tables. The metal umbrella shakes with the strength of the wind. I expect Simón to join me at the pool table, but he has a different idea.

"What are you doing?" I ask.

He jumps on one foot as he takes off a shoe, then repeats the motion with the other.

"Simón," I say.

"Maria Antonieta," he replies, teasing.

Soon it's shoes off, socks off, pants rolled up, and him lowering himself onto the gravel around the tiles. "Come on."

I laugh dryly. "No. The water must be freezing."

He leans over, dipping his hand in to make a little splash. "It is. It'll wake you up."

"I'm not tired," I retort.

He looks at me over his shoulder, patting the ground next to him with his still-wet hand. "Ven."

I hear the soft splash of his feet hitting the water, followed by a deep sigh. That's all it takes to convince me.

Damn it.

I kick the ground, still rubbing my arms, before I join him. Thank God I wore sandals today.

I put my feet in the water and let out a "Whoop!" when it touches my skin. It's so freaking cold. We're going to lose our toes after this. But Simón is grinning at me like a child. His eyes are wild with stars. Or maybe it's the million hotel room windows I see reflected in them. He looks absolutely beautiful. The wind has tousled his hair, but he hasn't bothered with fixing it. His shirt is wrinkled from having worn it all day. His beard seems a little longer than it was this morning. And then he sighs again, content.

I grin back.

My arm grazes his. We're skin to skin. I can't help but lean a little closer. Next to me, Simón's body goes rigid, supporting mine.

Thinking about how good it feels to be pressed against him, to lean on him, is not advisable. I focus on the water under my feet instead. It's soaking the hem of my jeans despite my having rolled them up.

In an alternate universe, I'm resting my head on his shoulder while holding his hands in my lap. I'm whispering my fears and doubts into the night. I'm admitting I'm scared I won't get the job at *Ethos*, and that I don't have another plan. I'm letting him comfort me. I'm letting myself depend on him.

"You'll get it," Simón rasps, reading my silence. "The job."

I sniff. The cold is making my nose itch. "You can't know that."

He pushes against my arm slightly. "No. But I know you. I'd hire you."

I snort, despite myself. I want to believe him, but the truth is there are a hundred other applicants better prepared for the job than me. The best thing I can do is manage my expectations.

"Hey." He turns to face me. "I mean it. If you don't get it, you can join the band. God knows you've rendered me useless. I'd be lost with you."

I still at those words.

Simón looks down at his hands, fidgeting with a loose thread on the inside of his jeans. Then he looks up and gives me a weak, almost pained smile, like he regrets saying anything.

I clear my throat. "What would I do?"

"Hm?"

"In the band," I clarify.

He shrugs. "Anything you want."

"Lead singer?" I volunteer.

Simón smiles, eyes twinkling. "Why not? We'll be an alternative pop band. Our songs will be spoken instead of sung. It's a whole concept."

"You haven't even heard me sing!" I playfully smack his arm with the back of my hand.

He laughs. "Yes, I have. At the karaoke bar."

God. That night. I got drunk for the first time in ages, sang Kelly Clarkson, and found out what Simón smells like. It feels like forever ago. I'd almost forgotten it happened.

"*And* you sing all the time at work," he adds.

"No, I don't!"

That makes him laugh even harder. "Yes, you do. The kids hate it. It's personally offensive to them."

I hide my face between my hands. "Oh my god!"

"You can't be good at everything, Marianto," he says, nudging his knee with mine. "It's not fair."

I sigh. "Ya sé. I hate it."

Simón laughs again, squinting at me adorably.

His watch beeps, signaling 8:00 p.m.

"I should go," I say.

"Mm," he says.

But neither of us moves. His eyes remain anchored to mine, like we're committing them to memory.

"I should go," I repeat.

He nods. "I agree."

But his gaze drops to my lips, then moves slowly back up to my eyes and parks there. My heart races, threatening to escape my chest.

This will end badly. I know it. There is no scenario in which shortening the space between us is a good idea, in which we both come out unscathed.

And then he says my name—a soft whisper, a plea. I've only ever seen the way he's looking at me in romance movies.

Blame it on my lack of self-restraint, or my desperation to merge this universe with the one in which we're together, or the fact that I'm simply done fighting this, but when his eyes meet mine again, it's almost like we've reached an agreement. The distance between us vanishes. For a split second we freeze, our lips millimeters from touching, as if giving ourselves the chance to back away if we want to.

The split second ends. Neither of us moves away. We move forward. The moment his lips touch mine feels like coming up for air after being underwater, like a veil is being torn and every bit of fear or anxiety or doubt I felt ten minutes ago goes up in smoke. My hands find Simón's neck, pulling him closer, and he responds without hesitation. Our kiss deepens instantly, more urgent and wild than tender, as if we're racing against time itself. Every inch of skin his touch encounters ignites a fiery heat inside me, melting away any icy reserve I might have been holding on to. His fingertips trail along my neck, sending shivers down my spine, then slide down to my waist, firm and possessive, drawing me closer until the space between us is nonexistent. I can't help but wonder—if I were a guitar in his hands, would his touch be as electric and commanding? A touch that's both gentle and powerful, capable of creating a symphony of sensations that make my heart sing and my body tremble with anticipation.

"Oh!" someone says behind us.

Simón and I startle apart. The person retreats, mumbling apologies, but neither of us pays attention.

It takes me about three seconds for the world to come back into focus, for my thoughts to fall back into their proper categories, before I realize the enormity of what I did.

Ever the mind reader, Simón begins to stand. "Marianto—"

"I'm so sorry." I jump to my feet, splashing his face in the process. "I shouldn't have." I gather my things, hugging them to my chest. "We shouldn't—I'm sorry."

I leave before he has a chance to follow me.

CHAPTER 29

"I KISSED SIMÓN." THE WORDS BURST OUT OF ME the second Blanca opens the door to her house.

Crickets chirp somewhere in Blanca's front garden as she gapes at me. Behind her, Gustavo leaps to his feet from the couch. I didn't even realize he was there.

"I'll make popcorn," he says before disappearing down the hall I know leads to the kitchen.

I fidget with my hands, fog coming out of my parted lips as I breathe. Blanca steps to the side, ushering me in. "I—What—When?"

I check my watch, stepping inside. "About ten minutes ago?"

"DON'T START WITHOUT ME," Gustavo yells from the kitchen, and Blanca's devilish little poodle starts barking somewhere in the house.

"What happened?" She shuts the door. "From the beginning."

I summarize the day as calmly as I can—getting the *Ethos* email while I was at work, Simón helping me, then staying with me, the cake, the pool, everything.

"And then you kissed Simón," Blanca finishes.

I nod. And then I kissed Simón. My body hits the couch unceremoniously. Blanca watches me almost in anguish, her face contorted in a painful wince.

"Am I awful?" I ask.

Blanca sits on the couch next to me and grabs both of my hands, clutching them tightly. "You are not awful." She squeezes my hands, as if to emphasize. "You're thoughtful, and caring, and you always think of others before you think of yourself. So you were selfish *once.* I'd say it's about damn time! It doesn't make you a bad person."

The smell of popcorn fills the living room as Gustavo returns, balancing three bowls in his arms.

"Bebé, tell Marianto she's not awful," Blanca commands.

He frowns at me, placing the bowls on the coffee table in front of us. "You are *not* awful. Why would you think that?"

"I don't know." I grab one of the bowls and hug it to my chest. "Because Ale and I broke up like three days ago? I should be sad. I shouldn't be kissing my boss."

"Did you like kissing your boss though?" he says, ignoring the first half of what I said.

I raise both eyebrows at the question. We're close, but are we this close? I don't think so.

Blanca seems to share the same thought because she says, "Bebé, I think you should leave."

Gustavo looks between us, all wounded puppy eyes, before he puts one bowl of popcorn under one arm and sets his attention on Blanca. "Tell me everything?"

She winks at him, beaming when he leans in for a goodbye kiss. The picture of true love. I hate them.

"Please bring that back." She points at the bowl.

"Yeah, I know," he says, walking toward the door. "I really

like Simón, by the way. He's so much more fun than Alejandro."

Of course he'd think that. He's met Simón once and that day he got onstage and sang Selena. Alejandro wouldn't even do that while drunk. His idea of fun was criticizing shows like *Grey's Anatomy* and eating at fancy restaurants. He likes a quiet life. I liked a quiet life too.

But Blanca hums her agreement despite knowing all this. Her disapproval was never a secret. Honestly, their encouragement warms my heart. Anyone I date is someone they'll be stuck double-dating, after all. Not that I'm planning to date Simón. I'm not. It's just nice to know that, if we lived in a different world, they wouldn't object to spending more time with him.

Blanca whirls in my direction as soon as Gustavo leaves. "But seriously, did you like it? How was it? Was it like you would do it again or was it meh?"

"Dude, the amount of stars I saw, it was like being in outer space," I tell her. Almost literally. "He was so gentle but still confident, like you *know* he knows what he's doing? And he seemed so . . . sure. Like it wasn't an accident. Like he meant it." Blanca grins at that. Not so fast, little speedster. "And I ruined it."

Her grin falls. "What do you mean?"

"I ran."

"You *ran*?" she repeats.

"Someone saw us and interrupted us, *thank God*. And then I apologized and ran away." I groan and hide my face between my hands.

"Oh, sweet summer child . . ."

"What else was I supposed to do?" I say. "He's Simón. From Caballo de Troya."

Blanca tilts her head to the right, watching me with smug eyes. "Like you would have a make-out session with Simón just because he's in Caballo de Troya. Give yourself some credit, Maria Antonieta. You didn't even go on a date with Alejandro until you were sure you liked him."

I also didn't kiss him until we were exclusive. But I was twenty-three.

"So you kissed him. Big deal," she continues. "You're a single twenty-seven-year-old woman. He's a single man. You've been spending every waking moment together for the past however many weeks. You like each other. It's not the end of the world." She offers me popcorn. I refuse. If I eat anything right now, I'll throw up all over the couch. Blanca shrugs and grabs a handful for herself. "You needed to get Alejandro out of your system anyway. I say go for it. Talk to him, see where he stands. Chances are he wants to kiss you again. Do *you* want to kiss him again?"

Warmth spreads through my body at the thought of being that close to Simón again. I can't stop replaying the moment in my head—the way his lips felt against mine, soft yet insistent, the expression on his face as I left. I can't pretend it didn't happen. What's worse, I'm not sure I want to.

CHAPTER 30

······

THE FOLLOWING MORNING, I ARRIVE AT WORK thirty minutes early.

Today we have a special session with the kids who are moving on to the live shows. We're leaving for Margarita in two days, and they're supposed to perform in front of the media to promote the show.

I'm in the rehearsal room, hoping Simón had the same thought I did and will arrive early too. While I wait, I make sure everything is ready—chairs arranged, electric piano on and working. I also try not to think about the kiss, but it's a much harder task.

I check the time on my phone. It reads 8:37 a.m. The rehearsal is scheduled for nine, so the kids will start arriving at any moment. I probably should have texted Simón first, given him a heads-up that I wanted to talk, but I couldn't bring myself to do it. I figured it would be better not to build anticipation. We're going to see each other today anyway, so it didn't feel necessary.

I'm regretting that decision now.

The door swings open and my heart jumps, but it's another one of the PAs, bringing in an approved list of songs.

"Buenos días," I tell him.

He gives me a sheepish smile, sets the list down on a table by the corner, and leaves.

Soon after, the kids start arriving one by one, like little drops of rain before a thunderstorm. Every time the door opens, I jump. And every time, I'm disappointed to see it's not him.

I check the time again. It is now 9:30 a.m. Exactly thirty minutes after we were supposed to begin the rehearsal. I do a head count to double-check all the children are here. Some of them are chatting among themselves, while others are doing warm-up exercises and competing to see who has better vocal range. When we first began, they hardly spoke to one another. Now they've become friends.

By the time 10:00 a.m. rolls around, the kids are growing impatient.

"Excuse me, Miss Camacho," one of the girls says. "Is Coach Simón going to be here soon? My mom said I can't stay past noon, we have a family thing."

"Uh—"

The door swings open and we all turn in its direction. Irina Montalbán marches in, her entourage in tow. Today, she's wearing a fur coat that's way too big on her and sunglasses. Her hair is styled like we're in the '50s, with a polka-dot bandana tied on top and everything.

The kids exchange amused glances, some wide-eyed, others trying to suppress a smile. A little boy with framed glasses is hiding his face but his shoulders are shaking, while the girl next to him nudges him with her elbow.

Irina claps twice. "Places, everybody!"

"Go back to your seat," I tell the girl I was talking to before I approach Irina.

She sees me and offers a condescending smile. "Thank you for looking after them. We'll take it from here."

Irina turns away from me and starts talking to one of her assistants. I tap her shoulder and she turns back around, clearly annoyed.

"I'm sorry, where is Simón?" I ask.

She pretends to check her watch and rolls her eyes. "He must be on an airplane heading to Colombia as we speak."

Colombia? I quickly check the schedule we all share, trying to see if this travel plan was on it, but I can't find it. He was supposed to be here today, coaching these kids, who *also* thought he was supposed to be here today, who were waiting for him and counting on him.

"It was terribly unexpected for me, I had other things to do. But alas, the show must go on. I wish other people would see it that way," Irina says with a dramatic sigh.

I glance toward the kids and see the amusement is gone from their faces, replaced now with confusion and a little bit of worry. Collectively, they all look to me, as if I have the answers. I don't. I'm as lost as they are.

"Anyway, you can leave," Irina says.

But these kids don't know Irina well, they've never been in a coaching session with her. They know Simón and they know me. And someone has to put them at ease.

"I think I'll stay."

Irina shrugs and marches toward the children. I head to my place in the back, where I always sit taking notes.

Blanca's words from last night come to mind. *Talk to him, see where he stands, see where it goes.* But it can't go anywhere. This proves it. I need someone I can rely on, and I don't have it in me to start dating for the hell of it. I know what I want.

Waiting for hours on someone who will not show is not what I want. I lived that life already as the daughter of Venezuela's sweetheart, and I don't plan on doing it again.

The kiss was a mistake. If he hadn't left today, he would have been gone a week from now. There is nothing to talk about. I just have to make sure it doesn't happen again.

Margarita itinerary:

- *Friday: 11:00 a.m.—Arrival*
- *Friday: 5:00 p.m.—Press*
- *Friday: 8:00 p.m.—Executives Dinner*
- *Saturday: 1:00 p.m.–4:00 p.m.—Press*
- *Saturday: 8:00 p.m.—Wrap Party*
- *Sunday: 1:00 p.m.—Departure*

"I thought we were flying first class," Irina says, trying to become as flat as a sheet of paper to avoid touching anyone else on the plane.

"It's a domestic flight, Irina," my mother says, pushing past to get to her seat. "There is no first class. You'll be lucky if they put ice in your 7UP."

Oh, God. This is already the longest flight of my life, and we haven't even taken off.

In between *Excuse me*s, *Thank you*s, *and So sorry*s, we manage to get to our seats. I take the window while, beside me, the seat Simón was meant to occupy remains empty. He's going to meet us in Margarita. At least that's what Mileidy told us. Apparently, it was easier for him to fly directly. We still haven't talked.

I sigh, adjusting my AirPods. In the row behind me, Mamá and one of the PAs chatter about her wardrobe sponsors for the live shows. The PA suggests asking local designer Arturo Goncalves.

"No, no," she says, *tsk*ing. "Arturo and I are not on speaking terms."

I select the "On Repeat" playlist on my Spotify. I don't have to listen to this story, I already lived it. Little fourteen-year-old me, stuck in a two-week-long battle between my mother and her brand-new husband. The short version: They had a big, blowout wedding, and two weeks later he told her he was gay. The long version is the one the PA is about to endure. It always ends in, "I'm not mad at him for being gay. I'm mad at him because he made me spend thousands on a sham wedding, and I didn't even get to pick my own dress." This flight is not long enough for her rant about the grudge she still holds over that incident.

The flight attendant walks us through the safety routine. I pretend to listen, but as soon as she's done, I close my eyes, focus on the music, and try not to think about how I am not ready to see Simón.

CHAPTER 31

••••••

WHEN I WAS IMAGINING THE PRESS STOP IN MARgarita, I was foolishly hoping for sunny days by the shore while ingesting unhealthy amounts of soda and Doritos. So far, the only sand I've seen is the kind that keeps getting into my shoes even though I haven't been to the beach.

I've been doing my job, laser focused on accomplishing every task. I know he arrived this morning. I know which PA went to pick him up at the airport. I know he's minutes, if not seconds, from sharing the same space as me again, after three days of silence. Which is why I don't allow my eyes to roam. If I do, and I see him, I don't know what it'll do to me. But the heart cannot be swayed. I turn to look over my shoulder. Almost by instinct, I find him among the crowd. My stomach drops, and a shot of electricity shoots across my nervous system. His back is to me; he's a full head taller than everyone else. He's wearing a brown leather jacket today, despite the heat. His hair is disheveled. He's stretching his neck, as if looking for something. And then he turns, and his gaze lands on me. He stops moving. The sight of him makes my heart flutter and ache all at once. It makes my heart clench with longing, despite everything. I still want. I still wish.

Simón starts toward me, but one of the producers claps loudly, breaking us out of our daze.

"Listen here, equipo," the producer says through a microphone. "We're going to split into two teams to make the most of our time. Irina and Federico, please follow the young man with the orange flag to your side of the set. Viviana and Simón, follow me. Today is all hands on deck so, PAs, pick a team and ask how you can be of help. Let's go."

I follow Simón and my mother, careful to stay well behind. In my professional opinion, Irina and Federico are the wrong pair to put in an interview together. Putting aside the fact that they have zero chemistry with each other, they're always bickering, and Federico never seems entirely awake. If *I'd* had to pair the teams up, I would have put Simón and Irina together because he's charming and good at compliments, which Irina loves, so she would have been more relaxed. Given the fact that my mother has chemistry with everyone and everything, she would have found a way to make it seem like Federico is brooding and mysterious instead of just boring.

"We need water for Simón and Viviana," the producer tells us. "For the reporters as well. They each get five minutes. We're going to be here for about three hours. I need someone at the front to receive them and guide them here, I need someone to stay here and guide them out when they're finished, and I need someone stationed there to replace the water bottle and complimentary bag before the next reporter comes."

"Marianto can do the water and bags," my mother says.

The producer's attention—as well as everyone else's—shifts to me. He raises both eyebrows, not in question exactly . . . more in judgment. Then he sighs and says, "Sure."

After everything is covered, I'm setting up a water-and-bag station, making a quick calculation of how many I'm going to need if each interviewer gets five minutes and we're going to be here for three hours. Twelve sounds low and I know from experience these things tend to last longer than anticipated, so I set up twenty. Just in case.

I take a peek at what's inside the bag—chocolate, an invitation to the first live show, and a brochure with additional information on the judges and the production. It's all in a mini tote stamped with the *Talento V* logo—two microphones crossed together to make a *V*, although to me it looks more like an *X*. Still, I want to keep one as a souvenir.

"You're lucky."

I turn to find one of the PAs beside me, grabbing a water bottle from the case under the table.

"Am I?" I say.

"Yeah," she says. "You get to sit through the interviews. Maybe if one of the judges quits, your mom will make them hire you for that too."

I gape at her, stunned.

"Why do you keep saying that?" It's not the first time this PA's made that accusation and it's frankly starting to get on my nerves. I did everything I could to make sure I didn't use my mother to get this job. It's another reason why I would never be happy in this industry, I would always question whether there was any merit to my achievements.

Irina's PA snickers, then parts her lips as if to say something, but a loud clap from our producer interrupts her.

"Positions, everybody!"

She rolls her eyes, turning away without a word.

I stand there for an extra second. The wind blows my hair into my face, individual strands sticking to my lipstick. Swatting it all away, I sigh. What she said isn't true. But I will never have to see these people, under these circumstances, again.

Thinking too much about how people perceive me here is only going to make me fall into a deep hole of anxiety that will be impossible to climb out of long after I'm gone.

When I face the set, I find Simón watching me with concern. The producer says something I can't hear and Simón's eyes shift from me to him, then back to me. He looks like he wants to walk up to me, clenching and unclenching one hand as he balances on his heels. I force myself to look away and focus on sitting at my water-and-goody-bags station and pretending I don't exist.

For the next three hours, my life consists of handing out the totes and trying not to feel jealous. Most of the interviewers are women, their ages ranging between eighteen and thirty. Every single one looks like she came straight out of Miss Venezuela—long, tanned legs clad in a minidress or shorts or a skirt; long, silky hair that belongs in a shampoo commercial; the face of a Victoria's Secret Angel. My mother, having been exactly this about twenty years ago, beams. They're all like the daughter she never had.

But I'm a rational person. That's not why I'm jealous. I'm not even jealous about the fact that they all ask Simón about his relationship status. (Single, if you were wondering. Which he's stated repeatedly and emphatically.) Or about the little pile of cards and coffee shop receipts with phone numbers messily jotted on them. No, that's normal. He's a handsome, single, talented man. I would probably be doing the same if I were the one sitting in that cushy chair, asking the questions. Really, *that's* why I'm jealous. I'm not the one in the comfortable chair. I'm the one in the plastic chair, by the plastic table, handing out water bottles when I have a degree sitting unused at home. I'm supposed to be qualified enough to *get* a water bottle and a goody bag.

I hate feeling like this. Because these women deserve it as

much as I think I do. And they probably have the good sense of knowing how to keep their jobs. Meanwhile, I'm being accused of being a nepo baby disguised as an assistant. It's a new low for me.

Daylight is quickly burning out, the once-blazing sun now barely a line over the horizon. Palm trees rustle, mere silhouettes by this point in the day. The faint smell of salt water coats the atmosphere. My skin is sticky, my hair tangled. Mosquitoes are starting to swarm with the temperature drop. I can't imagine we'll be here much longer, and I thank God for that. The urge to run to the bathroom to check my email about the *Ethos* job a million times is strong.

"Excuse me," a female voice says above me. I look up with a smile. The woman is tall, elegant, dressed in a suit composed of bright green shorts and a blazer. Her long hair falls in beautiful blonde waves down to the middle of her back. She returns the smile with a row of perfect white teeth. She has a card in her hand. It's not hard to figure out what's coming. "Didn't you use to work at *Ellas*?"

"Uh—" Definitely not what I was expecting her to say. "Yes."

Her expression goes from hesitant to elated in a matter of seconds. "I thought it was you! What are the chances? I started working three weeks ago. This is my first out-of-office assignment."

"Congratulations." I try to make it sound like a dismissal, but she doesn't leave.

"Thanks, I was so surprised to get the call because *Ellas* is iconic, but—"

Wait. "You're doing the column?"

She laughs, waving me off. "No, no. Oh my god, my love life's a mess. Like I said, this is my first assignment, but I'm in charge of covering events, concerts, premieres . . ."

I stop listening after that. Eugenia replaced me. Which, fine, I already knew and she had every right to do. But the fact that she also gave my dream job to someone else and sent them here, knowing how much it meant to me, is like a slap in the face.

I'm suddenly nauseous. A mix of emotions bubbles up inside me. Anger, betrayal, and disappointment are all vying for control.

Behind her, I see the crew is dismantling the set. My mother is standing still as a PA unwires her. Simón is deep in conversation with our producer, his back to me, as he's led away. We've wrapped up. This woman—my replacement—was the last reporter. The sun is gone, the sky is darkening. The hotel staff light up tiki torches to make a wide path from the pool to the beach. And I'm still sitting here.

"Anyway." The woman clears her throat, flipping her hair back. "I had to say hi, right? Oh—" She holds the card out. "A little birdie told me you could give this to Simón Arreaza?"

I stare at the piece of paper, force myself to take it. I took the others. She's no different. And Simón is a grown man, he doesn't need me policing who he gets phone numbers from. I'm not his manager.

I grab it with the tip of my fingers. "Of course."

She grins. I give her the water bottle and the bag and watch her leave, not missing a single step in her stilettos.

It shouldn't affect me, but a small sliver of my mind hoped Eugenia would overlook my failure to complete the article. After all, it was based on my personal life, and the job I aspire to has nothing to do with my personal life. I hoped that, after all these years, she would give me another shot. It's one thing to refuse, but to give the new girl the job I'd been after for so long is . . . I shake my head. *Don't think about it.* No one is irreplaceable, not in this industry. It was bound to happen eventually. I was given a task, and I didn't come through.

I'm gathering my things, ready to go up to my hotel room, when a familiar voice calls my name. She materializes beside me in less than two seconds, here to ruin all my wallowing-in-self-pity plans.

"There's mi reina," my mother says, cupping my cheeks.

I wiggle out of her hands. Not the right time.

"Something's wrong," she states. No doubts. "What is it?"

"Nothing's wrong," I lie.

I was simply reminded that there is always someone better standing in line to get what you want. And that people suck.

"You're my daughter, Maria Antonieta," Mamá says. "I know when something is bothering you."

I shoulder my purse, hugging the leftover goody bags to my chest. The irony to my mother's statement almost makes me laugh. She was always too busy to notice if something bothered me when I was growing up.

"Is it the breakup?" she asks. "Alejandro?"

I don't have time for this. "Sure, it's about Alejandro." Might as well be. My whole life falling apart began with him anyway.

"I knew it." She beams. "Mom powers."

"Right." If she really had Mom powers, she would have noticed that I haven't mentioned Alejandro in a while. She would have noticed me lusting after the man who was just sitting next to her for almost three hours straight. If she *really* had Mom powers, she would call me out on my lies, hug me, and tell me we should go get ice cream.

But she doesn't. When I lie again and tell her I'm tired, she lets me go.

CHAPTER 32

MY HANDS ARE COATED IN SAND AND MY PLASTIC cup is half full of seashells.

The waves crash against the shore, and together they meet with the force of two people who miss each other terribly. The sand welcomes the blow, crumbling little by little as the sea draws itself back. The moon hangs lonely from the cloudy sky. Somewhere in the distance, thunder roars. There are no stars visible tonight, but the moon is big and bright. If we were in the middle of the woods, I'd say it was a werewolf moon. But we're on an island, so it's more my finding-seashells luminary.

I walk along the shoreline, careful not to stray too far from the hotel. I can still hear the live band playing salsa at the restaurant and can still see the lights reflecting on the water, so I'm okay. A couple of young parents walk with their maybe four-year-old, one on each side of the boy, holding his hands and lifting him whenever there's a wave. The boy giggles and the parents look at each other and smile. I can't help but smile too, despite the pang of longing that comes with it.

I'm not sure if it's because I want to be the mom or because

I want to be the kid. Maybe both. Maybe I've been chasing not what I want, but what I lack. And I know it sounds like those are the same, but they're not.

Another seashell catches my eye (thank you, Luna), and I kneel to pick it up. It's shaped exactly like a guitar pick, almost as flat but a little dented. It's a blueish gray; maybe under good light it'll look different. I immediately know I'm going to give it to Simón. I doubt it'll work as a guitar pick, but it will work as a memento, a souvenir that reminds him of that one time he helped a fan try to get back together with her ex, only to end up . . .

I sigh, rubbing my arms against the cold, and decide it's time to head back.

Sunday is our last day on the island. We'll leave in the afternoon. I'll land in Caracas and quit. Simón will land in Bogotá, and we'll never talk again. Life will go on as planned.

I'm almost at the base of the stairs leading up to the pool when I halt. A few feet away, Simón stands on the bottom step, in his signature outfit. His hands are hidden in his hoodie's front pocket. His chin is tilted up, looking at the starless sky. It gives his jaw a sharp edge, but his shoulders are relaxed. He sighs with his entire body, almost as if he's trying to drink the ocean air in, fill himself with it.

And then he sees me. The sound of my racing heartbeat fills my ears, drowning out all other noise—waves, laughter, music—as I stand frozen by his gaze. The world seems to hold its breath, waiting for what will happen next.

Simón's gaze is open and inviting, expectant even. I move closer. His eyes stay on me the whole time. They only shift to the waves crashing on the shore when I'm safely standing beside him.

"Couldn't sleep?" His voice is low and raspy, the way I know it gets when he's tired.

I shake my head. "Too much on my mind. I can't sleep when I'm overthinking."

Simón inches closer, warmth oozing from his body. I immediately need him to step away. I'm cold and I want him to hug me. I'm cold and I want him to kiss me in front of another body of water. I want to pull that sweater off of him and keep it for myself.

I lean away.

"If it makes you feel any better, I also can't sleep when I'm overthinking," he says.

"Is that why you're down here?"

He sits on the steps. "No, I'm down here because someone in that band is off-key and I was on my way to tell them."

"I'm sure they'll appreciate your honesty." I dust the wooden step before I take a seat next to him. "You judge singers for a living, after all."

"Don't remind me." He leans back on his elbows. "I didn't have 'Becoming Colombia's Adam Levine' on my list of life aspirations."

"I think that's Sebastián Yatra," I say.

Simón laughs next to me, and I feel it in every cell. His body loosens, a leg stretched out to rest on the sand, a hand draped across his middle, his neck stretched back so he's looking at the sky again.

His eyes find mine as his laughter dissolves. "Marianto, I'm so sorry."

I shake my head. "It's okay." The words come out automatically.

"It's not okay," he says, shifting so we're face-to-face, our knees touching. "I had to go back home to record a new song we're releasing with another artist. It's a big deal and they couldn't reschedule. I completely forgot about it. I almost missed my flight because I slept in. I was swept up with work as soon as I arrived because it was only meant to be a day, but then I had a family emergency, and I was focused on *that*, and I figured at that point it was better to just wait until I saw you, because I was seeing you today. But it's clearly not better and—"

"Is everything okay with your family?" I ask, my voice small, as I trace the shape of a seashell with my index finger.

Simón nods. He's almost panting from speaking so fast.

"I'm glad," I say.

"Marianto, about that night—"

"Simón." I close my eyes. I don't want to hear it. It doesn't change anything. Of course he had a legitimate reason; legitimate reasons abound in this industry. That's not the point. There is no point. "It was just a kiss. It's okay. Who cares if we kissed once?"

He pushes to his feet, and when I open my eyes again, I see hurt reflected on his face.

"I do," he says. "And I think you do too. Do you know why I almost missed my flight?"

My chest feels heavy, like a weight I can't shake off. "It doesn't matter."

"It does matter." He pushes his hair back, looking away. "I understand you're angry—"

I shake my head. "I'm not angry."

"You are." He nods. "And you're disappointed. And you have every right to be. But you can't tell me what I've been feeling is all in my head."

"It doesn't matter," I repeat.

Simón throws his hands up, taking a step back. "Why do you keep saying that?"

Because I'm trying to convince myself. Maybe if I say it enough, it'll come true. Maybe if I say it enough, my heart will catch up to what my mind already understood.

"Because we're never going to see each other again after this anyway," I say. "I'm not coming back for the live shows."

"Great!" Simón says. "Get that job you interviewed for, live your dreams, don't come back to the show. What does that have to do with anything?"

"You're leaving," I remind him.

"I'm coming back," he says. "I can come back as many times as necessary."

The live band playing at the restaurant seems to have finished for the night, replaced by old-fashioned speakers. The family walking the shoreline is gone. Somewhere on the hotel premises, people talk over the music, their voices carried by the wind. I wonder if it carries our voices too. If anyone is interested enough in the couple by the mouth of the beach to pick up bits and pieces of our conversation.

"Listen," Simón continues. "I want to see you. I want to spend more time with you. I want to get to know you better. I like you. *A lot.* And forgive my boldness but I suspect you like me too."

My heart skips a beat, I feel my cheeks flush. God, I do. I really do. But even if I wanted to shout it out from the rooftops, what good will it do to admit it?

"Simón—"

"I told you what I want," he cuts me off. "What do *you* want?"

I stand, intent on running. I can't do this right now. I have feelings for him, that much is true. But everything else I've said is also true. He's leaving. He will always be leaving. And I will always be left behind, waiting.

He takes a step toward me. My brain screams *leave*, but my feet don't move an inch.

"What do you want?" he repeats, his voice low, little more than a whisper against the sound of the waves crashing on the shore.

The question feels like an accusation, even though I know it's not. Doing something because I want to and not because it fits the plan isn't how I'm wired. People make plans to stay on track, to have structure, to know what to expect. When you just let life happen to you, when you don't plan ahead, when you do what you want at every whim, then you end up with a string of broken relationships, leaving people behind, alone and heartbroken. If I can plan ahead and base my decisions on those plans, the pain risk is minimum.

"Ask me, then." He almost begs when I don't speak. "I'll say it again. I'll say it as many times as you need to hear it."

He's so close I could count his eyelashes, play connect the dots with his freckles. Simón is a work of art in so many senses. Beautiful inside and out, but also out of reach, forbidden. Okay to admire, maybe even touch, but not to take home. It occurs to me that *that's* what I want. If my mind wasn't my mind, if my life wasn't my life, if I wasn't the way I am, I would grab this particular work of art and run away with it. And here he is, in front of me, offering it.

My hands ache with the need to reach out, to touch him. The sound of the waves crashing on the shore is a distant memory. I'm only aware of Simón, his pleading eyes, his challenging stance. I lean closer, just an inch, maybe less. An imperceptible sigh escapes his lips, almost in relief, but he's waiting. When was the last time I did something because I wanted to? When was the last time my life wasn't dictated by a formula, a step-by-step? I can't even remember.

"What do you want, Simón?" I whisper.

His gaze flickers from my eyes to my lips, then back up. He swallows, inching closer. "A ti."

I want him too.

He doesn't close the space between us. I can hear the silent condition. *The choice is yours.* So, I don't think. I just do.

Before I have a chance to regret it, I take his jaw in my hands and kiss him. Because I want to.

CHAPTER 33

I WAKE UP THE NEXT MORNING TO THE SUN streaming in through my hotel window, dolphins bobbing in and out of the water miles and miles away, and my phone ringing. I almost knock over a cup on the bedside table in my sleepy attempt to get it.

Mamá, my screen reads.

"Aló?" Through the phone I hear waves crashing on sand and the happy beat of merengue playing in the background. "Where are you?"

"Hotel bar, eating shrimp," Mamá says. "Do you want to come?"

"Allergic, remember?"

What time is it?

I check my phone. Almost noon. I slept through like three different alarms. My eyes latch on the plastic cup I almost spilled a minute ago—a beat-up, slightly broken little thing with sand at the bottom, topped with seashells in various shapes and sizes. I recall last night, Simón and I on the beach, our lips . . . his hands . . . And my mother is still talking.

"—dinner tonight," she's saying. "Fancy dinner, so you have to dress up."

"What about the wrap party?" I ask. I don't have a fancy dinner in my schedule. No one has emailed me about it. Having my mother tell me doesn't sound like Mileidy.

"Oh, we can go to that after dinner," she says. I can practically hear her waving my question away. "It'll cheer you up. Trust me."

Why does that make me not want to trust her?

"Who's going to this dinner?"

"Oh, you know." Somewhere on the hotel premises, she's shrugging. "Family."

"So, us?" I ask.

"Yes. Family," she repeats. "It's our last night. I want to have a nice dinner before we head back. God knows we haven't had a moment to ourselves the entire time we've been here."

"Okay, sure," I say. "That sounds nice."

"Great! I'll text you the details," she says. "See you later, mamita."

"Okay, see you—"

She hangs up. Why do I feel like I just made a deal with the devil?

BECAUSE I AM nothing if not prepared, I have three different fancy dresses to choose from. I settle for a navy blue, long-sleeved, knee-length dress that hugs my waist like it was made for me especially—important, when you have zero curves—and makes me look put together in an effortless way.

I decide to curl my hair at the end. There's not much versatility to this length. All I do for makeup is put on mascara, eyeliner, and a wine-red lipstick. Last night in Margarita and all.

When I'm finished, my eyes roam the full-body mirror in

the bathroom one last time. The lipstick probably wasn't the best idea. I should have gone with lip gloss, something less flashy. What does one wear to a pre-wrap-party dinner? What does one wear to pre-seeing-the-guy-I-made-out-with-last-night dinner?

"Don't overthink it." I pull the hem of my dress down, smoothing invisible wrinkles only my anxiety can see.

Before I can talk myself into an outfit change, I leave the room.

The hallway is empty except for me and a housekeeper. I shift uncomfortably from one foot to the other, waiting in front of the elevator. The last few days have been an escape from reality. I haven't thought about *Ethos* not calling me back, haven't thought about Alejandro. I'm convinced the only reason I thought about Eugenia was because I ran into my replacement here, otherwise her name wouldn't have crossed my mind either. I've had little thoughts beyond what I can see and touch. Beyond Simón.

Ding, goes the elevator. Its doors creak as they slide open.

As if I've summoned him, Simón looks up from inside the elevator. His almost bored expression changes the moment he sees me. First a spark of surprise in his eyes, then a grin. His eyes move slowly over every inch of my body, setting my face aflame, until they finally land again on my face.

The elevator starts to close, and he shoots forward, stopping it with one hand in what has to be the sexiest thing I've ever seen a man do. In a matter of nanoseconds his face is ten inches closer.

"Maria Antonieta," he says, still grinning.

"Simón, I'm just going down to—"

"Me too."

I try not to laugh. Of course my mother invited him. She would not be Viviana Camacho without an ulterior motive.

The sound of my sandals clicking echoes as I step inside the elevator. I clutch my purse tighter, holding my breath.

"We could walk there together." He backs away from the doors.

I settle into a corner. "Sure."

The elevator slides shut. I don't know who moves first. One second, we're on opposite sides and the next, his hands are clasping the back of my neck, his thumbs tilting my chin up. My temperature skyrockets the second his hands are on me. My fists close on the lapels of his blazer. His lips seal mine. Or mine seal his. I don't know. But his body is pressing against me, his grip on my neck is steady, and his mouth is on mine. That's all that matters. I can breathe again. My ever-flowing mind is quiet and I'm aware of nothing but this moment—this moment in a frankly rusty elevator, where his hands move down to my waist, tracing the silhouette of my dress, where my arms close around his neck, pulling him closer until there is no space between us.

I feel myself growing greedy, wanting more. I let myself be truly selfish for the first time in I don't know how long. Let myself be free. It's incredible. I knew there was a reason I shouldn't have worn the red lipstick.

SIMÓN AND I stand side by side, staring at what appears to be a booked restaurant. But this is not out of the ordinary for my mother. What's out of the ordinary is the fact that there is a table for two people with floating red candles as centerpieces, right in the middle. Romantic music plays in the background, some bolero I've never heard before, and it drowns the soft splash of seawater against the rock this restaurant is built on.

"Are we the first to arrive?" Simón asks.

"I think we're the only ones coming," I say.

The waiters beam when they notice us by the entrance. They rush to greet us. I want to squirm away when they grab us by our arms and lead us to the one table, practically shoving us down until we're seated.

"I'm a little confused," Simón says.

"My mother," I explain.

"Your mother?" he repeats. "Did you tell—"

The thought almost gives me a wave of nausea. "God, no."

"I thought you were leading me to the wrap party," he says.

"I thought you . . . were coming to dinner with my mother," I say.

Simón details the table, the ambience. "I guess I should thank Viviana for setting up an improvised first date?"

I laugh. "You know, I can see her doing that."

Amusement shines in his eyes. Juan Luis Guerra plays softly from invisible speakers, tropical metals and drums casting a spell on us. He stands and offers me a hand. "Dance with me?"

I look at him, drinking him in. There is nothing I would like more than to dance with him. But we're still here for work, and we're in public.

I shake my head. "We can't."

Simón sighs. "Do you want to dance?"

"That's beside the point," I say.

"There's no one here."

"*We* are here," I remind him.

"Well, I'm not going to tell anyone," he says. "Are you?"

His hand doesn't waver, doesn't even shake, the man could be a neurosurgeon. If I say no again, he'll sit back down, the subject dropped. If I say no again, he'll pretend he never asked, this much I know. But when my gaze moves up and I'm looking at him, he lifts both eyebrows in a silent challenge.

I'm trying to think of a good reason why we shouldn't, a reason why tomorrow I will regret dancing with Simón now. None come to mind, even though I know that from a realistic point of view, there must be many. But for an exhilarating second, I don't care. I accept his hand. A grin splits Simón's face at the exact moment the opening notes of "Tus Besos" play from the speakers.

Talk about an appropriate song for the pair of us.

He tugs at my hands softly, pulling me up from my chair with a glint of mischief in his smile. I narrow my eyes at him as he leads me to an empty corner of the restaurant. The wooden floors beneath us are speckled with salt water, which bobs up and down around the rocks below.

And then we're moving. One, two, three, stop to the right. One, two, three, stop to the left. With each movement, we get closer and closer until he's holding my right hand against his chest. His rests at the curve of my back, pressing me closer. My free hand comes up to his neck. I feel Simón smile against my cheek as he spins us, never losing our step. My entire body is buzzing from being this close to him.

"Did I say you look very beautiful tonight yet?" he rasps.

I give my head the softest of shakes. He hasn't. I didn't know much I wanted him to until right this second.

The song ends. Simón takes a step back, putting a little distance between us, but doesn't let go of my hand. Instead, he squeezes gently and smiles.

"You look very beautiful tonight, Marianto," he says, his voice a soft murmur, matching the distant waves. "And every day of the past two months. The most devastatingly beautiful woman in any room we've been in."

Suddenly, it's hard to swallow. This thing between us . . . It's too soon to give it a name, but the way he's looking at me, like nothing else matters, like the world could be burning and he wouldn't notice as long as we're here together? He won't say it. I won't say it. But I don't think we have to. I think he knows.

And then I'm smiling. "Simón, you—"

"Maria Antonieta," a familiar voice says.

I freeze.

Simón's eyes follow the direction of the voice, and his face turns to ash. His eyes flicker back to me, a mixture of regret and dread clouding them. He takes a step back, then another.

I turn to find my mother, but that's not the worst part. Beside her, Alejandro is holding a bouquet of roses, surrounded by mariachi. His usually imposing demeanor is reduced to dust before my eyes. His arms hang lifeless at his sides, his shoulders hunch. He's looking at me like I'm a stranger.

Blood drains from my face so fast I feel lightheaded, nauseated. His presence here is jarring. Wrong. We broke up. *I* broke up with him. I'm away for work. He should not be here. He should be in Caracas, too busy saving lives to answer a text.

Next to him, my mother stares at me with a mixture of confusion and something else . . . regret, maybe? That's how I know: This is her doing. The nausea and guilt evaporate, making way for anger, but I don't have time to focus on my mother because Alejandro is here.

His emerald eyes shift from me to Simón, and back to me. "Are you serious? Him?"

My airways have shut, I can't breathe. Ale's expression hardens. "I never would have pegged you for vengeful, but—"

He shrugs, gesturing to us. I feel Simón straighten, feel him tense. All I can do is stare, let him accuse me of . . . what? We broke up.

Simón takes a step forward. "Hey, man—"

"You stay out of this," Alejandro snaps, before turning back to me. "He's exactly what you've always said you don't want—"

"Ale, stop—" I beg.

"What was it you used to say?" he continues. "No actors, no models, no musicians. That you wanted someone you could count on. Someone who didn't live half his life on an airplane or a bus. And now you're with my favorite musician. Am I supposed to believe you aren't trying to get back at me?"

"Alejandro, that's not—" I turn to Simón. "That's not—"

He fixes his attention on Simón. "I'd get out now. She planned this. She's a planner. That's what she does."

The words land on my chest like a string of bullets, each one cutting deeper than the last. If this is what he thinks of me, of my plans, why did he put up with it for four years? Why not save me the trouble, set me free? Maybe I would have found someone who appreciated it. But it seems even the one thing we had in common was an inconvenience to him.

Alejandro shakes his head with a bitter laugh. He turns his back on us and tosses the bouquet of roses through the open windows and into the sea. The sound of his heavy footsteps on the wood is loud as thunder.

I start toward him but halt. I have to go after him. I know I do. I have to . . . I don't know, explain, talk, make sure he's okay?

I turn to Simón, heaving, panicked. What Alejandro said to him was horrible. I need to talk to him as well. Explain. Make sure *he's* okay. But . . . "I have to go."

"I know," he says. His voice is barely more than a whisper. "It's okay."

My eyes mist. Burn. "I'm sorry."

"It's okay," he repeats.

I hesitate for an everlasting second in which my heart breaks. My carelessness falls heavy on my shoulders. I could have avoided this. If I hadn't been so blinded by what I wanted, if I hadn't been selfish with him. I knew better. The first tear falls. I wipe it away and take off running after Alejandro. I reach him when he's rounding the pool. People turn their heads in my direction when I rush past them.

"Alejandro!" I call out, panting.

He doesn't stop. "Congrats on your conquest!"

"Would you please stop for one second?" I say. "Please."

He whirls toward me, a tornado of fury and hurt. "Why? So you can make me look like an even bigger fool than I already do?"

"No." I reach for him, but he takes a step back, keeping the distance.

"Entonces, qué?" He throws his arms up. "What is it you want? You got your revenge. Congratulations."

"This isn't about revenge." Does he really have such a sour opinion of me that he thinks I would date someone in order to hurt him?

Alejandro's snicker tells me he does, his humorless laugh drips venom. "No, you're right. What do you have to get revenge for, anyway? All I did was try to make us the best we could be before we jumped into a lifelong commitment—"

I stagger back like he punched me. My voice is barely a whisper. "Excuse me?"

He doesn't hear me. Or he ignores me. "—trying to fix our relationship, while you—"

"Trying to *fix* our relationship?" I think of him telling me he's not sure he wants to marry me, of him calling me to ask for a favor after he broke my heart. I think of him deciding he wanted me back only because he didn't want someone else to have me. And I'm supposed to believe all that was for my benefit?

I'm too aware of the people trying to enjoy their pool time, who are now getting a spectacle they didn't ask for. I grab Alejandro's hand and lead him far from the prying eyes and curious ears of hotel guests. I'm surprised he doesn't shake out of my grip the second I touch him. His breathing is heavy, like he can't get air into his lungs fast enough.

I whisper while we walk. "You told me you needed time, you told me you weren't sure about me. I gave you the space you needed."

Alejandro does step away then, facing me. "And what's so bad about that?"

"You broke my heart!" I sob. I can't contain it anymore. I made a fool of myself over and over, trying to get him to love me again. I dragged Simón into this. I lost every shred of dignity I had chasing after him over the past few months. "You hurt me. You only changed your mind when I'd had enough of living in your purgatory, when I'd had enough of waiting around to finally be good enough."

Alejandro's fight leaves his body at once. He simply stares. I never thought I'd be telling him all this. When I broke up with him, I figured we would go our separate ways. I would not see him again, I would forget about the four years we spent together, like I'd done with every other relationship that hurt me. Be it a boyfriend, a friend, my mother . . . I'm not used to talking. I'm used to nursing myself back to health, picking up my own pieces and rearranging them into something that resembles a whole person.

But I'm talking now. And it's . . . freeing.

"Listen," I say. "Maybe I shouldn't have left the restaurant the way I did. Maybe I should have stayed and talked like you asked me to. That's on me." I put both hands over my chest, looking him straight in the eyes so he knows I mean every word. "But you don't get to stand here and tell me the pain you put me through was for us." Alejandro looks away. I don't stop. "I wanted us to work, Ale. I did everything I could think of. I modeled myself into the woman I thought you wanted, the woman your family wanted, and it was still not enough. I was never going to be enough."

I wipe the tears streaming down my face, the weight I've been carrying for the past two months lifting with every piece of truth that tumbles out of my mouth. It's messy and it's ugly, but it's out now. I can't take it back, and I don't want to.

"We were together four years, Alejandro," I continue. "Four years. Do you really think I would use Simón to hurt you? That I'm not heartbroken things went down like this between us?"

The realization hits me as soon as I say it. It was always going to end. I tried so hard to grasp the ashes of our burning relationship. I clung to the skeleton, tried to bring a corpse back to life, but deep down I knew there was nothing left to do. Where would I be, had I loved myself enough to accept his "break"? Where would I be if I'd ended things when he gave me the first sign that we had run our course?

It was all for nothing—the list, the humiliation. I was always going to end up here. We were always going to end up here, kneeling in front of our lifeless relationship, me declaring the time of death and zipping the bag closed. Alejandro wouldn't have done it. He would have gladly kept us in a coma for eternity.

I expect Alejandro to yell some more, to blame me, to wash

his hands of the responsibility, because I'm learning that's just what he does. But what he says surprises me.

"Of course not."

My eyes sting again and for a fraction of a second I allow the Marianto that fell in love with him when she was twenty-three to come out, to look at him one last time. She was young and she was hurt and she was angry and she wanted the security she lacked all her life. She did love him, but she loved him for all the wrong reasons. I take a step closer to him. "I'm sorry I hurt you. And I'm sorry you felt like you couldn't talk to me or be yourself. I'm mostly sorry I never gave you the chance to love the real me because I was trying too hard to be exactly what you wanted. That's what I should have said at the restaurant, but . . ." I breathe in, then out. "I don't think what worked between us four years ago works now. And I think you know it too."

Alejandro swallows, nodding. "I'm sorry I hurt you too."

A moment passes between us where we remain like that, staring at each other, knowing there is nothing else to be said.

Alejandro sighs. "I'm going to—"

He gestures vaguely to the hotel and beyond.

I nod. I don't trust my voice to speak.

"Goodbye, Marianto," he says.

I nod again.

People at the pool have forgotten about us. When Ale crosses the revolving glass doors to the lobby, no one pays attention to him. No one pays attention to the lonely girl by the bushes, hugging herself against the cold breeze.

Our last night in Margarita is one for the books. This island has a lot of making up to do.

CHAPTER 34

I'M STARING AT THE CEILING, FINDING SHAPES IN the shadows of every corner when I hear it.

Knock, knock, knock.

Simón. I went back to the restaurant to look for him, but he wasn't there. I stopped by his room too. Same story. The only other place I could think of was the wrap party, which made the most sense, since it would have been strange if he missed it. But I couldn't bring myself to go. There was no energy left in me to pretend in front of everyone.

I rush to the door and yank it open.

"You and Simón?" my mother says as soon as we're face-to-face.

I deflate.

She's in a sequin dress she wasn't wearing when the whole Alejandro-shows-up-out-of-nowhere disaster happened. For once, her makeup isn't intact, her forehead and cheekbones are a little bright.

I turn my back on her and walk back to the bed. I don't know why it bothers me that she clearly went to the wrap party, danced, ate, and *then* came to check on me. The wrap party wasn't optional for her or for Simón. It was as much part of her job as making the show and doing press. Logically, I know this. And I am nothing if not logical. So why does it piss me off that she's here *now*, and not before?

"Maria Antonieta," she calls after me, her voice stern. "You and Simón?"

I sit on the bed and grab a pillow to hug. "No. Not really. I don't know."

"It was all that time you spent together," she decides. "You can't spend that much time together with a man like him and not expect something to happen. Believe me."

I hug the pillow tighter as I stare at my mother. I do believe her. I saw it happen—our lives drastically changing over and over because she got a little too carried away with a co-star and had to get another divorce. She's a romantic, that's what she used to say. All artists are romantics. I guess I'm more like her than I'd like to admit. The thought makes me nauseous.

"He looked absolutely miserable at the party," she says. "If I'd known, I never would have—"

A knock on the door interrupts her. It's him. I know it's him. Before I can stand up, my mother is at the door. I can't see from where I'm sitting, but the look she gives me before walking out is enough to confirm.

Simón steps in two seconds later. He didn't change for the party, of course. He thought we were going to the party. The door clicks shut when he leans against it, hands hidden behind his back as if he has to restrain himself from touching me.

My hands fist in the pillow. "Hi."

"Hi," he replies, voice hoarse. "Are you okay?"

I shrug one shoulder. "Are you?"

"Yeah."

We stare at each other for one second . . . two . . . before he tips his head back and sighs.

"Say it," I plead. "I can take it."

Simón lowers his gaze to me, shaking his head. "I like you so much."

I'm nodding. "I like you too."

"Falling in love with you would be so easy," he says.

I agree. Falling in love with him would be too easy. As easy as quitting. As easy as taking an airplane to Colombia with him and letting him suck me into his world. I would be head over heels before we landed.

Simón swallows hard before he finally takes a step toward me.

"But?" I say.

"Last night, before you kissed me," he says. "I asked you what you wanted."

Yes. "I said I wanted you."

"But you didn't," Simón says. "You kissed me, sure, but you didn't say you wanted me."

"Simón—"

"I'm leaving," he continues. "And you just got out of a long-term relationship with someone you wanted to spend the rest of your life with. I know what that's like. It wouldn't be fair to you if we started something now. If something happens between us, I want to be there to figure it out with you." My throat tightens. "And . . . it wouldn't be fair to *me* to start something with you when you might still need to mourn your relationship."

I push to my feet. "Wait—"

"I know you think it's over," he cuts me off. "I know you think you're past it, but you were running after him just three hours ago."

"You told me—" I begin, pathetically.

"I know what I said," he replies. "I don't resent you for going after him, it's what you had to do. He wasn't a fling. *I* am a fling."

"You believed him." I blink tears away. "When he said I used you to get revenge on him. You believed that."

Simón shakes his head. "I know that's not who you are. I know you think you want me. Trust me, I want you too. But you wanted to marry *him*. And I am not him. I can't change my life. I can't change my profession. Neither can you. And you shouldn't, I don't want you to."

I'm crying. Again. Pressure grows in my chest. It hurts, like my heart is being crushed to pieces. I want to soothe it, but I'm numb.

Simón takes another step toward me, and another, until we're standing so close I need to look up to see his face. He places both hands on my neck, a feather touch. His thumbs graze my cheeks, catching my tears. "I would have loved for us to have a chance because I think you and I could be . . ."

He trails off, swallowing.

"I think so too," I confess.

"I just—" He clears his throat. "I can't be the man you're with when you realize you need to be alone. I don't want to have that conversation with you. I also don't want you to resent me for not being there. I don't want to resent you for demanding more than I can give. I can't do that again, Marianto."

I nod. I understand. I do. Logically, it makes sense. It's better to end things sooner rather than later, when our lives are tangled together, when our friends have followed one another on Instagram, and when our hearts have synced to beat at the same time. He's listing all the reasons why I knew it would never work. He's right. Isn't he? He's right.

I nod again, more emphatically.

Simón pulls me to him, circling my shoulders with his arms. I bury my face in his shirt, fighting sobs.

"I'm sorry I got in the way of everything you wanted," he whispers.

You're everything I wanted, I think. But I'm not brave enough to say it.

CHAPTER 35

THE PLANE LANDS IN THE SIMÓN BOLÍVAR INTERnational Airport with a jolt. Above us, another plane is taking off and I know, without a shadow of a doubt, that Simón is on it. I spent the entirety of the flight with my headphones on, pretending to sleep while I listened to Caballo de Troya over and over and tried not to cry. My mother tapped my shoulder once, but I continued my act and ignored her. I know there's a conversation we need to have, but I'm not ready to do it today, and I'm certainly not going to do it while we're stuck on a plane and Mileidy is sitting two rows away.

When the plane comes to a stop, I pretend to wake up. My mother does not wait five seconds before she's tapping my shoulder.

"Marianto, mamita, are you okay?" she says. "You look a little . . ."

She doesn't finish the sentence.

A little what? I want to push her to answer. A little worn-out? Sad? Like I don't know what I'm doing or where I'm going?

I unbuckle my seat belt and stand. "I'm fine."

"Are you sure?" she asks.

"Sí."

The door is open. I don't wait for most people to vacate the plane like I normally do but instead fling myself into the mass of moving limbs. If I don't get out of here soon, I'm going to have a panic attack.

I'm sitting on a bench next to a donut shop waiting for my mother so we can go home, luggage at my feet, when my phone chimes with a new notification.

It's an email. From Mileidy. No subject line.

I know it's bad the instant I see it. We just shared a weekend on an island. She's probably around this airport somewhere. Why does she need to send me an email without a subject line? My chest rises and falls rapidly, and my hand instantly opens and closes in an attempt to soothe myself.

The first thing I see when I open the email is a picture. My heart plummets. It's us. Simón and I. Kissing at the beach.

No. The airport starts spinning around me, my heartbeat is loud in my ears. If I wasn't sitting, I would have fallen to my knees. I shut my eyes instead, trying to get the ringing in my head to stop.

Of course we were seen. Of course. It was a public space, the only route to the beach, and we were staying at a hotel that, scarcely three hours prior, had been brimming with reporters. The picture is a screenshot from a gossip website. No, not a website. I recognize the color palette. The font, even if the source is cropped. The picture was published by *Ellas*. In the email, below the photo, there's a message. Short. Precise. It doesn't need clarification.

You're fired.

I remain there, sitting, eyes glued to the screen. I swallow hard. Mm-hm. Sounds about right.

I WAS GOING to quit anyway. I was going to quit anyway. I was going to quit anyway.

I repeat this in my head over and over, sitting in my living room, as my leg bounces up and down.

"She cannot do that," my mother says, pacing the living room, both hands perched on her hips. "I'll get *her* fired. See how she likes it."

I pinch the bridge of my nose, feigning calm. "Mamá. Stop," I say. "She can, and she did."

That's not what I care about. *I was going to quit anyway.* I just . . . I didn't want to get fired. I didn't want to burn possible bridges. I wanted to leave, not to be thrown out. All because of *Ellas*. And my own actions. Of course. I shouldn't have been publicly doing things I don't want people to know about in the first place. But *Ellas*. Eugenia had to approve it. And for it to come out on a *Sunday*? Like Simón and I are Taylor Swift and literally anyone on earth?

Blanca texted she had no idea Eugenia was going to run a story about how her former romance columnist, who posted a video of her breakup, was now dating the Caballo de Troya vocalist Simón Arreaza.

"Bueno, what does Simón have to say about this?" my mother asks. "He didn't get fired."

Simón didn't say anything about it because he doesn't know. He's probably still on the plane. And I sure as hell am not going to tell him.

I pinch the bridge of my nose. This is why I can't have a relationship with someone from the business. Because then *my* business becomes everyone's business. I knew this. I've been here before. I set the no-famous-people rule for a reason. When I lived by it, everything was fine. Rules are there to be followed. Especially rules that I planted with a clear head instead of a confused, smitten, silly little heart. Hearts can't be trusted. My heart is like a toddler with a marker.

"Simón is not an assistant," I say instead. "If they fire Simón, they'll have to reshoot the whole show. They're not going to lose all that money because his assistant was dumb enough to get involved with him before she had the good sense to quit."

Mamá shakes her head at me, disapprovingly.

"This wouldn't be happening if you listened to me," she says.

"No, Mamá." I push to my feet and head toward the kitchen, drawing a long, steady breath. She follows. "This wouldn't have happened if you listened to *me.* This wouldn't have happened if you hadn't helped Alejandro set up a romantic dinner while we were away for work."

"Disculpa, I'm not the one who was kissing Simón at the beach," Mamá reminds me, which only serves to make my blood boil hotter. "*That's* what got you fired."

"No, but you *are* the one who flew my ex-boyfriend in, which is why I can't talk to Simón right now."

"I was trying to support your choice!" she says behind me. "He reached out to me, he said he needed to talk, so I helped him. I thought that's what you wanted. What was I supposed to do?"

I turn around to face her. "I don't know! Leave it alone? Support my choice to break up with him?"

"You said you were upset about the breakup," she says.

"So what?" I laugh, but there's no humor in it. Only anger.

Twenty-seven years of it. "I was with the man for four years and all you did was tell me how bad you thought he was for me."

"Well, was I wrong?!" She opens her arms as if to say, *Look at the mess you're in.*

I need some water. But my hands are shaking so hard I'm sure I'll break a glass.

"That's not the point," I say. "The point is you only decided to support my choices after we'd broken up. God, that is *so* you."

I have a mini fridge in my room with a water bottle inside. I attempt to leave and go lie down, to forget this whole day happened before I say anything I'll regret. I sidestep around her. My door is right there. But her voice stops me.

"What," she says, "pray tell, is *so* me?"

I groan, my hands fisting, as I turn back to face her. "This. *You*, showing up for me when I don't need you to anymore. Making quasi-efforts only after it's too late. Ballet, college, Alejandro. You name it, you weren't there when I needed you to be and you've been trying to make up for it now that I'm an adult, but it doesn't work like that, Mamá!"

"Marianto—"

"No." The words flow out of me, causing wreckage like a swollen river, but I can't stop now that I've started. "I didn't need you to help patch things up between me and Alejandro, and I *don't* need you talking to Mileidy—"

"Well, the whole reason you even have a job to lose is *because* I talked to Mileidy."

I straighten. "You got me the job?"

Mamá looks away. I think back to the whispers, the little jabs from Irina's assistant, how I was brought in after being rejected.

"I didn't need you to do that," I say.

"Clearly, you did."

"No! *No.*" I'm so tired of her treating me like a child, of her good intentions messing up my life. "What I need is for you to stop casting judgment on my choices, take a step back, and let me screw up. Heaven knows *you* screwed up enough."

I regret the words as soon as they're out of my mouth. I'm frozen, eyes wide. *Take it back.* But my throat is tight, my eyes are burning, and no words come out. I should not have said that. I didn't want to say that. I love my mother. I love her so much the thought of hurting her is unbearable.

Mom blinks, swallowing. There's no taking it back. The damage is done. She should have let me go.

"I see." She sniffs without meeting my eyes. "I'll stay at a hotel tonight."

"Mamá." I take a step toward her, but she's already picking up her suitcase—still packed from our return—and walking toward the door.

She stops before she opens it. "I did the best I could," she says. "I'm still trying to do the best I can."

"Mamá, wait—" I choke on the words.

She doesn't wait. She walks through the door, slamming it on her way out.

I flinch, but don't move beyond that. I let her go.

CHAPTER 36

I'M A GHOST OF MY FORMER SELF. NO JOB. NO mom. Nothing to do for the first time in over ten years, except cry and sleep. So I revert to doing the only thing I know I'm good at: telling people what to do. It's not like I have a ton going on, having been fired. *Ethos* hasn't gotten back to me either. At this point, I'm pretty sure I didn't get the job. Xiomara said they wanted to fill the position fast. They would have told me already.

Still in my pajamas, with fingers dyed orange from inhaling Doritos three times a day, I go through a website where people post their questions and existential doubts and choose to answer the ones that don't send me into a pit of depression. Relationships are what I'm known for, the reason people sought me out at *Ellas*, but my life is such a mess that I can't bring myself to answer those.

Next to my laptop, my phone lights up with a text.

I half expect it to be Simón. He texted me a couple days ago, I'm guessing when he found out us kissing was now national news, but I didn't answer. The best thing he could have done was hit the brakes on us when he did. The worst thing *I* can do is open that door again.

But it's not Simón at all. I would be disappointed if I wasn't so surprised.

EUGENIA: Good morning, Maria Antonieta. Please stop by my office today at two. Don't be late.

My breath bottles up in my chest as I read the text over and over. She can't be serious. She ran a story about me and didn't even give me a heads-up. For her to text, out of nowhere, demanding that I go see her is so . . . Eugenia. I shouldn't even entertain the idea of going. I should block her. I'm not finishing the article, I'm not getting back together with Alejandro, and she's already given my job to someone else.

I lock and unlock my phone, trying to decide if I should text her back or not. Her words do not suggest she's awaiting a reply.

Ugh, who am I kidding? Eugenia wants to see me. Of course I'm going to go.

BLANCA JUMPS TO her feet the second she sees me walk into the office.

"First of all, you look gorgeous," she says. "Secondly, what are you doing here?"

Nervously, I look around for any sign of my ex-boss. "Eugenia asked me to come."

Blanca gasps. "Why?"

"I have no idea," I admit.

"Do you think she's going to offer you a job? After—" Blanca drops her voice as she scans the floor but no one else has noticed my presence. "The photos."

"I—"

"Is that Maria Antonieta?" Eugenia calls from her office, causing everyone to shift their attention from their laptops to me. "Send her in."

A soft murmur floats around the office as I follow Eugenia's command. What used to feel like creative freedom for me now feels like fear. Everyone walks on eggshells around here.

I halt when I reach what used to be my desk. Sure enough, my replacement sits there, impossibly long legs crossed, reapplying bloodred lipstick. She notices me through her pocket mirror and smiles, a catlike smile she hadn't shown in Margarita. Now *this* will be a perfect mini-Eugenia.

"Maria," she says with a grin. "So great to see you again so soon."

"Likewise," I lie.

"I take it you didn't give Simón my phone number," she says, her smile sharper.

The murmur around us grows.

"Maria Antonieta," Eugenia calls again.

"I have to—" I vaguely gesture to Eugenia's office and leave.

Dragging that conversation on isn't going to do either of us any good. With my luck, I'll end up confessing I no longer talk to Simón. Before I know it, there'll be a headline tomorrow claiming I'm Simón's groupie and that he left me because my toxic personality drives men away.

Eugenia's office looks exactly the same as when I left, and so does she. I don't know what I was expecting, it's only been two months, but it's like stepping into the past. If an iPad materialized under my arm and she asked me about my plans for the week, I wouldn't be surprised. It'd be like I was coming back after my annual vacation.

Eugenia perks up when she sees me, eyebrows raised to a level I didn't know her Botox allowed.

"Please, come in." She gestures to the chair across from her. "Long time no see."

Now, *that* is new. Usually, she leaves me standing by the door.

"How have you been?" she asks.

"I've been . . ." I blink. "I'm sorry, what am I doing here? You know I couldn't finish the article."

Never mind that everything I did with Simón proved to be helpful, if one did indeed want to get one's ex back.

She clicks her tongue, a wolfish smile on her lips. "Oh, yes. I do."

I know she's referencing the article she let my replacement write and publish. I can see in her black eyes she wants me to ask about it. I won't give her the satisfaction. After a beat of silence, she sighs with a roll of her eyes and leans forward in her chair.

"I'm writing a piece on *Talento V*," she says, like I should know this already. "But I don't want it to be a *here's this new talent show that could save Venezuelan TV from sinking deeper into the ocean* type of thing. I want the juicy details." She drums her fingernails on the glass surface of her desk. "Who better than you, a former employee in the production, to fill me in on those?"

She must be joking.

I wish I was surprised.

"I want to know it all," she continues. "The struggles of putting this show together, the rivalry between Irina Montalbán and Viviana Camacho, the burning romance happening behind the scenes . . ." A dramatic pause hangs between us at that. The burning romance. Me. "Tell me everything."

My hand tightens around my purse, resting on my lap. "Eugenia—"

"Help me with this little project and I will give you that promotion you want so badly," she says.

I never thought of Eugenia as the most ethical journalist out there, but this is unexpected. The offer keeps me in my seat. I don't have a job. I have money saved up from what I made on the show, but that won't last forever. I'm not going back to *Talento V* when the live shows start. I've stopped waiting for *Ethos* to contact me. It would solve a problem, but . . .

"You would do that?"

"Of course," she says. No hesitation. "I mean, I would rather keep you giving love advice, especially since you're now dating a celebrity, but if you're too tired of the glamour, you can join my staff in Arts and Culture."

"Huh."

Even after I begged, after I was willing to humiliate myself and Alejandro by writing a piece on our private affairs, she wouldn't promote me for my work ethic or talent or merit. I've wanted this job, this offer, more than anything for years. But I'm never going to grow if I come back here. I'll be a writer forever; she'll make sure of it. She won't promote me to editor because it wouldn't be convenient for her. I'd walk on eggshells, like the rest of the office, afraid of being fired again after the smallest mistake.

"I'm sorry, Eugenia, I can't," I say. "I signed an NDA."

"We're in Venezuela," she reminds me.

True. A lawless country where everyone does as they want, where justice is basically nonexistent. But if we all think like her, we will continue to be *that* Venezuela forever.

I shrug. "I can't. I'm sorry." I sigh, feeling the next words in my mouth before I pronounce them. I'm not going to regret this. "I would have loved to continue working for you, Eugenia, but if after five years of knowing each other the only reason you'd give me a promotion is if I screw someone else over, then I don't want it."

With that, I push myself to my feet and walk out, my phone already in my hand.

YO: Hola, Mileidy. I'm sure it's surprising to hear from me after what happened in Margarita. I wanted to let you know that a journalist approached me today to get inside information about the show. I think they were looking for dirt. Just thought you should know.

YO: I'm sorry if I made your life difficult, and I'm sorry for being unprofessional. Thank you for taking me on when I needed a job. Best of luck moving forward.

Blanca sprints up when she notices I'm out of Eugenia's office, her big doe eyes screaming, *What happened?!*

"I'm not coming back," I tell her. The full scoop of what happened today needs to be discussed over coffee.

Blanca leans over her desk, pulling me in for a hug. "I'm so happy for you!"

I giggle, hugging her back. "Right. Yay, unemployment!"

My phone vibrates again. I leave my former office with a promise to get together later and fill her in.

While I do have some savings, I'm not exactly swimming in money. But I can't resist stopping by the coffee shop downstairs, saying hello to my favorite barista, and getting a warm cup to go.

I check my texts as I wait in line.

MILEIDY: Oh, please, don't worry about that. I only hired you because your mother threatened to leave the show if I didn't.

She *what*?!

The man behind me clears his throat. I look up and realize two people have moved up while I was reading.

MILEIDY: Even your pay came from a chunk of hers. There's no such thing as a temporary assistant. But you did make our lives easier.

MILEIDY: Thank you for telling me. I appreciate it. Good luck with everything. Simón is a good kid.

Yes. He is. But I don't linger on that.

I owe my mother the biggest apology in history.

CHAPTER 37

I'VE HAD ENOUGH OF MY MOTHER NOT TALKING to me. In the four days since our fight, I've apologized a dozen times over text. I would apologize via phone or in person, if she deigned to talk to me. Was what I said untrue? No. Was it the right way to communicate a lifetime's worth of resentment? Also no. She had every right to leave and slam the door on her way out. I would have done the same. But I've apologized and she's still ignoring me.

I walk into the Meliá Caracas hotel like I own the place. My mother was briefly engaged to the owner forever ago. I got the room number from her husband, so I go straight up without stopping by the desk.

"It's about time you two patch things up," he told me in his thick French accent.

Luxury coats every corner of the lobby—soft lights reflect on perfectly polished marble floors; rich wooden details sprinkle the imperial staircase railings and baseboards; plants that seem to grow from the hotel itself adorn the hallways; bronze statues guard the entrance and its clear glass doors, framed with gold. I considered the Meliá for the wedding too. Seems like it was lifetimes ago.

The elevator ride is short. I march down the hall toward my mother's room, my steps muffled by the carpeted floors. The walls are lined with antique clocks, adding to the regal air that every room breathes.

My mother's hotel room door is like every single door beside it, nothing special other than the occupant, but now that I'm in front of it, I can't bring myself to knock. Ever since I was a child, I looked up to her. She was my hero. It was the two of us against the world. She wasn't perfect, but she showed how much she loved me. I never doubted that.

Come on, I think. *Knock.*

But the doorknob rattles before I have a chance to. My heart races in my chest. I should have called first. Never mind that she's not picking up my calls, I still should have tried. I hate when people show up unannounced. Maybe she has plans with someone. Maybe she's running late to something. Maybe I'm making an already complicated day even more complicated by showing up. Maybe—

The door opens. There she is, wearing a bright pink suit with needle-point heels. Every bit the diva she's always been, but her dark brown eyes—*my* eyes—are sad.

She blinks in surprise when she realizes it's me but doesn't shut the door in my face. Instead, she opens it wider.

My shoulders sag in relief. "Please, have lunch with me."

We stare at each other for what feels like forever. All around us, the clocks are ticking, until she finally nods and steps out.

We don't hug, but it's a start.

"YOU'LL LOVE THE food," Mamá says when the waiter leaves. The first words she's said to me since she left her room. "It's exquisite. I think I've put on ten kilos since I've been here."

She's speaking too fast, she's too ready to fill the silence. I don't doubt I'll love the food, but unlike her, I can't do small talk.

"Mamá."

I pin her with a look. That one word has never sounded so heavy coming from me.

She shakes her head as if to say she's not ready to talk. But then she sighs. "Okay. You said your piece. Would it be okay if I said mine?"

Though I'm expecting a long speech about how ungrateful I am, I nod. She wouldn't be wrong. However, when she begins to speak, she doesn't look like someone who is about to bite off her only child's head. Her eyes are soft, not the stormy way they get when I make her angry. Her features are relaxed. She's serene, like the sea before daybreak.

"The things you said to me . . ." I brace myself, my fingers fidgeting with the hem of the tablecloth. "Were not wrong."

My eyes snap up in surprise. Under the table my hands still.

My mother smiles, sadly. "Qué? You didn't think I was capable of admitting when I'm wrong?"

"Historically, no," I say, which makes her smile seem more genuine.

She shrugs. "Bueno, I didn't love the way you expressed your feelings, but you were right. I wasn't always there. *You* were always there when I needed you. You were more of a mom than I was."

My eyes fill with tears at the admission. I'm suddenly twelve, thirteen, fourteen again, running after my mother, making sure she eats on time, making sure she takes her vitamins, and making sure she catches her flights. Taking care of her. Taking care of everything.

"And you were so good at that, I never stopped to wonder if it bothered you," she continues. "You seemed happy. I thought you were happy. I'm sorry, Marianto. I missed so much of your childhood, and I *am* trying to make up for it now. But you're not a baby anymore, and you don't need me to take care of you." Mamá swallows, then breathes in with a smile. "You were so much better than me anyway. I was a desastre. Ask anyone." She pauses, grimacing for emphasis. "But I loved our little adventures. I loved having you on set, I loved watching you fall in love with entertainment. I loved that you seemed to be following in my footsteps."

Her playful smile becomes sadder. I know what she's thinking: I didn't. I didn't follow in her footsteps. I didn't study acting, I didn't go to the auditions she got for me, I didn't do any of it. I resented it so much it made me run away.

"But you went your own way," she says, her voice small. "And I'll be honest, it always felt like you were sticking it to me. And when you started working at *Ellas*, and you had no problem being in front of a camera for *them* . . . I suppose I felt that way even more. That might be the reason why I never . . . supported you. The way I should have. I'm sorry about that too."

"I wasn't," I confess. "I love entertainment, I love art and the way it makes people feel. I just never felt the desire to be famous like you."

"I know that now," Mamá says. "And I know you love Caracas, and that is why you decided to stay. You wanted a quiet life, so you made one for yourself. I support it now. You're living the life you intended to live."

I'm not, I think, but I can't admit it. Call it pride, call it cowardice. Maybe it's both. But I can't bring myself to admit that the quiet life I always thought I wanted might not be the life I want anymore. That, despite everything, I've missed our adventures, the chaos of it, of her and her world. The airport reunions, discovering new places and cultures. I miss it.

"Do you forgive me?" Mamá asks.

More tears spill from my eyes. I hate that she even has to ask. "Of course I forgive you. Do you forgive me?"

Mamá gives her head a single, firm shake. "Nothing to forgive."

We smile at each other across the table. I'm twelve, thirteen, fourteen again but for a different reason. A thousand restaurants, a thousand nights just like this one all over the country, then all over the world. Maybe more. Just the two of us and a restaurant table. Yes, not everything was bad.

But then she startles me by clapping. Once. *Loudly*. People turn to look at us. My mother doesn't notice or doesn't care.

"Now that *that's* out of the way," she says, "have you talked to Simón?"

Anxiety instantly flares at the mention of his name. I guess expecting her not to bring him up was a fool's hope.

My silence must be answer enough because she gives me a reproaching look. "Maria Antonieta." I don't say anything. "Don't tell me you would deny yourself the chance of love only because it doesn't fit into your plan." I open my mouth to defend myself but she's still talking. "Was it something I did? It was, wasn't it? It was all the husbands. I traumatized you."

"Mamá, it's not that," I say, even though it's a little bit that. "He's . . . gone."

Precious soul that he is, he was right about me needing time. He was right about the timing of it all. Anything we built surely would have crumbled.

"He's coming back," she says, like it's so simple.

"Okay, fine. He comes back, we get together, and then what happens?" I say. "Do I move to Colombia? Do I drop everything and become his groupie? Do I devote my life to supporting my music-sensation boyfriend while he's out there touring and living his dream? What about *my* dream?"

I can't go back to curating my life so that it can fit into someone else's. I can't go back to carrying all the weight, like I did with Alejandro. I can't be the one waiting by the phone, forcing myself to believe that his thing is so much bigger than *my* thing. The same way he can't go back to choosing between his love for someone and his love for his career.

Mamá frowns, shaking her head like I'm not making any sense. "Why do you have to do everything?" she asks. "What makes you think Simón won't meet you halfway?"

"Experience!" I've always been the one to do everything, to sacrifice. Giving, giving, giving without getting even half as much in return.

My mother reaches over the table, grasping my hand between both of hers. "Ay, Marianto." *Pat, pat, pat.* "Simón is different."

"What makes you so sure?" I ask.

"For one, he already excels at something I was never really good at," she says.

I huff. "And what's that?"

She squeezes my hand tighter. "Taking care of you."

The fight leaves my body all at once. I don't realize I'm crying until my mother reaches out and catches a tear trailing down my cheek.

I remember Simón editing my list because he knew I was headed for failure. He was constantly helping me, coming back to the office with me to sort through the scripts, sitting in the dark with me until I agreed to take the bed and give him the couch. I remember him making me feel safe, pulling smiles out of me, getting angry on my behalf. I think of him falling in love with me but refusing to start a relationship because he knew it would hurt both of us in the end.

He did take care of me. Around him, my mind could relax.

The waiter makes his way back to our table, now carrying our piping hot plates. I wipe the tears off my face before he reaches us. My mother pats my hand twice more.

"Think about it?" she says, sitting back against her chair. I nod. "The food really *is* amazing."

CHAPTER 38

······

"*PORQUE YA NO TE NECESITO*," I SING, PUTTING photos into boxes. "*Y si te llego a extrañar por un descuido, eso al rato se me pasa.*"

The last time I played this song, I was heartbroken. I was a different person than I am today. I reach up to touch the soft ends of my hair. I hadn't had collarbone-length hair in forever, mostly because Alejandro preferred women with long hair. But I've shed the Marianto I was back then. I'm grateful for her, grateful for Alejandro when he was exactly what I needed, grateful for the happy memories that will always stick with me. To curse it all would be unfair. Without the Marianto who stayed in a four-year relationship because it was safe, the Marianto I am today wouldn't be here, putting memories into boxes and rearranging her furniture while baking a cake from scratch.

Caballo de Troya's album has been playing on a loop all day. Simón's voice is soothing, like it's always been. More, actually. Now I can project his personality onto it, conjure illusions of what he'd look like singing any particular line with a certain amount of accuracy. I know the man behind the voice.

Lately I've been thinking about what it would be like to listen to these songs live, front row. Every fan's dream. I've been daydreaming about late-night FaceTimes, long flights, running through an airport to reach someone you love faster. Safety doesn't come from being anchored in a city, having a nine-to-five job, knowing what will happen every minute of every day. It comes from knowing your heart is secure, cared for. It comes from knowing you've found the place where you belong, a ground solid enough to build upon. No matter the distance, no matter the time difference, no matter the circumstances. When I think of it this way, the logistics seem manageable. Exciting even. I'm packing away the old Marianto too, and her fear-based beliefs.

I push to my feet, box under my arm, and scan the room. Surfaces that used to be covered in mementos are now flat and empty. I've dusted off my bookshelves and desk, removed picture frames on my coffee table for minimalist décor. I haven't been able to get a new couch because I'm still unemployed. Thank God for my mother deciding to split her *Talento V* paycheck with me; it's the only thing keeping me afloat. But I switched up the position of the TV, got a smaller coffee table, and laid out a soft new rug.

The apartment may always smell like it's been inside a closet for a decade, but at least it's more me now.

I put the box of pictures next to the others filled with items I've decided to throw away and come back to the last of the boxes; the one full of things not meant to be thrown away but to be returned—a couple of very expensive medical books Alejandro left behind, one of his favorite ties he thought long-lost, clothes he kept in my closet, a bottle of cologne. After one final scan around my bedroom, I decide it's time to close the box.

Blanca and her boyfriend offered to drop it off for me. Definitely a better idea than us seeing each other again.

At the last minute, I scribble a quick note and slip it in before taping it all up:

You were right. Gracias, Ale.

Even in the uncertainty I've been living in, I'm sure of this.

I SPEND THE rest of the morning in virtual interviews for different newspapers, none of which go well. At this point, I'm considering applying to be a news anchor or a talk show host for a random local channel. My experience at *Ellas* qualifies me to be in front of a camera, but my heart is set on writing, so I haven't brought myself to do it yet. I want to exhaust every other option first.

I'm ready to sit on my couch with a bowl of cereal and binge *New Girl* season 2 for some serotonin. But before shutting my laptop, I check my email for the umpteenth time today. I have a fresh new batch of applications ready to go out after I make lunch—the aforementioned cereal—and start the cycle of torture that is job hunting all over again.

When I type in my password, the screen unlocks to show me the document I'd been working on last night.

The Ex-Perimento (Or How I Fell in Love with a Member of Caballo de Troya)

Alexa, play mi canción favorita by Caballo de Troya.

I'm kidding. They're all my favorite . . .

I smile at the first line. Blanca was right, of course. The article was more of a story of how I fell in love with Simón, so I decided to go all the way. It's not finished. I'm not sure how to finish it. The IRL ending just seems too unsatisfying.

I hit save, just in case I forgot to last night. I'm logging in to my email when my phone starts ringing. I jump to grab it, sure Simón and I are connected telepathically, and he felt I wanted to talk to him. But no. It's an unknown number. I hesitate before picking up, but my mother decided to stay at the hotel until the end of the show. She could be calling from the room.

"Hello," a male voice says when I pick up. "Maria Antonieta Camacho?"

"Yes, this is she," I say.

"This is Miguel Vieira, I'm the editor in chief at *Ethos*," the man says.

Oh my god. Oh my god, *oh my god*, it's happening. "I'm sorry it took so long for us to get back to you. We had a minor setback in our schedule."

I toss my laptop to the side and stand, shaking.

"Hi! Hello. Hi," I say. "Nice to meet you. I completely understand."

"Wonderful," he says. I swear I can hear a smile in his voice. "Let me tell you a little bit about our vision."

Miguel Vieira paints a picture for me of what it would be like to work with them—talented Latin Americans from every cultural background, teams in every country of the continent, opportunities to collaborate between departments. It's a new company, which means it's a blank canvas where everyone has a brush. It's a dream environment. It sounds better than *Ellas* already.

"At *Ethos* we believe in investing in emerging talent, like you," he says. "We want your drive, your passion, your ideas.

We're not interested in hiring robots." He laughs and I can't help but join. "If this sounds at all like something you'd be interested in, we would love to have you on board as editor."

Editor.

At my side, my laptop still shows the email I was getting ready to send, applying for yet another job. But, as of fifteen seconds ago, I don't have to do that anymore. I'm employed. I'm an editor. It hurts to swallow. I realize it's because I'm crying. I'm an editor! An editor who hasn't said a word since getting the offer.

"Sí!" I blurt out. "Sí, I'm interested. I'm so interested."

"Amazing," Miguel says. "Welcome to the team, Maria Antonieta."

"Gracias." My voice is so small I'm not sure he hears me.

Before we hang up, Miguel tells me I'll get an email with next steps and that I'll probably need to drop by the office tomorrow to get paperwork started.

I squeal as soon as the call ends. I'm no longer unemployed! Laughter bubbles out of me. I'm alone in my living room, grocery bags are still in the kitchen, my shoes are in a heap next to the couch, and my laptop is dangerously close to falling on top of them. I'm a verifiable mess. But I have a job. I need to tell Simón. I—

I can't. I can't call Simón. According to my phone and the *Talento V* Google calendar I still haven't disabled, he's arriving today. In fact, he's on a plane on his way here. The flight from Bogotá is short, barely more than two hours, but I can't call him now. Though soon we'll be in the same city again and what will I do? I have no idea.

His absence grows heavier around me, replacing my laughter with long sighs. The lack of him is palpable. He's been one call or text or drive away for all these weeks, slowly sneaking into the cracks in my walls, making a home for himself. And I miss him.

A universe without Simón is worse than the alternative. He's worth the discomfort. He's worth the distance. He's worth the jet lag. He's worth back-and-forth travel. He's worth it.

And he should know.

I grab my laptop before I lose my nerve and stay glued to it until the article is finished. But when I read it over, calling it an article seems wrong. It's more than that. Our story, written out in my favorite way. Informative, brimming with details. Not a figment of my imagination, not a daydream, but a string of experiences woven together to let him know that every moment we shared together was genuine, real, one for the history books.

I stop at the last paragraph.

> *He asked me what I wanted, and I wasn't brave enough to give him a straight answer. I wish I could go back in time, to that beach, and spell it out on the sand. "You," a hundred times over, until it sinks in—"Tú, tú, tú."*

The email leaves my computer with a *swoosh*, but the sound is not as satisfactory as I hoped it would be. I think back to that night at the beach, to the certainty with which he told me he liked me, he *wanted* me. I remember his hands on my face as his lips claimed mine with urgency. He wasn't shy about his feelings for me, he wasn't vague, he didn't hide behind a screen. He deserves to hear it. He deserves to look into my eyes when I tell him. It's too late to undo the email now, but he should be arriving in about an hour. He won't see it until then. I push my chair back and stand, grabbing my car keys from my desk. If I leave now, I can make it in time.

On the road, I grip the steering wheel tightly, my knuckles white as I weave through the busy Caracas traffic. Every second feels like an eternity—my mind racing with thoughts of what I should say, how I should say it.

The city blurs past my windshield, but I focus only on the car up ahead, waiting at the red light. I press the accelerator a little more, my foot trembling with anticipation.

As I near the intersection, the light turns green—finally—but then, the cars ahead only inch forward until, suddenly, they come to a complete stop. My stomach drops. No, no, not now. Please, not now.

I hate Caracas, I find myself thinking. But the cars still don't move.

I make it to the airport two hours later and rush in, hoping his flight was delayed. I ask the first employee I see.

"That flight arrived about an hour ago," he tells me, without paying much attention.

There is no way Simón is still here. But I still walk in, walk the length of the airport, just in case. There are still people waiting for their ride. My heart sinks as I realize I could have missed him by mere minutes. He probably passed me on the road. As I walk back to my car, the silence feels deafening, echoing the emptiness inside.

CHAPTER 39

AS I RIDE THE ELEVATOR UP TO MY APARTMENT, I check my phone for the umpteenth time. There is nothing, from anyone. I almost miss Mileidy's constant texts asking me to carry out some ridiculous task just because she had to make it seem like I was an actual employee. Maybe Simón hasn't seen the email. Or maybe he saw it and he doesn't want to reply because he doesn't want to be with me anymore. Which is fine. It's fair. He has every right. Maybe he has a girlfriend.

The thought makes me want to throw up. I groan, letting my head rest against the mirrors behind me. The elevator dings and the metal doors screech as they slide open. I drag my feet out, then halt.

A tall figure sits right by my door. A black duffel bag sits beside him. It has a familiar logo, matching the signature hoodie he's wearing. He's a walking Caballo de Troya advertisement. Simón springs to his feet when he sees me. And even though he looks like he's been sitting there for hours, he's out of breath.

"Maria Antonieta," he says in his salutatory way, but his voice is hoarse.

"Simón."

Simón.

I'm not completely sure the sight before me isn't a figment of my imagination. Time seems to slow, every sound fading into a distant hum. My heart pounds so loudly I swear he can hear it.

A surge of warmth and longing swells inside me, so intense it's almost overwhelming. I feel a thousand emotions collide—joy, relief, a bittersweet ache of what we've lost, and a flicker of hope that maybe, just maybe, not everything is doomed.

"I was at the airport," I blurt out.

Simón's eyebrows shoot up. "The airport?"

"I wanted to tell you something," I add, as if that makes more sense. But it's now or never. I pull my phone out of the back pocket of my jeans and go through my email until I find the document. I clear my throat, suddenly nervous. Simón watches me expectantly. I clear my throat again and take a deep, quiet breath.

"*When I started the experiments, I didn't start with the idea of recruiting a coach, or want that coach to be my favorite singer . . . or want him to become . . .* " I look up at Simón. Who is kind-hearted, and responsible, and funny, and talented. Who in a matter of months made himself important to me, quickly becoming one of my best friends. Simón, who got off an airplane and the first thing he did was come find me. Reciting the article to him feels impersonal, in light of that. "Simón, I wanted to tell you that I got the job." Joy instantly enters his eyes. For me. I force myself to keep going. "And after I got that call, I realized the only person I wanted to tell was you. And that you were right, back at the beach." I swallow hard. "You asked me a question, and I didn't answer. I thought I did, but you deserve to hear me say it. I like you too. I want you too. I've never wanted to break all my rules so much in my life."

As I speak, the pressure in my chest grows lighter. It feels good to put this out there, to lay my feelings down at his feet and give him the choice to pick them up.

"I understand if your feelings have changed," I continue, as painful as that would be. "But you were brave in telling me. So I thought you should know."

Simón takes a step in my direction, then another, nodding. "I wanted to tell you something too." *Oh.* "What I said before I left—"

"No, no." I cut him off, lurching forward until my hands are on his forearms and I'm looking up at him. "Please, don't apologize for that. You did exactly what you had to do. You knew I needed time, and you gave it to me. You were so perfectly, selflessly you, and I'm so grateful to you for that."

He looks at me with a longing I've only ever seen in movies. I still can't believe he's here.

"I wasn't going to apologize," he says. "I meant what I said that night."

Oh.

I deflate. Coming all this way just to reiterate what he's already said seems a little unnecessary, if you ask me.

His hands cup the back of my neck, tilting my face up. His fingertips tap a slow rhythm on my skin. When he smiles with a sigh, my heart bursts. He looks at me like I'm fragile, made of porcelain, like I need to be treated with care. Like I deserve to be treated with care.

"I like you so much, Marianto," he whispers. "I meant everything I said. Falling in love with you would be so easy." *Oh.* "If we gave this a shot, I think you and I could be amazing." He produces a folded sheet of paper from his back pocket.

I immediately miss his touch. He unfolds the piece of paper with shaking hands, swallowing as his eyes bore into mine.

My heart grows when he shows me. A schedule. For the rest of the year. Where he'll be and for how long. Venezuela is scribbled in at least twenty times. At *least* twice a month. Every Venezuelan holiday is highlighted. Some of the squares are blank, and I realize they're for me to fill in.

"This is what I was doing the night before I almost missed my flight," he says. "I knew then, at that pool, before we even touched, that I wanted to try to make it work. It's going to be hard. There will be days when I won't be available and days when I'm traveling to other continents and our responsibilities are going to make it near impossible for us to talk. And there will be days when you will hate me for that." His plans rush out of his mouth so fast, I'm not even sure he's breathing. And I'm just staring. I can't believe he did this. "And now I know you just started a new job, so obviously you can't ask for a week off every month," he continues. "But Colombia is like a two-hour flight, so whenever you have a long weekend, I can fly you there and—"

I put my hands over his on the wonderful plan he made for us. Finally, he breathes.

"I know this isn't what you had in mind when you said you needed security." His voice is low, almost begging. His eyebrows are pinched together, like he's in pain. "And I know it might all be for nothing, and you might end up resenting me anyway . . . But I want to try."

It's like I can't stop nodding my head, and with every motion his shoulders seem to relax. "I can't believe you did this."

He shrugs one shoulder. "I know how much you love a plan."

I laugh. Which turns into one tear, then two, until I'm sobbing and Simón is immediately wrapping his arms around me.

"I want to try too," I mumble into his sweater.

Simón sighs heavily, his breath blowing into my hair. He pushes me away a little so he can see me, wiping the tears from my cheeks. "Do you think we'll regret it?"

I shrug, grinning through the tears. "No" is the first thing I say. But I pause to consider. Life is unexpected, and I have to stop convincing myself that it isn't. Trying to accommodate every single moment into color-coded squares could be a wasted effort in the end. "Maybe."

"Do you care?" he asks, leaning closer.

"Not one bit."

"Good," he rasps.

He pulls me closer in a single swift movement and seals my lips with his. For once, it doesn't feel daunting or scary. His touch is familiar. His breathing is in sync with mine, reminding me that I'm not stepping into nothing. That there is solid ground beneath me and a strong hand to steady me. And for all the talk of staying in one place, putting down roots not even God could pull out, I find that this might be all the security I need.

This is still a plan. It's just a new plan, one with room for adventures and traveling and stolen kisses in foreign alleyways with a man who isn't just my favorite musician, but my confidant, my safe haven. And it doesn't sound half bad.

EPILOGUE

SIX MONTHS LATER

BOGOTÁ REMINDS ME OF CARACAS, EXCEPT MUCH, much bigger, much colder, and infested with pigeons.

People own the most beautiful dogs I've ever seen. It's paradise for the gummy bear lover. The arepas may be plain and lifeless, but at least the bread is amazing. And don't even get me started on the coffee.

I wish we were having coffee instead of . . . what is it Simón said he's making? Chocolate con queso. That's right. Hot chocolate. With cheese.

In the six months that Simón and I have been together, today is the first time I've questioned my decision of dating a Colombiano. And I'm here for three whole months. I haven't admitted this out loud, but I'm scared. Who knows how many times they'll force this concoction on me while I'm here?

Maybe I can talk to Miguel and have him change my project to something else, something in México. Simón and I can have tacos every day. But even as I think about it, I know it's impossible. I arrived three days ago to get adjusted, to get used to sleeping in the Airbnb *Ethos* rented for me, and . . . to spend time with my boyfriend before I'm swamped with work?

"The Ex-Perimento (Or How I Fell in Love with a Member of Caballo de Troya—who are now on their way to becoming the biggest band in Latin America, by the way . . .)" article goes live next week in *Ethos Colombia*. I changed a couple things, of course. But Simón and I will always have the original.

A mug of steaming hot chocolate materializes in front of me. I look up to find Simón beaming at me, a mischievous glint shining in his eyes.

I grimace. "Do I have to?"

Simón sits across from me. "Sí," four Colombians say.

Fernando, aka "Fercho"—Caballo de Troya's lead guitar player and Simón's best friend—and Simón's sister, Montserrat, came to help me settle into the city. They're behind us in the living room, unpacking my books. Juan Sebastián, the final member of Caballo de Troya, is in the kitchen fixing everyone else's mugs. It's still surreal to call these people friends, to know their quirks, to have inside jokes, to watch them carefully unpack my life out of love, not just for Simón, but for me as well.

I grab the mug. "Fine."

Simón hands me a spoon. Fercho, Montse, and Juan leave their spots to watch me. I dip the spoon into the mug and fish out three cubes of melting cheese at once. I tip the spoon over until two cubes slide back in.

Then I eat it.

The chocolate itself is amazing. But the cheese . . . Who knew that gooey, sticky, melty cheese can be flavorless yet still offensive?

I hate it. But I love the man, so I try to keep a straight face. He looks too excited. Plus, I'm outnumbered.

"It's interesting," I say carefully.

Simón throws his head back and laughs. "Give me that, you hate it."

"Pfff . . . *no*," I say, which only makes him laugh harder.

I love the way he knows me. I love the way he shows it.

"Food's here," his sister announces.

Simón springs to his feet. He stops in front of me, cups my face between his hands, and plants a quick kiss on my lips. "Te quiero, 'mor."

Then he messes up my hair and turns to grab our dinner. I can't erase the smile on my face as I watch him; it's so wide my cheeks hurt.

I grab my mug of awful hot chocolate and cheese and gleefully eat another spoonful, content in this one moment. Even though I'm in a foreign city, eating something I never in a million years would have picked for myself, I still feel perfectly at home.

ACKNOWLEDGMENTS

The butterfly effect is wild because what do you mean this book wouldn't exist if I'd never met this wonderful group of people? All of you have shaped me and this book in one way or another, and while words can't describe the size of my gratitude, I'm sure as hell going to try.

To Gwen Beal, who has been my agent since 2020. Thank you for the phone call that changed my life. Thank you for giving me the peace of knowing you were going to be on my side. We took a chance on each other all those years ago, and boy, has it paid off. I can't wait to have that coffee with you in New York. To Geritza Carrasco, who later joined our team. Thank you for loving these characters as much as I do. Thank you for your excitement and your dedication to help me take this story to the next level. You are the best agents I could have asked for, and I'm so grateful to have you both in my corner. To Ciara Finan and Enrichetta Frezzato, who have taken *The Ex-Perimento* to places I could have only dreamed of, thank you. And thank you to the entire team at UTA and Curtis Brown. I'm proud to call these agencies my home.

I was sixteen years old when I decided I wanted to publish a book with Penguin Random House. Thank you to Angela

Kim at Berkley Romance for turning that dream into a reality. I still can't believe it. You understood Marianto and Simón like no one else, you understood exactly what I wanted to achieve, and you even loved Alejandro for all the reasons I love him too. The moment we hung up I knew, if by any chance you wanted to work with me, I would jump at the opportunity. And to Olamide Olatunji-Bello at Transworld for taking Marianto and Simón to the UK. Thank you for loving this book and seeing what it could be. Thank you for your enthusiasm, which has warmed my heart to no end. And thank you both for seeing beyond what I could see and guiding me through making it the best it could be. You are the best editors I could have asked for. To Kristin Cipolla, Yazmine Hassan, Jessica Mangicaro, Hillary Tacuri, and the rest of the Berkley team, thank you for working tirelessly to put *The Ex-Perimento* in the hands of readers. You are all a dream.

To Nessa Moulay, thank you. WE HAVE BEEN FRIENDS FOR TEN YEARS! It has been the joy of my life to share this wild publishing ride with you. If soulmates exist (and I think they do and that we can have more than one), you are one of mine. My first critique partner, my soul twin. Look at us! We're doing the thing.

To Carolina Flórez-Cerchiaro, thank you for telling me I was ready when I wasn't sure (multiple times). Thank you for championing not only my books but me. Thank you for your honesty; my books and I are better because of it. But above all, thank you for your genuine friendship. I'm so glad I get to share this journey with you.

To Gabriela Romero Lacruz, thank you for supporting me through the years. We found each other, two Venezuelans trying to break into this industry, and now we're both here. Thank you also for my beautiful cover, which I still can't stop staring at.

To Jessica Parra and Carolina Vilas, who read this book and told me this was the one. Turns out you were right! Thank you for helping me take it from messy first draft to what it is today. Your friendship is invaluable.

Dreaming in Venezuela can often be overwhelming, but if one only dares, then that person's dream becomes everyone's dream.

To my parents, gracias. Thank you for loving me, providing for me, encouraging me, and never telling me that I couldn't do it. To my siblings, gracias. Thank you for believing in me, for reading my Jonas Brothers fan fiction, for knowing that I was a little weird but never making me feel the full weight of it. Gracias, familia, for speaking about my dream never as an "if" but as a "when." Thank you to my abuela, my aunts and uncles, my cousins. We have dreamed together. We celebrate together.

Thank you to my niblings, Matias, Adrián, Verónica, and Francisco, for making me an aunt and draining my bank account. I love you to the moon and back.

To my friends, gracias. Thank you, Meli and Jonathan, for crying with me multiple times; that's how I know you love me. I love you too. Thank you, Diagnora and Gerardo, for telling people I'm a writer when I'm too embarrassed to do it myself. Thank you, José Manuel and Daniela, for showing your support in actions. Thank you, Celis family, for dreaming with me when I had no business calling myself a writer. Thank you, Gerlin and Ninoska, my best and oldest friends; I'm grateful for your support over the years. I love you and I hope we're friends until we die, even if we see each other less than once a year. Thank you, Laura, for answering my questions about

Caracas and for being one of my first readers in high school. Thank you, Leivys, for being a safe space and allowing me to be a safe space for you too. Thank you, Eliezer, for reminding me I deserve this and for understanding the assignment whenever I asked you a question from the male perspective. Thank you, Jhoselyn, Valeria, and Abby, for cheering me on every step of the way and for helping me spend money irresponsibly even when none of us had any. Thank you, Sam, Rosma, Xiori, Alfredo, Rosniel, Luzve, José, Pereira, Gabi, and the rest of Vida Friends, for being the best group of friends to exist. Thank you for the hugs, the laughter, the advice, the tears, the expensive meals on birthdays, and the improvised Sunday sandwiches. Thank you for having faith when mine had run out. I love you all more than words can express, and I'm so grateful for each of you.

To the amazing authors in the Berkley Discord, thank you for answering my questions. I still can't believe I'm one of you.

A special shout-out to that one teacher in uni who caught me writing in the middle of class and told me to thank her when I published my first book. Thank you.

Thank you to the One, who gave me a knack for romanticizing everything and for making people laugh. Te pasaste. Thank you for keeping life interesting. There is never a dull moment.

And last but not least, thank you, whoever you are, for making it this far. Thank you for giving Marianto and Simón a chance. Thank you for allowing me a few hours of your time. I hope you had as much fun reading *The Ex-Perimento* as I had writing it. I hope to see you again in the future.

Photo by Rosniel Acosta

Maria J. Morillo is a born and raised Venezuelan ESL teacher, translator, and author of love stories featuring Venezuelan women getting absolutely everything they've always wanted. A self-proclaimed fangirl since childhood, Maria draws inspiration from all her favorite things: pop culture, books, music, and celebrity interviews. When she's not writing, you can find her leading the choir at her local church. Maria currently lives in Maturín, Venezuela, with her family.

VISIT MARIA J. MORILLO ONLINE

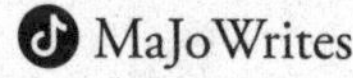

MariaJMorilloAuthor

MaJoWrites